Hunt the Straight Path Home

Rebekah Binkley Montgomery

Abundance Books

Published by Abundance Books LLC
Kalamazoo, Michigan

978-1-963377-09-5 ISBN (EBook)
978-1-963377-11-8 ISBN (Audio)
978-1-963377-05-7 ISBN(PB Print)

Contents

Hunt the Straight Path Home

A novel by Rebekah Binkley Montgomery

CHAPTER 1

Rural Mercer County, Ohio
Monday, February 3, 1915

Every fiber in Eliza urged her to run—to flee from the *Mahr*. She wanted to escape, but the creature sitting on her chest had her pinned, causing every breath to be painful. Eliza knew if the Mahr sat there long enough, she would run out of the strength to inhale and quit trying. Then what would happen to her?

In desperation born of exhaustion, she squeezed out a single word: "Jesus!"

The oppressive weight swept off her chest. She cautiously opened her eyes, fearful a smoke-colored imp might be leaning over her.

The full moon shone through the loft's window, illuminating some objects and casting deep shadows where anything might hide. Many times in the past she told her younger siblings, "There is nothing to be afraid of in the dark. There's nothing in the dark that isn't there in the light."

She knew that was no longer true.

After dark, a beast—which it seemed no one could reliably identify—was terrorizing Stringtown.

Lately, when Eliza walked to the Stringtown General Store to sell extra eggs, the beast's latest atrocity was the foremost topic of discussion; its kills and mutilations described in gory detail.

"It goes right for the jugular!" declared one of the gossips warming himself around the store's potbellied stove. This man was known to Eliza as a blowhard, prone to exaggeration. This time he actually understated the facts.

Some credited the beast with almost supernatural abilities.

"It killed one of my lambs. I followed the trail of blood for a ways, but then the carcass and blood trail disappeared. Explain that!"

Eliza heard the word Mahr bandied about by some with German accents. It took persistent wheedling on Eliza's part to coax an explanation out of Grandma Burger.

"I thought—hoped—we left all those superstitions in the old country."[1]

Eliza thought it weirdly coincidental that at the same time the Mahr haunted her dreams, a flesh-and-blood beast prowled the countryside. Like Satan, the beast looked for prey to devour.

Now, when greeting friends and neighbors, instead of waving they knocked on wood. Eliza found this curious and again went to Grandma Knapp for an explanation.

"The devil is supposed to be unable to touch oak. It's considered a holy tree. Knocking on wood proved you weren't the devil in disguise."

This information came with a warning from Grandma. "Eliza, don't get wrapped up in those old stories. They are delusions."

In a way, Eliza was glad for something else to be the focus of attention besides her family. In the past few months, her family gave the Stringtown residents plenty to discuss. Eliza did not miss the pitying glances and murmurs of sympathy.

Because of the stories and rumors of the marauding beast, Eliza no longer sent her twin brothers or her younger Ruthie to sell eggs to Charley, the store's owner. She feared they, too, would have nightmares if they heard the talk about the beast around the store's potbellied stove.

No one seemed to know what kind of beast was actually doing the killing. Nor had anyone actually seen the beast while evidence of the beast's savagery could be seen on many of the farms along Stringtown Road where the Burger homestead was located.

Stringtown Road received its unusual name when the area was settled by pioneers. They built cabins, farms, a church, and post office along a single path strung through the nearly impenetrable forest covering most of western Ohio. The Yankee Run stream, comprising the southern border of the Silas Burger farm, flowed into the Saint Marys River.

The pioneers who settled along Yankee Run were a tough, hearty group, but the killings had them unnerved and Eliza wasn't the only one having nightmares about the beast. Some neighbors were having them too.

Eliza wondered what she was supposed to do with her night-mares. Were these night visions warnings from God? Was she being given a glimpse of the future? Or were the dreams a natural reaction to the losses her family recently suffered combined with fear of what tomorrow may bring?

Some believed the dreams were from Eedhene, a spirit that warned that death was due to strike in the next twelve months.

There were whispers about an old woman living back in the woods who was said to have second sight, foretold the future, and interpreted dreams.

"She can even contact the dead," a neighbor whispered to Eliza. "But she won't do it for free 'cause if she's caught, she'll go to prison for practicing witchcraft. So she charges plenty."

Eliza was tempted to find the old woman and ask her to contact Mama, but she didn't have any money to offer her.

If only I could talk to Mama. She could tell me the meaning of these nightmares and how to make them go away.

Wherever Mama went, peace followed. Mama's calmness defused Papa's temper, something Eliza couldn't do and gave up trying long ago.

Mama also interpreted dreams. Like Joseph in the Bible who interpreted the prophetic dreams of the king's cupbearer and baker, Mama knew what dreams meant.

In the dark, Eliza saw she kicked the blankets off her little sisters when she fought the Mahr. She straightened the feather comforter over her two little sisters then snuggled into their warmth.

Eliza was almost asleep when the mantle clock chimed three times, and the early morning's silence was shattered by frantic barking from their guard dogs.

The beast!

She ran down the steps to wake Papa who was already pulling up his suspenders and stamping into his boots.

Outside, the barking was replaced by the snarling and yelping of a dogfight.

Eliza's hands shook as she lit the lantern. "What do you think is out there?"

Papa, a man of few words, answered her question by grabbing his shotgun housed above the door, opening the breech, eyeing down the barrels. Both chambers were loaded and ready.

As he clapped on his hat, panic rose up in Eliza.

"Papa, please don't go out there alone. Whatever is out there can see better in the dark than you. Wait until the sky gets lighter. Or until the boys or Mr. Altman can go with you."

Papa snorted in derision. "Let dogs protect the livestock while I hide in the house? You think I am a coward?" Grabbing a handful of shotgun shells, he stuffed them in his pocket. He paused by the door. "Have coffee ready when I get back."

He slammed the door as he disappeared into the night.

"Please be careful, Papa!" Eliza called after him.

Life is already hard without Mama. I don't know what I would do if we lost Papa too.

Eliza ran to the door and tried to look out the little window but found it frosted over. Using her fingernails, she scratched at the ice until she made a little peephole. Papa was nowhere to be seen.

Somewhere close to the house, a dog howled in pain. Other dogs barked frantic alarms. They knew something was out there and wanted Papa to know it too.

A blast from Papa's shotgun echoed over the snowy fields. A second shot followed.

Then came an ominous quiet. The dogs stopped barking. Papa was nowhere in sight.

Oh, Jesus! Please protect my papa!

As angry as she had been at God—and still was—she wouldn't blame Him if He completely ignored her.

CHAPTER 2

In her panic, Eliza forgot she was not speaking to Jesus. She couldn't forgive Him for Mama's death. At least not yet. Maybe never. Still, she hoped He was listening to her now. She wanted Him to feel guilt for taking Mama and leaving her to deal with her father and four younger siblings. Eliza was convinced Jesus had made a big mistake and she wanted *Him* to repent for a change.

The stillness worried Eliza more than all the barking and shotgun blasts. As long as Papa and the dogs were making noise, she knew they were alive. Prolonged quiet might mean the beast had its teeth in them.

Clad only in their long underwear, Eliza's younger brothers, twins John and Joshua, appeared at the top of the stairs.

"What's happening? What's all the ruckus about?"

"Something has the dogs all riled up. Papa went to see what it was."

"What is he shooting at?"

"How should I know? Get yourselves dressed and get out there and find out. Papa may need your help!"

She instantly regretted those words. *What was I thinking? After I begged Papa not to hunt the beast in the dark without backup, I tell the twins to go hunting when I know very well the two of them have no more sense than a couple of heads of cabbage! Now I have to try to talk them out of going.*

Disgusted with herself, she drew Mama's shawl tightly around her shoulders as if it could impart some of Mama's common-sense wisdom.

Eliza stepped out on the porch. The wind tugged at the shawl and lashed her with her own hair. Standing in the snow, her bare feet objecting to another reckless decision she had made, she yelled into the dark morning, "Papa! Papa! Are you alright? Papa! Where are you? Are you hurt? Do you need help? Answer me, Papa! The twins are coming out! Don't shoot them!"

She listened for his reply. All she heard was the wind moaning in the cedar break.

Papa should have heard me. Why doesn't he answer?

John and Joshua clumped down the steps, giddy with excitement. They hurriedly dressed against the cold.

"Wait! I think you boys should stay inside and let Papa handle the situation. Everyone is jumpy with all the livestock deaths. Papa won't know you are out there. Or where you are. He is liable to shoot you in the dark."

John patted her cheek as the boys went out the door. "Don't worry. We'll be careful."

She heard them hollering, "Pa! Where are you?"

Maybe they're not as foolish as I thought. Hopefully, Papa will know they are out there and won't shoot them.

Coffee. Papa said he wanted coffee ready.

She threw a handful of coffee beans into a small skillet reserved for roasting them and set it on the back of the stove to slowly brown.

Thoroughly chilled, she pulled the rocking chair close to the cookstove and wrapped herself in Mama's shawl. Crocheted from scraps of yarn, it was certainly no thing of beauty. But when Eliza held it close, the shawl smelled like Mama—a combination of cinnamon, coffee, and lemon verbena. The fragrance of Mama calmed her worries over Papa and the boys.

I'll never wash Mama's shawl. It's all I have left of her.

It was Monday. Laundry day. She wished with all her heart her grandmother and aunt would come to help her tackle the family's laundry.

In the chaotic aftermath of Mama's death, laundry was the last thing on Eliza's mind. Then one day, she awoke to find everyone in the family was experiencing a laundry emergency, which they blamed on Eliza. They assumed Eliza would wash their clothing. She was already doing all the cooking, baking, and housework. She was caring for Mama's chickens. She made sure her younger brothers and sisters did their homework, were clean, had their lunch pails, and were dressed warm enough for their walk to school. She hadn't realized everyone's laundry was also her responsibility too.

Papa's temper flared when he opened the wardrobe and found no clean shirts. Shaking his fist at Eliza, he thundered, "What are you doing with your time all day? When are you going to get me some clean shirts?"

The twins only owned a couple of shirts each. On the verge of manhood and awash in hormones, Grandma told them, "You two are as gamey as a deer in rut. You need to change your shirts often." So they did.

Ruthie spilled grape jelly on the only school dress that still fit her. She tried to wash it out, but it left a sticky stain, and she was ashamed to wear it like that.

After Mama died, little Betty started wetting the bed again. Ruthie and Eliza dried the bed coverings every morning, but a whiff of urine followed all three of them everywhere they went.

Barraged by a hail of complaints, Eliza prepared Sunday night for Monday's wash. Since she was washing all of their clothing except the dirty ones they were presently wearing, she thought they should help.

Ruthie and Betty were playing with their rag dolls at Papa's feet while he drowsed by the fire. The twins were engaged in a checker tournament.

"John and Josh, Mama's soap needs to be grated into a bucket of water. Will you two come do that?"

The twins folded up their checkerboard and started for table when Papa opened one eye. "Sit down, boys. That's women's work. Eliza, don't confuse the boys. They do plenty of work outside. Ruthie and Betty, go help your sister."

"I can't," Ruthie replied. "It's Sunday and we're not supposed to work on the Sabbath. It's in the Ten Commandments."

At that, Papa opened both eyes.

"Ruthie, my commandment is you best be grating soap, or you and I will be taking a trip out to the woodshed."

Before she dragged herself to bed, Eliza took a hatchet and filled the wash boiler and rinse tub with ice she chopped out of the rain barrel.

Since the wash would be hung outside to freeze dry, Eliza put the wooden clothespins in salt water so they wouldn't freeze to the clothes or the line.

"Lord Jesus, help me get the laundry washed. And please send Grandma and Aunt Cora ... No! I'm not going to ask You for any help. You don't listen to me anyway!

Eliza's attitude was in direct opposition to what Mama tried to impress upon her children.

"Jesus is your very present help in times of need," Mama told them. "He'll never leave you nor forsake you. The Bible says, 'I can do all things through Christ who strengthens me.' When you need help, you can depend on Jesus."

Up until Mama died in agony, Eliza firmly believed those words. What convinced her God was deaf to her prayers was when Mama was in torment Eliza earnestly prayed God would take away Mama's pain. But all of Eliza's prayers, their neighbors' prayers, and all the prayers of the church people didn't convince Jesus to alleviate Mama's pain. Or spare her life. Their prayers didn't do any good at all. She concluded Jesus wasn't listening to her.

The acrid smell of scorched coffee beans brought her back to the present.

Oh, no! I've burned them again! Eliza couldn't seem to get the timing right on roasting coffee beans. She either burnt them or ground them too green.

Papa will probably complain because I burned the beans. Well, I'm not going to put up with his criticism at all! If Papa hadn't scared off Ada, I wouldn't have to make coffee for him, and he would have plenty of clean shirts.

The Ada episode still made her cringe. And Eliza paid the largest price for Papa's actions.

Papa had definite ideas how a house should be run. Everything should be in its place. There should always be cookies in the pantry and hot meat-and-potato meals on the table at suppertime.

After Mama died and Eliza couldn't keep up with both school and housework, Papa hired Ada, a recent Irish immigrant and widow, to help out on Mondays with the laundry and Thursdays with the heavy cleaning and baking.

"I'm so glad to have your help!" Eliza greeted her with open arms.

Ada greeted Eliza with equally open arms. "I'm glad to be of any help I can. You poor child to lose your *mam*. You're just at the age where you need a mam most of all," Ada said in her charming Irish brogue.

For a week, Eliza and Ada worked together harmoniously and everyone was happy. With Ada helping, it looked like Eliza could continue to go to school and still keep house for the family.

It seemed too good to be true. And it was.

The following Monday, as soon as she came in the door from school, Eliza felt tension in the house. Something wasn't right with Ada. She was not her usual joyful self.

Accustomed to Papa's changeable moods, Eliza ignored both his elation and depression and went about her day. Papa would eventually get his equilibrium back and life would go on.

She assumed Ada was similarly constructed and the storm would pass.

Ada scrubbed the dirty knee of one of the twin's pants so violently Eliza was afraid she would find that pair in her mending basket with a hole in the knee.

Finally, Ada couldn't contain herself.

"Miss, I need to talk to you about your pa. Now I am a God-fearing woman. I was wed for five years, two months, and eight days to a good man, God rest his soul. Never once did my Tiernan give me a moment's fear he was anything less than faithful. And I the same to him."

Ada turned the pants over and went to work on the other knee.

"Even though we vowed to be wed until death us do part and Tiernan has passed, I am still his wife. And so I ever shall be."

Eliza was puzzled by Ada's soliloquy. "I don't understand. What brought this on?"

"Your pa! He doesn't take no for an answer! Your mam is not yet cold in the ground and your pa is trollin' to replace her—with me! Doesn't he have any decency?"

Eliza was thunderstruck. *What is Papa doing?*

"You tell your pa I'm here to work. He's not paying me to be courted by him!"

Ada put up with his advances for a while, but Papa became so aggressive she finally quit—but not quietly. She was vocal about her reasons why she wouldn't work for the Burgers anymore. No other woman wanted to work for them, and their neighbors looked askance at them.

Hopelessness overwhelmed Eliza when Papa went to school, withdrew her, then told her about it.

"You're needed at home," he told her flatly. "You will take Mama's place and run the household full-time."

She'd cried herself sick over Papa's actions. She contemplated running away, but where could she go? If she went to her grandparents, Papa would come and make her go home.

Eliza glanced at the clock. It read 4:15.

Papa and the boys have been out there for most of an hour, and they aren't back yet. I hope they're not hurt.

Jesus, please bring them back …

Eliza heard the little girls talking and laughing while dressing. Once ready for school, they would do their morning chores as Eliza did hers.

She lit the lantern and then filled a bucket with hot water from the cookstove reservoir, adding a splash of apple cider vinegar. This was for the chickens to drink.

Bundled in Mama's chore coat, she stepped out onto the front porch and briefly studied the eastern sky for hints to the day's weather. Although stars still shone, first light was on the horizon. The east was clear with streaks of pink dawn blushing both the heavens and the snowy fields. It looked like the day's weather would be cold but with winter sunshine.

For a moment, the veil between life and death seemed thinner. Eliza felt tantalizingly close to her mother.

She shut her eyes and whispered, "Mama?" Then listened with her heart expecting to find Mama. Instead bitterness arose along with a sense of outrage.

Most of her life, she and God had been friends, but now Eliza felt betrayed.

Mama loved You, God. But You let her suffer and die!

For that, Eliza had not forgiven Him and had no plans to. She hadn't felt truly safe since Mama died.

Back inside, Eliza stoked the cookstove with the last of the firewood, hefted the wash boiler full of ice over the fire. When the water came to a boil, beginning with the whites, each piece of laundry would be scrubbed on the washboard, rinsed, then hung outside on the clothesline to freeze dry.

It seemed to Eliza, Mama's, Grandma's and Aunt Cora's hands were impervious to the scalding hot wash water. Using the laundry paddle, they would fish a garment out of a simmering tub of water and wring it out with their bare hands.

"How do you do that?" Eliza often asked.

"You'll get used to it after wringing out a few pieces of hot laundry."

Eliza was certain she would never get used to it.

Chapter 3

As the wash boiler began to steam, she grew anxious for the safety of Papa and the twins. Eliza intended to wash and wait by the stove for them to come in. She weighed her options if any of them were hurt.

Then it dawned on her. *Bear Altman! He would know what to do!*

Papa once described Mr. Altman's appearance on their doorstep, declaring, "One day, all my prayers for a good farmhand were answered when Bear showed up!"

The neighbors were leery of the shaggy, giant stranger. Some influential people talked the sheriff into investigating Mr. Altman to see if he was an escaped prisoner or a criminal on the run. The sheriff found nothing amiss in Altman's background or in him. But in the two years he worked for the Burgers, the farm improved and became a showplace. First the neighboring farmers were jealous. Then they tried to hire him away from the Burgers.

Eliza's planned vigil was sabotaged by a combination of heat from the wood stove, Mama's shawl wrapped around her, and exhaustion. Despite her intentions, she nodded off.

Her repeating nightmare began as it always did with a sweeping sense of dread. Her heart pounded wildly. In her nightmare, she looked behind her. The mahr was hiding in thick underbrush. She knew it was stalking her, waiting for her to show any sign of weakness.

"I will be strong!" Eliza declared in her dream.

The mahr chose that moment to attack.

Dear God! Please save me!

CHAPTER 4

From the coop, the roosters seemed to be in a crowing contest reminding her to get her chores done.

The chickens had been Mama's special project. She read every scrap of information on chickens she could find, following whatever advice from the *Farm Journal* magazine made sense to her. Her chickens responded gratefully, stayed healthy, and laid eggs.

What eggs the family didn't eat, Mama sold to Charley at the Stringtown General Store a half-mile from their farm. From her income, Mama was careful to give ten percent to God plus special church offerings at Christmas and on each of her children's birthdays. Beyond that, she saved her egg money, using it to buy luxuries such as an occasional hair ribbon for one of the girls or a bit of candy for everyone to share.

Now Mama was gone.

The coop was dark when Eliza pushed open the door. The hens roosting in their cozy nests murmured a little greeting to her while roosters crowed up on the joists above. She took the lantern down from the ceiling hook and checked the kerosene level. Finding it sufficient, she lit the lantern and rehung it. The lantern's golden light illuminating the cracked corn and fresh water called to the hens. They hopped down, crowded around Eliza's feet, clucking, pecking, and bickering for room at the feeder and water pan.

Mama told her lighting the lantern early in the morning was one of the keys to the success of her flock. "Chickens like to see what they're eating. The more a hen eats, the more eggs she'll lay. So I wake 'em up early so they get busy and make eggs."

Her other secret was the one Mama said mattered the most. "Daily I pray a blessing on my chickens. You must do that, too. Promise me."

Eliza promised. Now, since she was mad at God, she regretted her promise. Watching the hens pecking at the corn, Eliza wondered what she could say to God that would bless the chickens without giving Him credit for the prosperity of the flock.

"Bless Mama's chickens," she muttered as she left the coop.

Back in the house, Eliza heard the little girls laughing and talking as they finished their inside chores, while Eliza sliced bacon then fried it in an iron skillet.

Then she stirred up a batch of cloud biscuits using Mama's recipe.[2]

To properly bake biscuits, the oven needed to be very hot. Eliza added two sticks of pine, which burns hot and fast, to the cookstove's firebox so the biscuits would be fluffy and light—if she didn't burn them. Of course, a hot fire also meant everything on top of the stove would have to be watched closely or it would boil over or scorch.

With the cloud biscuits in the oven, she decided to make gravy to go with them. Eliza poured off most of the bacon grease while retaining several tablespoons in the skillet, along with crispy bacon bits. She sprinkled flour on the grease until it was absorbed, then stirred the grease and flour mix constantly until the flour turned toasty brown. She added a generous amount of whole milk and cream, stirring as the gravy thickened.

In another skillet, bacon grease sizzled and popped as she cracked in a dozen fresh eggs.

Betty was sleepily setting the table. At five years old, this was her job at every meal, which she did without reminder. Her baby-fine blonde hair was tangled; her cheeks rosy from sleep and her dress buttoned crooked. She stopped next to Eliza, her chubby hands full of tinware, and turned her cherub face up to be kissed.

"Morning, Little Betty."

"Morning, Big 'Liza."

Eliza heard the scrape of boots and some stamping on the porch. She ran to the door and opened it. Her brothers and Papa were there, carrying pails of steaming milk while balancing their shotguns over their shoulders.

"Papa! I was so worried about you! What happened out there?"

"I'll tell you in a bit," he said cheerily. "Let me catch my breath. Coffee ready?"

Leaving his boots and snow-covered outerwear near the stove, he took his seat at the head of the table.

"Coffee, daughter."

She poured him a cup. He took a sip, wincing at the burned taste although he did not reprove her.

As she finished fixing breakfast, Eliza waited impatiently for her father to tell her what happened to the dogs.

Ruthie, dressed but also uncombed, poured the first buckets of milk through the separator. As soon as the buckets were empty, John and Joshua snatched them up and went out to finish milking before breakfast and school.

Anxious to hear what happened out there, Eliza studied her father. Clearly the events of the last several months aged him. Eliza felt a pang of guilt.

Maybe he is suffering Mama's loss but in different way than I am.

As the family ate breakfast, they heard in the distance the popping and coughing of Lulu, Grandpa Knapp's black Oldsmobile.

All Grandpa Knapp's buggy horses had been named Lulu, regardless of their gender, so it was only natural that his automobile would likewise be christened.

Lulu was his pride and joy, but it could only be driven if the weather and roads were perfect. Too wet and Lulu would be stuck up to her bumpers in mud. Too much snow, she was similarly incapacitated. Somehow on this frigid morning, Grandpa had coaxed ol' Lulu to life.

The little girls ran to the kitchen window and peered through the melting ice on the windowpane.

"It's Grandpa! And Grandma! Aunt Cora too!"

Eliza's heart leaped with joy. Grandpa sometimes brought the women to help Eliza with her chores. She hoped this was one of those days.

Betty opened the front door to let them in as Grandma, laden with baskets, struggled over snow-covered ruts in the yard to reach the porch.

"What did you bring me?" Betty hollered.

"Betty! Don't beg at Grandma! At least let her get in the house first."

Betty stuck her thumb in her mouth and began to sniffle.

As glad as she was to see her grandparents and aunt come, there was one thing they did that bothered Eliza: they undermined her newly assumed position of authority. Eliza would ask Betty to do something, and one of them would tell Betty she didn't have to do it.

Grandma grunted as she bustled through the door and bent down to embrace the little girl.

"Now, now. Don't cry. Everything is all right. You know Grammy always brings you treats, don't you? Well, I did this time too."

Grandma squeezed Betty into her ample bosom. The child buried her face in Grandma's breast and began to sob.

"It's all right, now," Grandma crooned.

She picked her up and carried her to the rocking chair. She sat down heavily and rocked Betty on her lap while patting her on the back.

That child knows if she is pitiful enough, Grandma will eventually give her a sweet to cheer her up.

"Eliza, I think this child is too young for school. She's all worn out. Maybe she should wait a year. Are you putting her to bed early enough?"

"I think so, Grandma. I tuck her in at 7:00."

"Well, I still think school is too much for her."

Eliza overheard Grandma whisper, "Here, honey. Here's a lemon drop. See if that doesn't help."

Like magic, Betty's tears stopped. She jumped off Grandma's lap and sorted through the paper bags, tins, and jars in the old lady's baskets.

"Betty! Stay out of Grandma's baskets unless you ask permission."

The little girl stuck out her lower lip and began to sniff again.

"Let her be, Eliza! Don't rag on her. She's not hurtin' anything," Grandma scolded.

"I brought you cookies," Grandma told Betty. "The kind you like with pink icing. Let's find them and you can have one on your way to school and a couple for in your lunch."

She's spoiling her! Grandma will give in to her every whim and then leave me with a child who thinks she's queen!

Grandma made large cookies measuring four inches in diameter. She cut them out with a stew can she repurposed as a cookie cutter. Her recipe, carried in her head, made so much dough she mixed it up in a dish pan.[3] No matter how often Eliza watched Grandma mix and roll, she couldn't get the proportions right. Grandma's cookies stayed soft; Eliza's cookies had what Grandma kindly referred to kindly as "body."

The family made room at the breakfast table for Grandpa and Grandma Knapp and Aunt Cora. They bowed their heads, and in German fashion, each child from the youngest to the oldest recited a few words of thanksgiving. Papa gave a final blessing.

As the food passed, Eliza hovered between the table and stove refilling dishes and pouring more coffee or milk as needed. Eliza hadn't counted on three extra mouths to feed this morning, and she was worried. Sometimes, Grandpa and Grandma and Aunt Cora ate before they came. Sometimes not. She closely watched the egg platter and realized that a dozen eggs among nine people would not go very far.

I should have known better. Nothing goes to waste around here anyway; not with two growing boys.

There was a sharp rap at the door. Before she could answer it, Mr. Altman stuck his head inside.

"Good morning, folks," he called cheerily in his rumbling baritone.

"Pull up a chair," Papa invited. "Eliza, another plate and utensils."

She forced a smile and fetched them from the cupboard. Now she knew without a doubt she hadn't made enough breakfast to feed this hungry man too. Mr. Altman frequently ate his meals with the family, so Eliza was well aware of his hearty appetite.

In desperation she did something she'd seen her mother do in similar circumstances. Slicing her last loaf of bread, Eliza scrambled several eggs in a flat bowl, added a pinch of nutmeg, a generous splash of milk, and a bit of vanilla. She melted fresh butter on the griddle. Then dipping the bread slices one at a time in the egg mixture, she fried them to a golden brown.

When Mr. Altman first arrived, he helped Papa on the farm one day a week as rent on the log cabin in the woods where Papa and his first wife and boys once lived. Over time, Mr. Altman had been working for Papa more and more. The farm was growing and prospering as a result.

In his better moments, Papa admitted much of his newfound success was due to Mr. Altman's encyclopedic knowledge of the natural world. He knew what and when to plant by the phases of the moon. He also understood weather and animal husbandry.

Papa was aware his neighboring farmers were envious of Mr. Altman's skills. He knew several were secretly offering Mr. Altman full-time work. Early on, Papa avoided paying him in silver dollars. Instead, Papa paid him generously in bread, eggs, ham, bacon, milk, garden and orchard produce in season, and meals. Sometime Mama sewed for him too. As competition for his skills grew, Papa reluctantly opened his wallet and augmented his wages with cash.

Since Eliza could see so little of his actual face, it was impossible for her to determine how old Mr. Altman was. He wore his black hair shoulder length. With his full beard, mustache, six-foot plus frame, and lumbering tread, local gossips described him as looking like a bear.

Soon Bear became the name most people called him. Eliza thought she heard his given name was Robert, but it didn't matter as she called him Mr. Altman anyway. His hands and fingers matched his size, but he was surprisingly agile with them. Occasionally, he would ask for a needle and thread to patch his clothing. It both surprised and amused Eliza he could effortlessly thread the needle and neatly sew.

Mr. Altman wasn't a local person. He had no family in the area. In fact, no one had ever heard him mention kinfolk or even where he originated. When questioned, he politely declined to answer. If pressed, he'd simply get up and leave.

Mama always called him a blessing sent from God. He not only raised the quality of the livestock and farm crops, but after supper, he would often discuss the Bible with her.

"More coffee, Eliza," Papa called from the table.

"Let me help." Grandma opened the drawer of the coffee grinder and sniffed remaining grounds suspiciously.

"I thought the coffee tasted funny," whispered Grandma. "You've got to watch the beans more closely, Eliza. Well, let's not be wasteful." Grandma poured the scorched grounds into the pot and started it perking.

Try as she might to be organized, Eliza just couldn't get everything done. She was still cooking breakfast when Aunt Cora offered to comb out the girls' hair and check the boys over before school.

As the crow flies, the elementary school was not far away. Although the ground was frozen hard enough for the children to walk on, deep snow lay across the fields, making it impossible to reach the schoolhouse. To travel by the roadway, the children needed to leave an hour early to walk two miles to school.

Eliza kissed each of the children as she checked them over to be sure they were dressed warm enough for their trek to school. Then they were gone.

Wearily, Eliza poured herself a cup of coffee. There was very little food left—only some crusts of bread on the girls' plates. As she cleared the dishes, she ate them so nothing would go to waste. Grandma set a plate of cookies on the table for the men to enjoy with their coffee, and Eliza hooked one of those too.

For a restful few minutes, Grandma and Aunt Cora took over the kitchen. They bustled about washing and drying the dishes. They knew keeping house was hard work for one as inexperienced as Eliza. They tried to help with the big chores like washing, baking, and canning. The day-to-day chores, Eliza could mostly muddle through alone—burning the coffee, not fixing enough food—but making progress, nevertheless.

Eliza had a secret dream she hoped would take her off the farm forever.

Mama knew her daughter's dream, but she was gone now, and her dream was something Eliza knew Papa would never understand.

He was already skeptical of educating women beyond eighth grade. He thought women should marry young. Since Eliza was seventeen, he considered her well on her way to spinsterhood.

From time to time, Papa pointed out several single, young farmers to Eliza. It was no secret that he wanted her to marry one of them. Papa had a grand vision for his farm. He lived in terror one of his neighbors would tempt Mr. Altman away, and then where would he be? When Papa took stock of his assets, he figured Eliza's value was to give him another farmhand on a permanent basis.

Eliza had no desire to marry a farmer and spend the rest of her life working hard and dying young. Too much drudgery was assigned to a farmer's wife, especially when Eliza had a dream of her own.

Time and time again, Eliza heard Papa expound on the evils and dangers of women working outside the home.

"No daughter of mine will ever work outside the home, except over my cold, stiff body."

He was particularly against women filling the job that was Eliza's secret ambition: to become a nurse.

"Nurses are degenerates," he preached at them. "They lack decency and modesty and any sense of shame when they see and handle the bodies of diseased men. Who knows how some of these illnesses are passed from one person to the next?"

He had examples of nurses who caught diseases from their patents too. He knew nurses who contracted polio, TB, typhoid, the whole Pandora's box of pestilence from their patients.

"I suppose midwives and granny ladies are necessary when babies are born, and the family don't have kinfolk handy. Other than that, the risk to life and limb is a gamble not worth taking. No daughter of mine will ever become a nurse."

When Mama was alive, she tried to soften his viewpoint on the subject. But Pa's mind was set in stone.

However, Eliza enjoyed caring for the sick. Even as a little girl, she brought home wounded birds and other creatures she either nursed back to health or buried in the garden. She was painfully aware of how little real knowledge of the healing arts she possessed. If she had only known more, she often thought maybe she could have saved Mama. But Mama's death only pushed Eliza's dream further away than ever.

When she attended school, she had been close friends with several girls, but she had a crush on the same boy since first grade. Glen Franklin was her idea of a boy who could grow up to be the perfect man for her. He was good-looking, smart, athletic, and ambitious. He made her laugh with his funny stories and observations. Although his father was a farmer and he helped out, Glen confided to her that farming was not for him.

"I was doing some spring plowing behind Jack, our mule, when something occurred to me. I said, 'Jack, you are stronger than me, you pull the plow better than me, you can work harder than me, and you don't mind looking at the south end of a north-facing mule all day. As soon as I'm able, I'll leave the farming to you, and I'm going to become a railroad engineer and see the world.' And wonder of wonders, Jack looked at me and said, 'That's fine with me! I don't see an angel with a sword blocking your way.'"

At the time, Eliza laughed with delight at his tale. She knew Glen was referring to the Bible story of Naaman, whose donkey spoke a warning to him. She also noticed he was choosing a career that wouldn't hitch his wife to a plow the way farming did.

As she sat at the breakfast table, she wished she was back in school making plans to meet Glen so they could eat their lunches together. It had been so long since she saw him. She supposed Glen had forgotten her, and another girl had caught his eye. At the thought of what she was missing, a tear ran down her face.

Eliza felt Bear Altman's dark eyes upon her. Feeling guilty for resting, she looked through the errant wisps of red hair that always escaped while she cooked.

"More coffee, Mr. Altman?"

He shook his head, but his look was piercing. "I'm just wondering if you're getting enough to eat. You cook for everybody, but you hardly eat a thing. You're fading away before our eyes."

Papa laughed heartily, but his laughter had a false ring. "Not Eliza. She's strong. She's like her mother, built for work and babies. Why, Margaret could work all day without stopping and Eliza's the same way. Margaret loved to work around the house, and when she was done in here, she'd pull on her boots and come out and help me with chores. My! How I miss her!"

Grandma sniffed and wiped away a tear. "Mr. Altman is right, Silas. Eliza is thin, and kind of pale, too. There's a lot of work here for one little girl."

Papa jumped up angrily. His chair tipped over backwards, hitting the floor with a bang.

"What am I supposed to do about it? I don't make her help on the farm. If I could make life easier for her, I would, but I can't. And I have to think about the rest of the children and providing for them too."

At his outburst, Eliza noticed Grandma and Grandpa exchange a long, questioning glance. They knew that typically Papa was even-tempered except when he was drinking. Then he was unpredictable and explosive. She supposed they would take her aside and ask her privately if Papa was drinking and she dreaded it. Eliza was conflicted how to honestly answer their questions. It felt like a betrayal to tattle on Papa, but she knew Grandpa would have a heart-to-heart conversation with him about the effect alcohol had on his self-control. Eliza and the rest of the children needed that talk to happen soon.

"You are a good provider, Silas," Grandpa chimed in, trying to mollify Papa's ruffled feelings. "I think Eliza will eventually grow into the job. And of course, we'll continue to help out when we can."

"Of course, we will, honey," said Grandma, patting Eliza's hand. "Now let me fry you an egg. Have you eaten today?"

Eliza, embarrassed by all the attention, shook her head.

"You just sit there a bit, 'Liza said. Cora, you start the bread and I'll fry Eliza an egg," Grandma said.

Cora silently began the process of baking the bread for the family. Since it was Monday, they would do laundry and make six loaves of bread, a big batch of cookies, and three or four pies—just enough baked goods to last the family through to Thursday when Eliza would do a big baking to get them through the weekend.

As Eliza ate her egg, she listened to Papa, Grandpa, and Bear Altman discuss the series of livestock killings. There was a difference of opinion among their neighbors. Some thought there was a feral dog in the area. Others were sure it was a wolf.

"I could tell you positively if I could see a clean footprint."

"You can tell the difference?" asked Papa. "Something set off my dogs early this morning. I don't know if whatever was out there is what has been killing livestock, but I scared it away with a shotgun blast and tracked it for a while. You want to look at the prints?"

"Yes, I do. I think I can identify what animal is out there. It's all in the way the joints in the paws fit together," said Mr. Altman. "And the number of prints confirms it. Take wolves, for instance. They live, travel, and hunt in packs. If there is one wolf, there will be at least two, usually a male and a female. And soon, there will be more. So, if you are hunting one, you should plan on hunting two or more."

"I suppose we should put together a hunting party, don't you think?"

"No, I think it's too dangerous," said Mr. Altman. "These farmers don't know wolves. Having them running around in the woods with live ammo makes me nervous. They're liable to shoot at anything that moves, such as somebody's cow or each other."

"But we have to do something. We can't afford to let whatever it is continue to eat little pigs and chickens and calves. Next thing you know, somebody's child is going to come up missing."

"I didn't say you should let it continue to kill; I think a hunting party would be ill-advised," said Mr. Altman.

A knock sounded on the kitchen door. Eliza sprang to open it. Several Springtown farmers stood there, hats in hand. She was surprised to see them. Evidently Papa was not. He came to the door and stood behind her.

"Hello, McMillen, Zizelman," Papa said. "Come in."

The men swept past Eliza, handing her their hats and coats as they came through the door.

"Coffee?" Papa asked them.

They nodded and seated themselves at the table.

While Eliza poured coffee, more wagons pulled into the yard. Papa admitted the men to the kitchen where they drew up to the table, talking crops and livestock, laughing and joking among themselves, and to Eliza's embarrassment, making grimaces of alarm as they sipped her coffee.

"Everybody here?" Papa asked.

"I don't see Ed Moeller," one of the men volunteered.

"Should we wait?"

"He maybe got held up. He's lost chickens, so he ought to be here," said the same man.

"I got work to do," said Hiram McMillen. "I say we go on without him."

Most of the rest murmured agreement. The kitchen, fragrant with unwashed men, manure, bacon, and scorched coffee, grew silent.

Papa began. "As you all know, we have something killing livestock in the Stringtown area. Bear Altman here … " He jerked his thumb in the big man's direction. "Believes it could be a wolf. Tell them why, Bear."

The men turned their attention to Mr. Altman.

He briefly explained what he knew about the hunting habits of wolves verses dogs. "What I really need is to see a footprint. I can tell some of what we need to know by that. A clean set of footprints would be ideal. Then we would know if we were dealing with one or two animals or a pack. And as I told Silas, where there is one wolf, there generally are two. And where there are two there will soon be more. I suggest you address this issue before it gets out of hand."

The men murmured to each other as they contemplated this grim information.

"The frequency of the attacks makes me think we may have a nursing female with cubs or a pack of animals," concluded Mr. Altman.

"Do you have a suggestion as to what we can do to stop the killing?" Tom McCaley said.

"Me?" Mr. Altman seemed amused. "I don't think most of you are ready to hear my suggestion."

"Come on, Bear. You've brought us this far, acting like you got all the answers. At least tell us what you'd do if you were in our boots," demanded one of the farmers.

The room grew silent with anticipation. Mr. Altman stood up, strode over to the window ledge and looked out the pane.

Suddenly, he turned around and addressed them. "Let me do the hunting. I'll get him. Or her. Or them."

The men looked at Mr. Altman in surprise.

"Why you, Bear?" Tom McCaley asked.

"Because I know how to hunt." Mr. Altman gazed levelly at them. "I know how to hunt wolves."

"I think we should form a hunting party and let Altman lead it," suggested Hiram McMillen.

A murmur of approval swept over the room.

Mr. Altman shook his shaggy head.

"I won't do that. You men are farmers, not hunters. Some of you may be both, but I won't take responsibility for leading untrained men with guns onto other people's property. You're likely to shoot somebody's livestock. Or each other. Your lives would be at risk. So would mine."

At this, the farmers grumbled.

"It makes no difference to me," Mr. Altman told them. "You asked and I told you. And while you're at it, here's something else you probably won't like. I would expect to be paid."

The farmers sat in stunned silence.

"Why, Bear Altman! I can't believe you'd charge your neighbors!" Hiram McMillen burst out.

"Mr. McMillen, I have no stake in any of this. I own no livestock or land. I hire out to others for my livelihood. You may hire me to go alone to hunt this menace. Or not. It doesn't matter either way to me. But if you men decide to form a hunting party, I do think you should publish public notice of your intent so no schoolboy checking his traps gets shot by accident. Now I have chores to do."

"I won't run from a fight, and I don't need you to fight for me," said Pete Zizelman. "I'll protect my own family."

Mr. Altman lifted his coat and hat off the peg where he had hung them.

"Wait a bit, Altman," Papa urged. "Don't be too hasty.

"Friends," Papa addressed the assemblage, "I, for one, don't have time to hunt for wolves or dogs or bogeys. Neither can I afford losses. For the last two years, Altman has done a great deal of work for me. I know him to be reliable and honest and competent. If he says he can do the job, I say, let him traipse around in the snow and cold and hunt this thing. We'll guard our homes and protect our families and livestock. I don't think anyone should consider that cowardly. I would say it is a wise plan."

Once Papa put it that way, it appealed to the majority of the men.

"Altman, what do you figure on charging us?" asked Zizelman.

"A week's wages. Five dollars."

"Do you think it will take you that long?" asked McMillen.

"I'm risking my life," said Altman, "and my life is worth more than five dollars to me. Furthermore, you can divide my fee among all of you."

"That's fair."

"Well, I didn't have much of a crop last fall and I don't have as many animals as some of you do, so I shouldn't have to chip in as much as Silas should," Hiram McMillen said. "Or none at all."

He turned to Altman. "Can't you hunt it out of neighborliness? The Good Book says, 'Love your neighbor.' Here's your opportunity."

Altman laughed. "McMillen, the Bible also says, 'A workman is worthy of his hire.' If you want to hire me at my price, which is a reasonable one, do so. If not, don't. I'm not a beggar. I earn my keep."

The discussion was brought to a rapid conclusion when they heard the creaking of Ed Moeller's farm wagon as it pulled into the yard and parked close to the kitchen door.

Moeller didn't knock or come in the kitchen. Instead, he opened the door and stood in the doorway, briefly listening to the arguments.

He broke in. "Wanna see the work of this monster? Come look in my wagon."

Leaving their coats and hats, the men filed outside. In the back of his wagon lay a mutilated dog.

McMillen broke the silence. "We got to do something. And quick. How soon can you go after that beast, Altman?"

"I could start tonight," said Altman, "while all of you are safely in your beds asleep. And for heaven's sake, keep your livestock and children inside."

CHAPTER 5

For the remainder of the day, Papa, Grandpa, and Mr. Altman chopped firewood from timbers stretching along Yankee Run, the little clear water creek meandering through miles of fields and trees on its way to join the St. Marys River. The timbers were part of the vast woodland that still covered much of the Ohio countryside.

Some twenty-five years earlier, Papa and his first wife, Ellen Coppess Burger, built a log cabin in those woods bordering the creek. Moving west from hilly Pennsylvania, they were impressed by how flat the land was. Thinking it would be easier to farm, they purchased eighty acres of mostly clay-laden swampland covered by giant trees with impressive circumferences and growing so close together in some places, it was impossible for a man to walk between them. Where there weren't clay beds, the soil was rich and productive.

Trees were felled, scrappy pines and cedars burned outright. Hardwoods, such as walnut, chestnut, and hickory were cut, sold, and floated down the waterways, destined to decorate mansions for wealthy easterners. The rest was chopped, split, and made into firewood. Every cleared half acre begged to have tree roots grubbed out, swampland drained, and planted with wheat or corn.

Silas added livestock until he had a fine herd of dairy cattle. He built the first section of the barn up near the road almost three-quarters of a mile from the cabin. The cabin site was chosen because it was close to the water from Yankee Run. Silas discovered it was too far back in the trees to sell milk.

While Ellen and their growing family stayed in the cabin, Silas lived in the barn, sleeping there at night to protect his precious cows. He had plans to eventually build a house by the barn, but there just weren't enough hours in a day to get it all done.

His wife bore him three sons. One died at birth and was buried, unnamed, with only a wooden cross for a marker. The other two boys, Silas Jr. and Coppess, looked like promising farmhands to their father.

Ellen didn't live to see her boys plow the sod or milk cows. She died of "milk fever" and was buried next to her anonymous newborn son.

Ellen's death left Silas in a predicament. He couldn't have two little boys sleeping in the barn and he couldn't leave them back in the woods by themselves.

Kindly neighbors, the Knapps, living on the next farm west had two daughters, Margaret and Cora, who cared for Silas's little boys in their home.

Cora was the oldest. She had beautiful dark hair but was quiet and plain with a hint of a mustache.

Margaret was younger, red-headed, spunky, and energetic. Young men all over the county watched this pretty girl with interest while largely ignoring Cora.

Marrying Margaret Knapp became something of a horse race. To compete with a wealthy man who had a lovely home, Silas hurriedly built a new clapboard house behind the barn.

Silas's own considerable charm or Margaret's love for the two motherless boys, or some combination of those factors, convinced her she should become Mrs. Burger.

She might have chosen differently if she had known Silas's secret: He was a mean drunk.

With her parents living just a mile down the road, the first time Silas hit Margaret, she took his two boys and went home. When Silas sobered up, he discovered Margaret was not as willing to overlook his occasional sprees as Ellen had been. She refused to go home with him or let him have Silas Junior or Coppess unless he proved he was sober and would stay that way. He spent every evening for the next six months at her parents' house proving he could stay sober.

For the next nineteen years, the log cabin stood lonely and abandoned beside Yankee Run with only two graves for companionship. When Bear Altman showed up looking for work, he preferred the solitary little shack to sleeping in the loft of the barn.

Although Pa and Mr. Altman had come up to the house to a hearty lunch, Eliza knew working in the timber stimulates a man's appetite. About three in the afternoon, Eliza and Cora bundled up and took a hot snack of freshly baked rolls, cookies, fried ham, macaroni and cheese, and a stone jug of hot coffee back to the men.

Mr. Altman has done a good job fixing up the old cabin, Eliza thought as she stirred up the ashes in the cabin's stone fireplace to warm the food and coffee. *It's snugger than our house.*

Stomping the snow off their boots on the porch, the men came inside the cabin to eat. With ravenous appetites, they fell upon the snack. While waiting on the men to finish eating, Eliza studied the snowy woods through the cabin's one window. She noticed a large pile of trimmed logs and recognized by the bark that they were oaks which Papa used to frame out buildings.

"Papa, what are you planning to build?" Eliza asked.

"What makes you think I'm planning to build something, little girl?" Papa asked, his mouth full of ham.

"The oak logs, Papa. I know why you cut oak."

Silas grunted. "I cut oak because there's money in them trees. I've been cutting oak out of these woods since before you were born. Nicely seasoned oak brings good money, and this is the time of year to cut it."

He shoveled in another mouthful. "This ham is good, if I have to say so myself. Come on, Altman. Back to work. Daylight is wasting."

As they left, Eliza glanced at him sharply. She knew Papa wasn't telling her the truth about selling the oak.

He's planning to put up a new building. I wonder why he won't say what it is.

She would have been shocked if she had known the truth.

CHAPTER 6

"You send your pa or one of the boys over if you need me," said Grandma.

She stood on the kitchen step, bundled against the gathering cold and anxious to get home before it got any darker. But her face was creased with concern for Eliza.

"I can spare Cora if need be. Lot of work here for just one girl."

"Ugah!" sounded ol' Lulu's horn.

"Come on, Esther!" shouted Grandpa from the Oldsmobile. "Junior and Coppess are going to be wanting their supper."

Junior and Coppess, Papa's sons by his first marriage, were now young men in their early twenties. They still lived with Grandpa and Grandma Knapp and did their farming. Papa would have liked to have the boys help him instead, but Papa was a difficult taskmaster, and they didn't get along with him.

Eliza stood in the kitchen, the air fragrant with laundry soap and fresh-from-the-oven bread and cookies. It was wonderful to have the laundry washed and the baking done for a few days at least. Now, she only had supper to fix, dishes to wash up, chickens to feed, and frozen laundry to bring in off the clothesline to be ironed on Tuesday.

Then the blessedness of bedtime.

Every task took longer to complete than she planned. It wasn't until a few minutes before ten o'clock she did a final check on the chicken house.

Carrying a shotgun as Papa dictated, along with a lantern, Eliza wearily trudged toward the coop.

Something isn't right.

By the lantern's flickering light, she saw the board blocking the ramp to the chicken yard was dislodged.

That's strange.

Cautiously, she opened the door of the coop a crack and peeked in. Eliza gasped. Bloody feathers and crushed eggs were scattered over the floor. Even with her limited vision she could see the coop was in total disarray.

She ran for the house. Papa was dozing by the stove.

"Papa! Something's been in the chickens!"

Papa pulled on his boots, grabbed his shotgun and followed her out to the coop.

In a hoarse whisper, he said, "I'm going to count to three and when I say, 'Now!' point the lantern into the coop. It may be that we can temporarily blind whatever is in there and I can get a shot off. Think you can do that?"

Eliza trembled as the memory flooded back of the Mahr. If a demon did this, a shotgun won't stop it.

Then another thought popped in her head: *Is God punishing me because I'm mad at Him?*

"Can you do that, daughter?" Papa's voice held an undertone of impatience.

"Yes, Papa," she whispered.

"One, two, three," he said softly.

Then he shouted, "Now!" Together they burst through the door. Eliza flashed the lantern. With one motion, Papa cocked the shotgun and sighted down the barrel.

The startled chickens panicked. Squawking and beating their wings, they flew upward, adding to the chaos of death inside the coop.

Holding the lantern aloft, Eliza and Papa surveyed the damage. Five hens were gone. Two more lay half eaten on the floor.

Papa took the lantern from Eliza and scouted around the outside of the coop.

Still trembling, Eliza stood in the dark coop and reflected on her losses. Not only had she lost hens but after a scare like this, she knew it would be several days before the remaining chickens would lay.

This was a financial loss for her and would be a hardship for the family. They counted on eggs as the basis for breakfast and some of their baking.

Papa, holding the lantern, stuck his head inside the coop. "Come here and look at this."

He held the lantern so she could see where the board had once been propped. Dark spots of blood lay on the glistening snow. There were several distinct sets of animal footprints.

Papa picked up the board and jammed it in place with his fist.

"It looks like the other attacks," he said soberly. "But it's strange a wild animal would enter a coop so close to the house. Whatever it is, it's getting comfortable and bold."

"Or hungry," added Eliza. "What should I do with the dead chickens?"

"Leave them until morning. Go back to the house and stay there but get your brothers out of bed. Tell them to bring lanterns and my coat and get out here. We'll check the rest of the livestock. Someone will have to go back to the woods to get Altman. He'll have a fresh trail to follow."

"Papa, I've got to clean up the mess in there."

"Not tonight. The mess will be there in the morning. I want you inside the house, so I won't have to worry about you or one of the little girls going outside or being attacked by whatever tore up the coop. It could still be out here, watching and waiting to finish off the rest of the chickens."

Eliza hadn't thought that far ahead. The beast could be watching them right now.

Eliza ran to the house. She was still trembling as she moved Betty over into the middle of the bed. Fully clothed, she laid down on top of the quilts.

Through the walls, she could hear Papa and the boys calling to one another as they searched through the farm buildings to verify the livestock was uninjured.

She heard Josh shout, "The pigs seem to be alright!"

"Oh, Mama. I'm sorry about your chickens," she whispered into the darkness. "I'm so sorry."

The idea Bear Altman was going to hunt down this creature and kill it pleased her. She wanted vengeance.

A chilling thought occurred to her. *Might the beast kill Bear instead?*

Chapter 7

As if in a dream, she heard someone come into the kitchen. She heard the scraping of two chairs on the floor as they sat at the table. She recognized Papa's voice and the rumbling baritone of Bear Altman. She knew she was expected to get up to see if they needed anything to eat, but she was tired from the day's work, and it was nice to get off her feet.

I'll get up in a moment …

It seemed like only a second later, the clock chimed four times, signaling the beginning of a new day. She realized she slept soundly all night. It was the first night since the killings started that she didn't have the nightmare.

Stiff from cold, she found herself on top of the quilts and still dressed.

The attack on the chicken coop seemed unreal, like a nightmare. And losing those hens made her feel like she'd failed her mother.

What will I find when I look in the chicken coop today?

She fervently hoped Mr. Altman found whatever it was and shot it dead.

She heard voices at the foot of the stairs and smelled a faint whiff of coffee. Eliza hurriedly washed, dressed, then came down the stairs to find Pa and Mr. Altman sitting at the kitchen table, each with a cup of coffee, discussing Mr. Altman's hunt of the night before.

"You got it then, Mr. Altman?" Eliza asked as she helped herself to the coffee.

"That I did, Miss Eliza. You'll find your chicken thief skinned, and her hide nailed to the side of the barn."

"A wolf?" asked Eliza.

He nodded.

"Only one?"

"No, it was a big female—the biggest I've ever seen—with pups. She had eight of them, almost big enough to start hunting on their own. It's no wonder she had to kill so often to feed them."

"What did you do with the pups, Mr. Altman?"

"Only what I had to do."

"You faced all of those animals at once? They didn't hurt you, did they?"

"No, ma'am, but thank you for inquiring."

Through his dark beard, Eliza caught a flash of white teeth she presumed was a smile.

His smile was a sight she was seeing more often. When he first knocked on their door, he was moody and withdrawn, hiding out in the little cabin, and refusing all invitations to join the family for meals or to sit in front of the stove and warm up. He said little in those early days. Eliza thought he was just shy and unaccustomed to being around people.

In the night, a southerly breeze had blown in a warm weather front.

When Eliza stepped out on the porch, she heard icicles crashing to the earth and melting snow sliding off the roofs of the house and outbuildings as the sun warmed the shakes.

How quickly everything changed! Yesterday, it had been winter with all its icy fury. Today, spring was in the air. Yesterday, the whole county was gripped with fear over a monster. Today, the monster's hide and that of her offspring was nailed to the barn wall and no longer a threat.

She glanced in the direction of the barn. It was too dark to see the skins.

I wonder what can be made from wolf pelts. Mama might have known, but Mr. Altman will know.

One of the harsh realities of farm life was some creatures had to die so others could live. The farm once belonged to the wolves, panthers, rattlesnakes, and other dangerous creatures. Now it belonged to chickens, cows, pigs, and people. Wolves had to die so other animals could live.

After breakfast, Papa and Mr. Altman drove the children to school on the buckboard, and then headed to town to deliver the milk to the cheese factory while spreading the good news of the successful hunt to the Stringtown farmers and collecting Bear Altman's wages.

They were home around noon. Eliza had made a pot of ham and bean soup with cornbread for lunch. As she ladled the soup into bowls, Eliza heard all about their morning.

"Can you believe that old skinflint McMillen? The rest of the farmers paid up and were glad to do it. They appreciate you got the wolf and her pups before there were any more killings. When I knocked on McMillen's door and told him it was time to pay up, he said he didn't owe anything because he hadn't agreed to your fee. Why, I believe he'd skin a flea for its hide."

Mr. Altman laughed. "Forget about it. No need to waste good energy on hard feelings, Silas. Old McMillen has to shave his own face every morning. As close as he cuts corners, maybe one of these days, he'll cut off his own nose."

As spring and warmer weather approached, Ruthie started talking about new summer dresses. In years gone by, Mama made each of the girls a new Sunday dress for Easter, which they wore all summer. Eliza knew only too well that she was not nearly the accomplished seamstress that her mother was, but she didn't want to see the girls disappointed. Furthermore, she thought it would be nice to have a new Easter dress too.

"Please, Papa. Oh, please," begged Ruthie and Betty. "Can't we have new Easter dresses?"

"No," said Papa, with a little more heat than was necessary. "We don't have the money."

"But Papa, my everyday dress is too small for me. It pinches under my arms. See?" Ruthie lifted her arms to show her sleeves cutting under her arms.

"It's so tight I can't put my arms up. And my Sunday dress is the same. I can pass them down to Betty, and then she'll have dresses. Eliza can wear Mama's clothes, but Eliza's hand-me-down will be too big for me. But I'll save them until I can fit them. Don't you see, Papa? You'll save money because you'll only have to buy two new dresses just for me."

"Ruthie!" Eliza scolded. "How can you be so thoughtless and selfish? Betty and I need new clothing too. Your everyday dress is scarcely more than a rag. And you burnt a hole in your Sunday dress. You can't be serious that you are the only one who needs new clothing. And what about John and Josh? They are growing so fast I can scarcely keep them in food. They're going to need new clothing too."

Papa grudgingly gave in. "Eliza, you can come into town with me in the morning to pick out fabric when I take the milk to the dairy."

That night, Eliza was so excited she barely slept at all. Not only were there no monsters in her dreams, but she hadn't been to Rockford since Mama's funeral, or anywhere for that matter. Only occasionally, when she could get everyone to cooperate, did they go to church.

Papa drove to town daily to deliver milk to the cheese factory. He thought someone should always stay with the farm to watch the stoves and care for the livestock. Because the boys were in school, usually, that person was Eliza. But with more and more signs of spring, Eliza was restless to go somewhere, anywhere. Traveling to Rockford to buy fabric seemed a golden adventure. Since Aunt Cora was there to help for several days, it seemed a good opportunity to slip out of the harness and go into town.

While some of the students dropped out of school after eighth grade, many of her classmates who graduated from the one-room schoolhouse attended high school in Rockford. She had barely seen any of them except at church since Mama died and her Papa pulled her out of school.

Just in case she ran into some of them, Glen Franklin in particular, she wanted to look good. Eliza arranged her hair with more care than usual and put on her Sunday dress for the trip. She hadn't worn it much since Mama's funeral. She was dismayed to discover it was almost too short. Maybe she could add a ruffle on the hem.

Even to her own eyes, her image in the mirror looked young, girlish and a little faded. Her green eyes seemed too large for her thin, heart-shaped face. She pinched her cheeks and bit her lips trying to bring back a little color. She wanted to look mature, so she composed her face to look serious and older, but she thought she looked silly, like a child trying to be an adult.

She had only one piece of jewelry: Mama's gold watch. It hung on a black velvet ribbon and had an intricate design engraved on the back. Eliza tied it around her neck and tucked it inside her dress. Just having it close to her gave her courage and hope.

It felt strange to have Cora take total charge of the kitchen for breakfast. Odder still to walk out of the kitchen, leaving work undone, and climb on the wagon full of milk for the cheese factory. But Eliza enjoyed the novelty of it.

The children clambered into the wagon. The roads were muddy and almost impassable, so Papa would drop them off at school on their way into town. For a moment, it seemed like the old days when Mama was still alive, and every day was an adventure instead of a drudgery.

Eliza was surprised to see hilltops and ditches blushed with green. Tiny leaves were budding out on the ends of the twigs. Although the spring breezes were chilly, contradicting the bright morning sunshine, Eliza was joyful as she arranged the wool blanket around her legs and feet.

Rockford was a three-mile drive from the Burger farm; however, it took the fully loaded wagon almost an hour to navigate the thawing roads and ruts. As they got closer to town, Eliza saw more wagons and people, but the most amazing sight was the automobiles. Eliza had heard Papa say that there were lots more horseless carriages now, but she could scarcely believe how many. Fortunately, Papa's team of horses were accustomed to the popping and coughing engines, but Eliza saw some drivers struggling to keep their horses from bolting and running away from the strange automobile sounds.

As they arrived in Rockford, she was amazed to see so many electric lights. Nearly all the stores had a brightly burning bulb hanging down on a wire from the ceiling. Eliza had seen electric lights before, but she was always fascinated and a little fearful of them.

What will they think of next? I don't think I'll ever get used to these newfangled inventions.

Papa pulled up to the hitching post across the street from the dry goods store. He helped her down from the wagon. Reluctantly, he reached in his pocket and gave her five quarters—$1.25.

"This is what I always gave your mother. You need to get your thread, buttons and notions out of this too."

Eliza didn't believe him. She knew Mama wheedled more money out of him and she intended to do the same.

"I don't know how much the piece goods is going to cost. And since everyone has grown this year, it's going to take more fabric and thus more money," she reminded him, still holding out her hand. "Last year, Mama said percale was nineteen cents a yard and cotton was nine cents a yard. A dollar and a quarter won't come near to dressing us all."

She smiled up at him, her hand still open.

Papa grumbled under his breath. He dug in his pocket until he found his wallet. Eliza caught a glimpse of more than a few paper dollars and some coins in it. He selected two more dollar bills and laid them on Eliza's hand. She quickly put the money in her pocket before he changed his mind.

"Don't worry, Papa. I'll give you back any change, but don't expect much. Besides, I have a little money of my own. John and Josh have been selling our extra eggs to Charley at the store, and I think I can make the money stretch. That's what Mama did too."

He narrowed his eyes. "How much money do you got?"

"I'm not telling. Just a little bit for some sweets for the girls and …" she continued playfully, "if you're good, I'll give you a sweet, too."

Papa snorted as if receiving a piece of candy was beneath his dignity, but a flash of a smile showed through his beard. "You women are beyond figuring. Always full of surprises. You be careful, now. There have been some rowdy types hanging around Little Oklahoma of late. They come into town during the day and some of the ladies have been bothered by them."

He crawled into the wagon. "I'll be back in about an hour. Don't make me wait." He slapped the reins. "Get up!"

As Eliza watched him drive off, she realized that she was alone in town without any family. This was a new experience for her.

Rockford was crowded, bustling with horses, wagons, automobiles, and people. Papa's mention of Little Oklahoma revived her curiosity about the place the preacher called "a den of sin." She looked north, past the stores in Rockford's downtown to a brightly painted building. Supported by pylons, it stood on a muddy island in the St. Marys River channel. It was a law unto itself.

What went on in Little Oklahoma was something preachers railed against without naming the sin, adults spoke of in whispers, and a mystery schoolchildren tried to solve. Little Oklahoma was quiet just then, but with nearly three dollars in her pocket, she resolved to be wary. What she really wanted to do was go down there and look in the windows to see what was so bad.

People said "wild things" happened there. Eliza and her classmates discussed this at length. Since none of them had any knowledge of the seamier side of life, they had nothing to give substance to their imagining.

Papa and Mama knew. They made the children—including Eliza—cover their eyes when they drove the wagon past Little Oklahoma. Covering her eyes didn't block out the loud music, laughter, and shouting. Eliza stole a few peeks between her fingers but saw nothing to explain what wild things were.

There was so much to see that Eliza found it hard to keep an eye on the traffic as she crossed the brick-lined street. Modestly hiking her skirt up to keep it out of the mud, she stepped off the boardwalk and onto the street. In low spots, tired skiffs of ice lay on grimy puddles. Wagons and autos splashed through them, flinging freezing dirty water onto pedestrians.

A bell tingled announcing her entry to the dry goods store. The candy stall stood at the front greeting customers with temptation. Behind shining panes of glass were luscious-looking confections. Brightly colored jellybeans, licorice whips and buttons, all manner of chocolates, saltwater taffy, packs of chewing gum, NECCO wafers, peppermint disks, caramels, and more—all competed for attention and money. Eliza was captivated by the sight. In the past, Mama always hurried her past the candy to the fabric at the back of the store. With no Mama there to rush her, she wanted to stare at the candies all day and sniff the sweet flavors emanating from them.

Her candy worship was interrupted by a squawky male voice. "Eliza! Is it really you?"

Eliza reluctantly tore her eyes away from the candy. When she looked up, her heart skipped a beat. The one person she hoped to see in town—Glen Franklin—stood beside her.

Glenn was a few years older, and he had matured considerably since the last time she saw him. His complexion had cleared up. He looked less like an awkward kid and more like a man. He even had a start of a mustache.

"Oh, Glen! How nice to see you! When did you begin working here?"

"At Christmas and I've been here ever since. My pa said we needed the money. It's good to see you, too, Eliza!"

"Did you get your diploma?"

"No, but I'm going to. Look," he said, showing her some books under the counter. "I study when I don't have customers. At night too. I'm going to take a special test and get my diploma and then …" He paused and glanced around to make certain no one overheard. "If you promise not to tell, I'll let you in on a secret."

Eliza leaned inward over the jaw breakers. "Of course, I'll keep your secret."

"I'm going to join the army. I think America is going to war against the Hun and I want to fight."

"Oh, no, Glen. America doesn't stick her nose in other countries' affairs. I hear the army is a fine place for young men, but we won't go to war in Germany. That Pancho Villa thing in Mexico is different because he's directly attacking us, but Germany can't get to us. President Wilson will keep us out of it. Besides, I don't think American boys would fight against their German cousins." At least that's what Papa told us.

"You haven't been reading the papers out there in the country, have you?"

"No, not much. Papa sometimes reads them to us. I only hear what he says."

"I'll tell you something, Eliza, I have been following this thing closely and we are going to war with the ol' kaiser. If we don't, I'm going to join the French Foreign Legion and see the world. I'm not going to be stuck in Rockford all my life."

"But," he said, lowering his voice, "don't tell my pa. He thinks I'm nothing but a workhorse. He doesn't care that I don't want to farm, and I sure don't want to pass my life selling sweets and buttons."

Eliza nodded. She understood what Glen was saying.

"I thought you were going to see the world as a railroad engineer. Remember?"

They both laughed at the memory.

He blushed a little. "So, you remember that. Well, yes, I thought I would see the world that way, but it's too limiting for me. As an engineer, all I would see is the same ol' train track day in and day out. I want more."

Eliza was captivated by Glen's spirit of adventure. Maybe someday, he would ask her to see the world with him and she would tell him "Yes!"

"What are you doing since you quit school?"

"Speaking of being a workhorse, I am taking care of my family. You knew my mama died?"

He nodded. "I'm real sorry about that."

"I just cook and clean and wash and mend, day in and day out. That's all I do. My Papa took me out of school and so I'm trapped. But since you told me your secret, I'll tell you mine. I want to go back to school and get my diploma too."

He studied her quizzically. "Why? What do you need with a diploma? Women don't need a diploma to keep house. Or do you just want to get off the farm? Maybe teach?"

"I want to get off the farm, that's for sure. But I also want to go to nurses' training. I want to be a nurse."

For a moment, he regarded her with surprise. Then he had a flash of understanding.

"You know something, Eliza, I think you would make a terrific nurse! I remember the time Bertha Lewis fell off the schoolhouse roof and cracked her head open. You did a better job of taking care of her than ol' Miss Bush did. She went all to pieces, but you kept your wits about you and were calm. And Bertha was a mess. Blood everywhere but you didn't panic. You just patched her up until Doc Jackson got there and took over."

"You know, Bertha was in here the other day, acting all snooty like she didn't even know me."

"Must have been that crack on her head that made her forget you."

They both laughed.

It is so good to talk to someone near my own age. I knew I missed it, but I didn't know how much.

"Look here, Eliza. You can go down to the high school and rent books like I did. You can study at home, take a test, and if you pass, get your diploma. And then, if you can scrape together some money, maybe you can go to nurses' college. But you have to get your high school diploma first, right?"

"Oh, Glen! That would be a dream come true!"

Nurses' college was a long way off, but she remembered a verse from Proverbs Miss Bush made them copy over and over again on their slates when Eliza was but a pig-tailed girl in second grade: "Ponder the path of thy feet and let all thy ways be established. Turn not to the right hand nor to the left."

She thought long and hard about being a nurse, questioning whether it was the right path for her. She was sure it was. She wouldn't allow herself to be turned to the right or the left. A step forward on that path would be to get her high school diploma.

"Glen, you are one smart candy-and-button salesman! I'll do it! I've got to convince Papa to allow me, but I will take one step at a time.

She smiled up at him.

For a long moment, Glen looked into her eyes.

He might kiss me. Eliza felt weak in the knees.

"Now, would you like to sell me some fabric and some candy?"

He offered her his arm. "M'lady, it would be an honor to show you our wide selection of quality fabrics and notions."

Eliza laughed and slipped her arm in his.

Glen was surprisingly knowledgeable about fabrics and notions. He knew which buttons and ribbons went well with various clothing designs and the latest patterns. Under his expert guidance, she bought enough material for one new dress each for herself and the girls and a new shirt apiece for Pa, John and Josh. He even pointed out the spring gingham prints that were marked down from seven cents to six cents per yard, so she bought some of those too. Finally, she picked out a sack of candy for the girls, John, and Josh, then paid for it all and had a little money to spare.

Time flew by, and when she glanced at Mama's little clock around her neck, she realized that Pa would be back in less than ten minutes.

"Eliza, you can stay here and talk to me. Or if my employer will allow me, I'd be happy to escort you outside to see the sights until your father returns. There're some bad sorts in town now and again. I really don't think it's safe for you to walk around without a man to keep you company." His dark eyes searched hers for encouragement.

The store suddenly seemed very hot. Eliza realized Glen no longer considered her solely a schoolmate but as a woman. The thought made her blush.

"Oh, Glen, do you think he would let you? I don't want to get you into trouble or cost you your job. May I leave my purchases here until Papa comes for me?"

"Of course, Eliza. Leave your packages here and I'll go ask him now."

Eliza stepped out onto the sidewalk while Glen talked with his boss. It was the first time she could remember a man treating her as a woman rather than a girl. Because that man was Glen, the knowledge was intimidating and exciting all at the same time.

As she waited, a stylishly dressed group of men came up the sidewalk. They wore brightly colored derbies with garters on their sleeves. Although it was chilly, they were coatless. As they approached, Eliza shrunk back against the building and tried to disappear. As they passed by, they raised their derbies to her and continued on their way. She heard one of them say, "That little redheaded gal back there would be a nice piece of merchandise."

Eliza didn't know what he meant. She wondered who she could ask.

"Eliza Burger!"

She startled. At first, she didn't see who called her name. Then she saw Dr. Jackson coming out of the pharmacy. His handsome face lit up with a smile as he approached her. He tipped his hat to her as he came up the walk. As always, in spite of the mud everywhere, his black suit was impeccable and his shirt so snowy it made Eliza feel shoddy and ill-kept.

"Hello, Dr. Jackson."

"What brings you to town today, Miss Eliza?"

"I've been shopping for fabric to make Easter dresses." She grinned. "I'm planning to go to the high school and rent books so I can earn my diploma."

"Most admirable! By the way, Miss Eliza, I was planning to stop by your house sometime on one of my rounds, but since here you are, I'll ask you now. Would you be interested in a position here in town that would allow you to attend school, have a place to stay, and a little spending money on top? I remember how competent you were during your mother's illness, and I've been looking for a young woman who might serve as a companion to my wife and help out in the office in exchange for room and board and a salary."

Eliza's heart almost stopped.

That would be perfect! But what about my family? If I don't take care of them, who will? I doubt Papa would let me consider it.

Eliza swallowed hard. "Thank you for the offer, Dr. Jackson. I would love a position like that, but I have so many family responsibilities that there is no way possible I can leave home."

"Of course. Of course. Such a shame about your mother. She was a good woman. But I thought your father …" Dr. Jackson stopped in mid-sentence. He was about to say something more but changed his mind.

"Well, never mind, my dear. However, if your situation changes, and I still haven't found anyone, would you consider it?"

"Oh, I would! But honestly, Doctor, I don't think there is much of a chance of that."

"One never knows, Miss Eliza. Tell me why a pretty girl like you wants a diploma?"

Eliza blushed. It was almost too revealing for her to tell two people her secret the same day.

"I would like to go to Ft. Wayne to nurses' college. My father does not approve and will not support me, but I very much want to go. I know I will need a diploma for admission, so I'm letting my way be established."

Dr. Jackson laughed, but not unkindly. "That's a very noble way to put it, Miss Eliza, and I salute you for your efforts. I hope someday you'll achieve your dream and come back to Rockford to be my nurse."

His eyes traveled down the street to her father's approaching team.

"There's your father now. Who knows? Perhaps your situation will change sooner than you guess. Good luck to you and do remember my offer if something should change." The doctor bowed slightly.

"Don't wait on me, Doctor. Nothing much is likely to change for me," she said as she stepped back into the dry goods store to collect her purchases.

As she prepared to climb into the wagon, Glen pulled her aside.

"Eliza, I need to ask you an important question. If I go away to fight, will you write me?"

"Of course, Glen, if you want me to. Why wouldn't I? But I hope war is a long way away."

"Maybe not as far off as people think. But if I go, I'd very much like to hear from you. You won't forget me, will you?"

"No, Glen. How could I?"

Glen helped her up on the wagon. "Goodbye for now, Eliza."

"What did that skinny weakling want?" Pa demanded as soon as they were out of earshot. "He isn't asking to come courting, is he?"

Eliza laughed. "No, Pa. He's a schoolmate of mine. He was asking me to keep in touch. If he asked to come calling, you would let him, wouldn't you?"

"No! Forget about him! He isn't the right kind of man for you."

He's just the right kind of man for me!

It took some wheedling to convince Papa to stop at the high school so Eliza could rent some books. He thought the whole business was foolishness, but after a few pieces of candy, he pulled the team up to the high school and waited impatiently in the wagon while Eliza ran to the principal's office.

Before Papa took her out of school, Eliza heard Principal Cook address the subject of students requesting to finish their high school education at home. In the chaos around Mama's death, she had forgotten about it until Glen mentioned it to her.

Eliza knocked on the principal's door.

"Enter!" he gruffly called out.

"Mr. Cook, I want to go to nurses' college and become a registered nurse. But first I need a high school diploma. I've been told I can borrow books, study at home, take a test, and get a diploma. Is that true?" She held her breath as she awaited his reply.

What if Mr. Cook only let boys borrow books? Then what?

"Young woman, I do not know your character. Why should I loan books to you? Schoolbooks are very expensive to replace. The books I have here are used, thus I cannot ask the entire purchase price for them. Neither can I loan them out without assurance that they will be returned in the same shape as you see them now or you will have to replace them. I need that assurance. What can you offer?"

Eliza's fabric and candy purchases left her only eighteen cents in her pocket. She wasn't sure what schoolbooks cost to rent, but she was certain it was far more than eighteen cents.

Disappointed, she looked down. Through the fabric of her dress, she caught a gleam from her mother's watch. She slid it off her neck and quietly laid it on the principal's desk. "It was my mother's. It's gold."

Mr. Cook picked up the watch and silently studied it. "You must want an education very much."

"Oh yes, sir, I do!"

Mr. Cook turned the watch over in his hand as if weighing it. He vaguely remembered reading the obituary of a Burger woman who passed away. He remembered that one of her children had been forced to drop out of high school. Perhaps this was she.

He swallowed hard and shook himself back to his professional demeanor.

"Well, then, Miss Burger, shall we write out a contract between us? I will hold your mother's watch in my desk. In exchange, you may borrow and return books. When you return the books in good repair, you will then take the proficiency test. When—and if—you pass and I hand you your diploma, I shall also return your mother's watch. How will that be?"

"That will be wonderful, Mr. Cook!"

He questioned her as to her last completed level in school, then dispatched his secretary to fetch the appropriate books while he wrote out an agreement between the two of them. He signed it, as did Eliza. Then he turned the paper over to her.

"There you are, Miss Burger. You keep the paper. I'll keep the watch."

"Oh, thank you, Mr. Cook! You don't know what this means to me. I…"

"That'll do, Miss Burger."

Abashed but excited, she left the principal's office with an armful of books.

Although she had been inside no more than fifteen minutes, Papa was in a foul humor over the wasted time.

"I don't have time to fritter away my day while you have tea with some dandified schoolteacher. I've got a farm to run, and you've got clothing to make. I don't know why you think you need them books anyway. Don't you have enough to do? If you got time on your hands, you could come out and help with the chores rather than waste your time learning stuff dead people did."

"Yes, Papa." She settled down to read in the back of the wagon next to her fabric purchases while Papa grumbled under his breath as he drove the team home. She occasionally glanced up at her father, his back stiff with disapproval, as the wagon lurched toward the farm.

What roadblocks will Papa throw my way? I can already see him planning to sabotage my efforts. I'll have to keep my books out of his way. Otherwise, he might start a fire with them.

CHAPTER 8

It was a cold Monday morning in mid-April when Eliza saw the blue and purple heads of Mama's crocuses poking through the ice around the foot of the rain barrel.

She poured a kettle of boiling water on the thick cake of ice at the top of the barrel and let it melt a bit before she hacked out ice chunks. Rain, snow, and runoff from the roof kept the barrel full of water for laundry and was exactly what she needed to wash the printed flour sacks she had been saving all winter.

The wash boiler had just begun to steam when Cora and Grandma Knapp's wagon pulled into the yard.

"We're here!" Grandma announced as she and Cora burst through the door. As always, they came laden with baskets full of cookies, treats, interesting little tidbits, and gossip.

They brought the flour sacks they saved all winter.

The women heaped the flour sacks in the middle of the kitchen table. Some of the sacks were bright and pretty, lavishly decorated with flowers, others were rather plain, but every scrap was usable if they could get the advertising printing out without wrecking the fabric. Even if the ink didn't come out, the fabric could be made into underwear or bloomers, or used as a towel.

"I thought maybe we could do some swapping around for prints that match. We might end up with enough of a few designs to make everyday dresses for the little girls." Grandma said.

Settling into chairs around the table, they turned the sacks inside out, pulled out the stitches, shook out every bit of embedded flour they could, then deposited them in the copper wash boiler.

Eliza added some softened soap, borax, and powdered bleach to the simmering wash water, then stirred the sacks with the wooden paddle. When she judged a piece of fabric to be clean and the lettering washed out, she lifted it into another simmering tub—this one containing some vinegar to neutralize the soap. The piece of fabric got its final rinse in a tub of ice, which cooled the flour sacks enough to be wrung out and hung on the clothesline.

When the last of the sacks were merrily boiling, Eliza poured each of them a cup of hot coffee, added a thick dollop of cream, and placed them beside Grandma, Cora, and herself.

"Did you see I brought you the newspaper, Eliza?" Grandma asked.

"Yes, thank you. I look forward to reading it."

"Well, there's a story in there about the sinking of a big ship—the Lusitania. Just a terrible thing! All those lives lost! Germany is going to have to answer for their actions."

Eliza immediately thought of Glen.

I hope I see him again before he goes off to fight.

"There's another bit in there you must read. It's a write-up about education for women. They had a doin's at the school in Rockford. County teachers put it on."

"What does it say, Grandma?"

Eliza wanted to know anything that was going on at school. It made her feel a little bit more like she belonged.

Grandma smiled. "I was hoping you'd ask. Cora, hand me my glasses."

Grandma rattled through the pages until she found the article. "Here 'tis."

First, Grandma read aloud an account of a sewing demonstration by Miss Crockett, teacher of domestic science, and her pupils. When she finished that section, Grandma cleared her throat. "Now here's the part I want you to hear."

Mrs. Geachie then delivered an address which should have been heard by every girl and her mother as well. She had for her subject "Home Making."

"There are two words in the English language which cannot be dissociated," said Mrs. Geachie. "Those are home and woman. Wherever there is a true home, a woman's hands and brain have made it such. Since homemaking is the prime vocation of womanhood, the girl should early be taught the proper way to cook, bake, wash, and mend. The kindergarten age is none too young to begin this training; sixteen is too late. Eighty-five percent of divorces are caused by poor cooking."

"I can cook!"

"I know you can, dear, and you're getting better at it, too. I just wanted to remind you of what is important. Don't fret about not going to school. As you can see, even the teachers would tell you that learning to keep a home is more important than the other subjects. You can learn everything you need to know to lead a happy life right here at home. I'm here to help you and Cora is too. Knowing science and arithmetic and history are fine as far as they can take you, but cooking and cleaning and sewing, now they are what's going to make your future husband happy and your life too." Grandma slapped her palm upon the tabletop to emphasize the point. The coffee cups jumped and slopped over.

Eliza was stunned and hurt. She never felt more alone. She assumed Grandma and Cora were in league with her and her plans. Now she knew better.

"Excuse me," she murmured. "I need to check on the chickens."

She slipped into her coat and stepped out the door. Once outside, she ran full tilt into the chicken house, startling the hens into wildly flying about. She threw herself onto a bale of hay and wept with abandon.

Nothing in my life will ever be right now that Mama's gone. Why, God, didn't You let her live?

At this moment, Eliza wished she could march into God's heavenly throne room and have it out with Him.

How dare He sit up there and make decisions without regard to the plans of others! Just because He was all powerful didn't mean He could mess up everyone's lives and then have the audacity to expect people to worship Him!

Eliza was startled by a creak of the chicken house door. Bear Altman's shaggy head ducked under the frame as he surveyed into the interior.

Eliza stared up at him, her face streaked with tears.

"Everything all right, Miss Burger? We saw you running across the yard and your pa sent me to check."

"Everything's fine. Please tell him I'm fine." She turned her face away, hoping he hadn't seen her tears.

"I can't do that, Miss Burger," he said softly, his low voice rumbling.

"Why not?"

"Because it would be a lie. You're not all right." He moved a straw bale a respectful distance from her and sat on it, his large hands resting lightly on his knees. "Can I help?"

"How could you help? Nobody can help!"

"You're probably right." He stood, his hands traveling up his thighs and resting on his hips. He looked at her until, against her will, her eyes were forced to meet his.

They glared at each another for a moment. Suddenly Eliza smiled. "I'm sorry, Mr. Altman. You did not deserve that, and I apologize."

"Apology accepted. I, on the other hand, did not intend to pry. I want you to know that I wish you well and I would be honored to have you consider me a friend."

Eliza was a bit taken back. "That's very kind of you, Mr. Altman. I am unaccustomed to such generous offers."

"The pleasure, I assure you, would be all mine. Let me speak frankly, Miss Burger. I can't help but notice that you have a fine, questioning mind, and I've seen the schoolbooks you brought home. With proper education, you could accomplish as much as any man. I also realize that you have very heavy responsibilities for one so young. Life must be difficult for you just now."

"Why, yes, it is. How did you guess?"

Mr. Altman's smile, all but invisible through his heavy black beard, showed in his eyes.

"I try to pay attention to what is going on around me, Miss Burger. Now, I have a suggestion and an offer. Will you hear them?"

Eliza nodded.

"I know you have very little time to study. After supper, you have sewing, mending, and various chores. Would it help you to have someone read out loud your textbooks while you continue your work? Someone with whom you could discuss the lessons? A private tutor if you will."

His dark eyes searched her face as she thought this through.

"That would be wonderful! But who would do something like that for me?"

Mr. Altman modestly bowed his head.

"You can read? I mean…" she stammered. "What sort of education …"

He laughed ruefully. "Please give me a little credit, Miss Burger. I'm not entirely illiterate."

"I didn't mean to imply that," she said with false indignation to cover up her slip of the tongue.

"I think the truth is you didn't intend to say it out loud, but you certainly thought it. Let's be honest with one another. Hitherto, you have considered me the big, hairy lout who helps your father with the cows and pigs, causing you more cooking and cleaning, and carves funny little wooden things because he has nothing better to do. Right?"

She felt her cheeks redden as she glanced around the coop, searching for something to relieve her embarrassment. "Well, I … What do I have to lose? Let's give it a try."

"We may not get a great deal done every evening, but each little bit will help you toward your goal and eventually you'll make it."

"Turn not to the right hand nor to the left."

"Ah! A verse from Proverbs. So right, Miss Burger. We'll stay on the path at all times. And before you know it, you'll have your diploma and be further down the road."

"Nurses' college," she blurted out. "I want to be a nurse. I don't want to work like a draft horse day in and day out. I want to be in town and clean and be where there are other people to talk to. You know, boys and girls my own age. I like taking care of the sick. I think I'm good at helping people get well."

"I believe that. You are very attentive to the needs of others. But a nurse's job is difficult and dangerous and not nearly as clean as you think."

"You sound just like Papa!"

"Has your Pa volunteered to help you with your studies?"

"No. He thinks being a nurse is an awful occupation for a woman." She lowered her voice, "He thinks it's only for bad girls."

"I guess I don't agree with your pa on that point. Furthermore, I'm willing to help you study to become one. I know a little about science and medicine, and I even have some medical textbooks we can read. How would that be?"

Eliza could hardly believe her luck. She had schoolbooks plus access to medical texts, and someone to read them to her while she continued her work. It was almost too good to be true. It was as if everything was being planned by an Invisible Hand.

Eliza looked up at Mr. Altman. His disheveled black hair and beard had bits of straw in it from working in the barn, but his dark eyes were intelligent. He seemed eager to help her.

What if he can't read very well and stumbles over the bigger words? How will I tell him that it's not going to work without humiliating him? And what will Papa say if I spend evenings listening to Mr. Altman read? He might demand that I return the schoolbooks and spend every waking minute tending to the house and farm. It's a gamble but what do I have to lose?

Eliza realized Mr. Altman's offer could make her dreams come true—or kill them altogether.

CHAPTER 9

"Come on, Grandpa. I guess we better get home so I can start supper," Grandma said.

Cora stayed an extra day to help with stitching up the new clothing. Eliza was surprised to have Cora volunteer to remain to sew, especially since she knew Cora didn't particularly enjoy it.

Eliza nervously watched the door all through supper, but Bear Altman didn't appear. By the time the table was cleared, she almost convinced herself that he had forgotten and wasn't coming.

The women, along with Ruthie and Betty, finished the dishes while Pa lingered over his pie. "Tomorrow, I'm going to haul the oak logs Bear and I cut to the sawmill. I'm going to have them made into two by fours for the new house.

"New house? Who's getting a new house?"

"We are, Eliza."

"Why, Papa! You never mentioned a new house before. What made you decide to build?"

She remembered the oak timbers seasoning on the wood lot, but she thought they were for a farm building rather than a house.

He shrugged. "Just thought it might make life a little easier for you girls. With the kids growing up, we need a little more space, and I think you need a room of your own. I'm thinking four bedrooms upstairs, and one bedroom downstairs. A kitchen, of course, with a pitcher pump in the sink, and a dining room, and parlor."

"A water pump—inside. And a parlor!" Eliza was shocked but pleased. Every time she spilled cold water into her shoes when dragging in a heavy bucket from the outside pump, she dreamed of an indoor pump in the sink. It would be a thing of beauty to her. Mama always wanted a parlor to entertain company, but Pa had dismissed it as a "frill." Now the family was going to get one plus an indoor water pump.

"Pa, tell us more! Where are you going to put the new house?"

Even Aunt Cora appeared interested.

"Not so many questions! I'll show you tomorrow. In fact, I'll walk off the foundations so you can get an idea how spacious it will be. By the way, it will be a brick house, not clapboard. Not another word about it, now. The kids have studies."

Eliza was excited but she did as he asked and gave up questioning Papa. She knew he only told you what he wanted you to know and not one word more. But he had given her plenty to chew over and digest.

The boys carried a brightly burning caboose lantern to the table, and Ruthie joined them with her books too. It was the best light in the house and the one they used for their homework and Eliza used for sewing. She and Cora each took up a bit of sewing and pulled in close to the bright white light.

They had not sewn but a few stitches when a knock sounded at the kitchen door.

Papa opened it and admitted Bear Altman. He, too, had a caboose lantern in his hand.

"I mentioned to your Pa I was going to help you with your studies, Eliza, and he recommended that we go to the other side of the room where we will not disturb the others while they study. This lantern, I might mention, is a gift from your Pa. His contribution to your education." Altman nodded toward Papa who blushed a little.

First a new house and then a caboose lantern to use as a study light. I did not expect Papa to cooperate. He's full of surprises.

"Oh, Papa!" Eliza hugged him around the neck.

"Go on, now," he said gruffly. "I want to hear what them books say that's so interesting."

Papa and Mr. Altman moved extra chairs around behind the chimney to the far side of the downstairs into the area where Papa slept. Eliza and Cora put the lantern between them and Mr. Altman. They began to sew while he read aloud from the volume on American history.

Eliza was surprised and pleased to hear him read so well. His expressive baritone rumbled through the events of the Civil War States and made the narrative come to life. They all listened with rapt attention.

Small Betty, dressed for bed, brought her blanket in to be cuddled on Papa's lap. Even though she was tired, she struggled to stay awake, so she did not miss what happened next. Ruthie soon joined them, and then Josh and John. When they came to the review questions, everyone wanted to answer them.

"Eliza must answer these questions in order to pass the examination. We need to help her get them right," Mr. Altman insisted.

Papa agreed, and they all listened to Eliza's answers. Everyone ready to prompt her if she hesitated.

At 7:30, Papa carried the sleeping Betty up to bed. Aunt Cora trailed up behind him to make sure the little girl was tucked in properly. Usually, that was Eliza's responsibility, but Aunt Cora offered to do it so that Eliza could continue with her studies.

When Eliza sent Ruthie up to join her little sister, she resisted.

"Eliza, you come tuck me in and hear my prayers, please?" Ruthie begged.

"I'm studying with Mr. Altman just now, and I'm sewing your clothing. Go on, now. Aunt Cora is already upstairs. She said she'd tuck you in."

"I don't want Aunt Cora to tuck me in! Betty calls her 'Mama' and she doesn't correct her for that or nothing. She's not Mama!"

"Of course, she's not. She's not trying to be. Besides, Betty sometimes calls me Mama too. I don't fuss at her about it. If I did, it would just remind her that Mama is gone. Don't be so silly, now. Go to bed."

"Please, Eliza!" Ruthie begged. "Just because you have a beau doesn't mean you can't tuck me in."

Eliza blushed but was firm. "I don't have a beau. Go to bed!"

"You are a mean, mean person, Eliza Burger!" Ruthie stamped up the stairs.

"I'm sorry," Eliza apologized to Mr. Altman. "I don't know what gets into her. Aunt Cora is trying to help. I don't understand Ruthie at all."

"Really?" His eyebrows raised quizzically, his dark eyes piercing. "As someone who wishes to be a nurse, you may have to determine what is going on in a patient's mind as well as their body."

"Why would that be?"

"It is a strange thing about the human mind. No doctor in the world knows much about it, but most believe what the Bible says about the mind: 'As a man thinketh in his heart, so is he.' In other words, if a man thinks of himself as sick, he can truly make himself ill. Not all illness comes from the mind, of course, but sometimes to treat the body, you have to know what the mind is thinking. A proper diagnosis may depend upon it."

"So, what do you think Ruthie is thinking?"

"I think she misses her mother's attention, and you seem to be the one person in the world who is most like her. Therefore, she wants your attention. My guess is that she looks at Miss Knapp as an interloper and nothing at all like her mother."

"Well, that's true. Aunt Cora isn't much like Mama. She doesn't really look much like her, and Mama was…" Eliza searched for the right words. "Mama was lively. She laughed a lot and had a twinkle about her. Aunt Cora is a great help, but sometimes, I, too, wish she was a little more like Mama."

They stopped talking as they heard Aunt Cora coming down the stairs. She came in and picked up her sewing, her eyes troubled. Aunt Cora sat down with a sigh.

"Eliza, you better see to Ruthie. She says she's got a stomachache, but I don't think she's running a fever. She wouldn't let me hear her prayers either."

"Aunty," said Eliza, "it is good of you to stay and help with the sewing. You really have been wonderful to pitch in since Mama's gone. I don't know what I would have done without you."

Eliza gave Cora a warm hug. Cora brightened and smiled; her heavy face lifted. For a second, she was almost pretty. Eliza ran upstairs to tend to Ruthie,

In the morning, Silas took Eliza and Cora out to a section of field that stood between the chicken house and the road. Excited as a boy, he stepped off the dimensions of the new house. It would basically be a square two-story building with a single gable roof. There would be four rooms on the first floor and four on the second.

He pointed out the vein of clay stretching along the north fork of Yankee Run. While a bane in farming, it was perfect for making bricks. Papa said he'd hired a man and his boys to dig the clay, make the bricks, and fire them on the site. They would use some of the wood he had cut last winter for firing the bricks, augmented by a small natural gas deposit discovered on the farm.

The house was to be framed in oak, but the floors and wood-work would be made from imported yellow pine, a wood with almost no grain.

"It'll be a deluxe house. The nicest on Stringtown Road. You know how I feel: Nothing's too good for my girls."

"Papa, you've been planning this house for a long time. How come you never said anything?"

"You got your own dreams to fret over," he told her affection-ately. "I didn't want you to feel badly if mine didn't work out."

He mentioned that after he, the boys, and Bear Altman hauled the seasoned logs up from the woods, if the weather held, they'd get the joists and stringers cut and maybe part of the foundation dug before the week was up. It was a little too early and wet to be plowing or planting, so it was the perfect time.

"I've hired some neighbor boys to help out, so you and Cora will have a few more mouths to feed, probably beginning to-morrow." He pushed his hat back and stared at the sky for some indication of the next day's weather.

This is all happening very fast.

The weather held, and six strapping young men, along with Junior and Coppess, arrived at daybreak to begin digging and hauling foundation flagstone and logs, all from the banks of

Yankee Run. Eliza begged Cora to stay a few extra days and the two women cooked and baked on a grand scale to feed the hungry workers.

John and Josh dropped out of school for the remainder of the year to help with the new house and later with the plowing and planting. Ruthie and Betty pitched in, too, when they got back from their day in the classroom.

The next few weeks were the busiest Eliza had ever known. As the sunshine hours grew longer, and there were tender bits of green grass to peck at, the hens laid more eggs. However, some hens went broody, producing explosions of fluffy little yellow chicks.

The pigs farrowed successfully, except for one old sow who ate all but four of her piglets. Innocent of housebreaking and the rules of polite behavior, they were temporarily housed in a wooden box behind the kitchen cook stove and assigned to Eliza's list of responsibilities, adding an earthy quality to the aroma of cooking.

Cows began calving producing a flood of fresh milk to be separated. Even the cat showed up at the back door with a newborn kitten in her mouth, begging to share the warmth of the stove with the piglets.

Papa, Bear Altman, John, and Josh worked long hours turning up the fields. Because they were gone all day, the little eat-often baby animals scattered over the farm also became Eliza's to care for. Eliza felt she literally ran through the day, from one chore to the next.

One morning in mid-May, Papa stuck his head through the back door and announced he'd turned over the garden and that it was ready to plant. Eliza sat down at the kitchen table, held her head in her hands, and cried. If they planned to eat next winter, she knew she needed to make a garden.

In the loft, Eliza opened the cream can where Mama packed seeds she'd gathered from last year's garden. Wrapped in paper and labeled with Mama's neat handwriting were seeds for summer's bounty, autumn's harvest, and winter's groceries. She tearfully sorted through the packages, and for the first time in nearly six months, she prayed for strength.

In the bottom of the cream can, Eliza found six small books all with different dates, filled with Mama's script. She'd often seen her mother writing in them and wondered what they were all about.

Curious, Eliza opened one. It read, *'Tis early yet, Lord. My children and husband are asleep. Today I hold before Your throne this child who is yet unborn. You know this child and have planned every day of its life. If this child will not love and serve you, take it back to heaven before it has a chance to sin so that its soul might be saved.*

Eliza noted the date: Oct. 1, 1912. That was just before Betty's birthday. Mama was praying for baby Betty! A thrill of horror swept through Eliza. Mama wanted her children to love God so much she was willing for them to die as infants rather than grow up and go to hell. Eliza was stunned. She couldn't bear to read any more. She shut the little book, gathered up the notebook diaries, put them back in the cream can then replaced the lid.

Those books of Mama's would have to wait for another day to be read. Someday when Eliza could bear to see what Mama had prayed for her. She carried the cream can upstairs and hid it as far back into the eaves as she could.

Bear Altman was as good as his word about helping with Eliza's studies. He, too, was working long hours on the farm or on the new house. On the rare days Pa didn't need him, he hired himself out for other farmers needing help. But regardless of how tired he and Eliza were, by the light of the caboose lantern, they continuing to work their way through algebra, spelling, geography, English, and history, occasionally reading from some of his medical textbooks for variety. When the days lengthened and the light lingered, Eliza took her work outside and they continued studying in the cool of the evening.

Eliza was not the only one who benefited from the nightly reading sessions. All of the children's grades improved. When Mr. Altman's throat grew tired from reading, one of the boys would take over. Now Eliza was going to need the evenings to work the garden. She was disappointed to suspend her studies for the spring and summer, but she didn't know how to squeeze any more life out of the day.

That night, Eliza and Mr. Altman set up a little later than the rest to finish a chapter in the English grammar book. Papa had already turned in and was snoring softly from the bedstead behind them.

When she reluctantly told him that she would be gardening in the evenings and couldn't continue her studies for a while, it surprised Eliza to notice Altman frowning, deep in thought.

"Look, two pairs of hands are better than one. I'll help you get the garden work done and we'll still squeeze in a little school. Maybe only a half hour, but 'turn not to the right hand or to the left…'" he began. Then smiled at her.

"I couldn't ask you to help with the garden after working all day in the fields!"

"You didn't ask. I volunteered. Besides, it's a science lesson."

Eliza laughed, but she was uneasy. She had never planned a garden. In all the years before, Mama knew just where she wanted things and Eliza planted them where she was told.

"Mr. Altman, I'm worried about planting the garden. I've never planned one and I don't know what to do. If I don't do it right, there won't be enough food put up to get through next winter. I'm more than worried. I'm frightened."

"Let's look the situation over," suggested Mr. Altman. They moved to the kitchen table and Eliza got her seed packages from the pantry. Sitting side by side, they diagrammed the garden space on a slate and decided where and when to plant the vegetables.

It hadn't previously occurred to Eliza that Mama made successive plantings of certain crops to keep the table filled with fresh vegetables and to space out her canning. As Mr. Altman explained, it was important to plan so everything didn't ripen at once. It would be wasteful to have bushels of green beans ready to pick, nip, and can at the same time corn and tomatoes needed to be put up. They made a list of the fruits and vegetables needing to be canned or dried, approximated their growing and ripening cycles, and planned their planting calendar.

"Of course, I don't have to tell you that Mother Nature has a way of rearranging things by not cooperating with the right kind of weather, but we can try to work with her and pray for the best," he said as they surveyed their diagram and planting dates.

As Eliza transferred their notes onto the proper spaces on the picture calendar, she was overwhelmed at the amount of food that would have to be stored for winter and fervently hoped she was up to the task. It seemed a little less daunting to have it planned, and hopefully, spaced out, but she still knew nearly every day would be filled with strenuous preserving.

"How do you know so much about all of this? Who taught you how to plan a garden?"

Mr. Altman smiled. "I read. A lot. And not only high school textbooks."

His eyes took on a faraway look. He fell quiet. To her surprise, she saw his cheeks were wet with tears.

"What is it, Mr. Altman?"

"When I was a boy, I knew women who literally worked themselves to death to feed and clothe their families. My mother was one. If she only had the knowledge how to plan her efforts to coincide with nature's rhythms, life still might have been difficult for her, but the work wouldn't have killed her. I knew there had to be a better way to do things, so I started reading to find out all I could on the subject."

"Mama did that, too. She read everything she could find on caring for children, sewing, gardening, and raising chickens."

"Your mother was a wise woman. She wasn't afraid to learn and challenge conventional wisdom. In many respects, you appear to be a good deal like her."

"I hope so."

"A woman has to know so much. She has to be a doctor and nurse, seamstress and carpenter, cook and baker, farmer and canner, teacher, mathematician—so many things to be a wife and mother. I admire a woman who can keep it all straight. I think any woman who can smoothly run a household could manage anything in the world. And that's another reason why I believe in educating women. The more a woman knows, the easier her life can be."

"Do you really think so? Papa doesn't think a woman needs any learning."

"I suspect your pa thinks women just naturally know how to care for a home by virtue of their gender. But I've noticed it takes a tremendous amount of skill and energy and intelligence to make a home. It is not something that can be learned overnight. It requires a lifetime of learning.

"You're very young to have such a big house full of people to care for. Most women start housekeeping with just a husband and a house and maybe a small farm, and then add babies one or two at a time. Overnight, you inherited a house, four children, and a fair-sized farming operation. That would be quite a bit for an experienced housewife to manage, let alone a girl of seventeen."

His brown eyes smiled warmly at her above his bushy black beard. Eliza suddenly found herself wondering what he looked like under it.

"I can be of some help to you, but God was your mother's strength, and He will be for you, too."

Eliza sighed. "I used to trust God, but He betrayed me when Mama died. I'm so angry at Him, I don't want to talk to Him, or think about Him. And I certainly don't trust Him to help me. If He had wanted to be helpful, He would have let Mama live. But to be completely honest, I miss Him."

"I know what it's like to be angry with God. Some of the anger comes from the pain of a loss like you've suffered. But faith means that we trust God even when we don't understand what He's allowed."

"Why were you angry with God?" Eliza asked.

"It's very late, Eliza. You need some rest and so do I," said Mr. Altman, avoiding her eyes.

When he left for the night to walk back to the woods in the dark, Eliza realized that she knew almost nothing about this big man who befriended her family—only that he loved God, could do most anything, and seemed to know something about everything. Eliza lay awake a long time wondering what his secret was and why he wouldn't tell it.

With the help of Betty and Ruthie, Mr. Altman and Eliza planted the acre garden. Roughly half of it was set aside for sweet corn to be planted in four one-week intervals. Pumpkin hills were planted between the rows. Squash would be planted on the far side of the barn so the bees would not cross-pollinate the squash blossoms with the pumpkins and ruin the seed for the following year. Melons were planted on a sand patch down near Yankee Run where they would get plenty of water, but not mongrelize either the squash or pumpkin seed. Popcorn had to be planted well away from other varieties of corn, too, or its seed would be lost.

They dug a trench the length of the garden and filled it with a combination of sand and chicken manure, where they planted the root crops of carrots, beets, and onions. A large potato bed was laid and thickly covered with dirt and straw.

It was too early to put tomatoes and peppers directly into the garden, but they could be started in the cold frame. Eliza had never used the cold frame herself, but she understood the principle. Placed on a high, well-drained area of the yard, it was built on the order of a door and jam laid on the ground. A pane of glass took the place of the wood on the door. To become an effective nursery for tender seedlings, it needed to sit over a specially prepared shallow pit.

After Eliza dug out the cold frame's soil from the previous year to a depth of about three feet below the surface of the ground. She laid down a layer of fresh horse manure. The manure produced heat as it decomposed, speeding germination and warming the roots of the plants during chilly spring nights. Over top the manure, she spaded in a thick layer of garden soil well mixed with a little sand to make the soil light and prevent muddiness.

During the day, she propped open the glass to correspond with the whims of the weather. If it was warm and sunny, the frame door could be opened wide. If it was chilly, it might be propped opened only a crack to let out the moisture.

Along with the other baby lives on the farm, Eliza diligently tended the delicate young plants in the cold frame several times a day. One mistake, and the plants could freeze or roast, severely limiting the variety of food she would have to place on the table both this summer and all through the winter.

Once the new plants pushed through the soil, Eliza found beauty in the shiny green ribbons of corn and carrots' lacy fronds. She kept her hoe by the door and took it with her in the mornings when she went out to feed the chickens. The sun was up earlier and there was enough light by 5:30 a.m. so she could differentiate between weeds and garden plants.

Dew dampened her skirts as she hacked out intruding weeds and loosened the soil around the tender plants. Fortunately, there had been plenty of rain to get the garden off to a good start, but the outside pump still stood sentinel to provide water if the skies refused, only that had to be carried by the bucketful.

She enjoyed caring for the little plants and was surprised to find herself praying for them as she worked the hoe. A whole year's worth of groceries lay at her feet to be coaxed and cared for. But for the first time in her life, she was aware of how much their entire existence was dependent upon the goodness of God.

The brick makers were digging, forming, and firing brick for several weeks. The wood fires heating the kilns left a smoky pallor over the yard and farm. The laundry she and the girls hung on the line smelled like smoke. On the bright side, mosquitoes avoided the smoky yard so Eliza and her sisters could work in the garden or orchard any time of day or evening without being bothered.

The rhubarb and asparagus, planted in established beds, came on first. Each plant needed daily feedings with manure water to prolong their bearing cycles. After eating canned foods all winter, the family and workers were so hungry for fresh fruit and vegetables, Eliza questioned if there would be any extra rhubarb to can. But augmented by fresh dandelion greens, peas, and lettuces that were soon ready, Eliza managed to can several quarts for winter pies.

At the same time the rhubarb was ripe, Mama's chickens produced a flood of eggs. All of the neighbor's flocks were laying heavily, too, so the price was too low to make the eggs worth selling. Eliza made rhubarb custard by combining beaten eggs and rhubarb with molasses and a few dashes of vanilla, cinnamon, and nutmeg. She poured all of this into a buttered pan and baked it until it was puffy and lightly browned. The family poured cream over the top of the hot custard and ate it by the bowlfuls with every meal.

Eliza used the extra eggs for noodles.[4] She rolled the dough until it was paper thin, cut fine or wide strands, then thoroughly dried them. What the family didn't immediately eat, she sewed into a double layer of clean flour sacking. Although the air could circulate freely around the noodles to keep them from going bad, the extra bags prevented flies from landing on the noodles. She hung the bags of noodles in the rafters for winter.

The first of the sour cherries ripened while the last of the rhubarb was still on. When the slugs found the rhubarb as they inevitably did every year, Eliza boiled the stalks with unpitted ripe cherries until they released their juices. She strained the juice through cheesecloth to remove the pulp. Each batch tasted different because the proportions of cherries to rhubarb changed. Regardless, sweetened with a little sugar, this made a refreshing, tangy beverage similar to lemonade, but with a beautiful rosy color. Kept in a stone pitcher in the spring house, it didn't last long because it quenched thirst on a hot day like nothing else.

Canning cherries was a time-consuming process. Eliza and the girls picked bucketsful first thing in the morning while it was cool and the sugar content in the cherries was at the highest. They set the buckets in the spring house until evening. When other chores were finished, they could rest while pitting and listening to Mr. Altman read from Eliza's textbooks as the fireflies flirted in the twilight. It was a sticky job to plunge the round end of a hairpin into the cherries, one at a time, and fish out the pit. Juice ran down their arms, which flies and sweat bees found irresistible.

They saved the pits and boiled them with the water that they used to fill the quart jars before canning. The pits gave off an almond flavor and improved the color and taste of the canned cherries. The pits were boiled a second time in a little bleach and laid in the sunshine to dry. They blanched to a pretty pale gold color, and Betty and Ruthie threaded them on a heavy string to make necklaces for themselves and their dolls. When they wanted pink pits, Eliza boiled the pits with a few slices of red onion.

Watching the progress of the new house was exciting. Papa made several sketches of his plans and Eliza could see his dream come to reality right before her eyes.

There were many decisions that needed to be made for the house. Eliza noticed Papa must believe all women thought alike. Often as not, he asked Cora to choose items for the house rather than Eliza.

It was Cora who chose the single spray of wheat design for the face plate trims on the woodwork, which was okay with Eliza. Had she been asked; she would have chosen something a little fancier. It was also Cora who decided on what color to stain the floors and paint each of the rooms.

Cora spent much of the summer at the house, and Eliza was so grateful for her help with the gardening and canning. She felt she really couldn't complain when Papa let her select a few frills for the house.

"I want to get gaslight fixtures for the house today," Pa told Eliza and Aunt Cora over breakfast on a late August morning. "I need one of you girls to go with me to Celina on the eight o'clock train to pick them out. What do you have planned for the day?"

Eliza fumed. *Papa knows perfectly well what I have planned for the day!*

Eliza stayed up late the night before washing the bushels of windfall apples they collected along Yankee Run. Then, while

Mr. Altman read to her, she cored and quartered the apples, cutting out the worms and rotten spots. She divided the apples into several kettles and added a dash of vinegar to each, a scant handful of salt, and a quart of cider. With the lids on tightly, she put the kettles on the back of the stove to slowly simmer all night.

By morning, the apples were thoroughly cooked and ready to be finished first into jelly, then into apple butter. The tripod and huge cast iron kettle were assembled and standing in the yard, awaiting the apple pulp. There was no possible way she could drop everything and go to Celina. In the summer's heat, the apples would ferment.

"Papa, you know we're making jelly and apple butter today. It is an all-day job! I can't leave it until tomorrow or we'll lose the whole batch."

Silas turned to Aunt Cora. "Well, I need somebody to come with me and do the choosing. Cora, how about you?"

Eliza saw that Cora was thrilled with the possibility but hesitant. "I don't want to leave Eliza here alone to do everything."

Papa said, "Ruthie will be here, and so will John and Josh. Tell you what, Eliza, if it'll be any help, we'll take Betty with us, so she'll be out of your hair."

Little Betty was beside herself with joy. "I've never ridden on a train before!" She jumped up and down with excitement as Eliza helped her into her Sunday dress.

Struggling not to contaminate the child's excitement with her own resentment, Eliza said, "When you get to Celina, hang onto Aunty Cora's hand the whole time. We don't want you to get lost in such a big place."

Betty's eyes grew large and round. "Is Celina bigger than Rockford?"

"A lot bigger. You'll see electric lights everywhere and automobiles and crowds of people."

"Eliza, come with me! They might lose me!"

"Aunty Cora will keep track of you. But you keep track of Aunty Cora, too."

Eliza braided Betty's fine blonde hair and tied one of her own hair ribbons around the end. "See here, Betty. I'm putting my ribbon in your hair. It will be like I'm going with you. Remember everything you see so when you come home you can tell Ruthie and I all about it."

The girls heard Silas outside on the wagon shouting for Cora and Betty to hurry and come.

"Go on, now. Papa's waiting."

Betty scampered down the stairs and out the kitchen door. As Eliza watched from the upstairs window, Papa extended his arm to Betty and lifted her onto the buckboard. She squirmed in between Papa and Cora.

They would drive the wagon into Rockford, board the horse at the livery stable, and catch the train that would take them the thirteen miles to Celina.

Eliza sighed when she heard Ruthie banging around downstairs in the kitchen. Ruthie could be a lot of help when she wanted to be, but if she didn't, heaven help them all.

Downstairs, Eliza lined a large crock with cheesecloth. She piled fragrant cooked apples into the food mill, turned the handle, and squeezed it through a screen. The peel and seeds stayed inside the mill, but the apple's goodness was mashed and put into the cheesecloth-lined crock.

Once the cheesecloth was nearly full, Eliza gathered up the edges and twisted it gently. Sweet apple juice ran out of the cheesecloth into the crock. The apple juice was full of natural pectin, and once sweetened and boiled down, it would become jelly.

The pulp that remained in the cheesecloth was turned into the outside kettle and simmered and stirred all day until Eliza judged it was thick enough for apple butter. Into this, Eliza added brown sugar and cinnamon, and then ladled it into jars to be sealed in the canner.

As Eliza and Ruthie worked side by side in the steamy kitchen, they were tempted to prop open the back door for ventilation. But that would have extended an invitation to flies that had recently visited the manure pile.

Once John and Josh had the fire started under the tripod, they carried out the apple pulp and dumped it into the kettle. Ruthie fed the low fire under the kettle all day, frequently stirring the butter while Eliza made jelly and sealed it with paraffin in scalded glass jars.

Papa, Aunt Cora, and Betty still weren't home at suppertime, so the boys did the milking and chores while Eliza and Ruthie finished processing the quart jars of apple butter.

Bear Altman had been working on the house most of the day, but after supper, he came to the kitchen and pulled up to read to Eliza while she washed the dishes.

"Mr. Altman, I am so tired this evening that I'm not sure that it is worth your effort to read to me. My mind won't think!"

"Full of apple butter?"

"Partially," Eliza admitted with a smile. "But the rest of me is just plan worn out and angry. How could Papa take Cora and just abandon me here with all of the work to finish? I don't know what he is thinking!"

"I believe your pa thinks he is doing something special for you and your brothers and sisters. It's costing him a lot of money and time."

"I know building a new house is expensive. It's just that it is costing all of us right now, especially me!" Eliza was almost in tears.

"Be patient, Eliza. This new house might work out better than you think. But enough of that. You need a little fun to sweeten all of the work. Let me help you clean up, then let's take the boys and Ruthie down to the McCaleys. They're going to have a singing tonight."

"Oh! That would be fun!"

Eliza loved to sing but since she quit going to church, she really didn't have much of a chance.

Mr. Altman filled the sticky, empty kettle with soapy water and set it back on the fire to boil out the apple butter residue while Eliza and Ruthie finished the dishes and put away the food. John and Josh were enthusiastic about going anywhere, and when the dishes were done, they scrubbed themselves clean in the sink and slicked down their hair.

Eliza and Ruthie put on their good dresses. Ruthie begged to use Eliza's hairpins and put her hair up on top of her head. Ruthie thought it would make her look older, and Eliza was surprised to see with her hair upswept, the twelve-year-old looked more like a young woman than a girl. Since Eliza had loaned her hair ribbon to Betty, she brushed out her own hair and let it hang over her shoulders. It made her look even younger than Ruthie, but she was so happy to be going somewhere she really didn't care.

When Mr. Altman finished cleaning the kettle, his face was streaked with soot. He washed his arms and hands in the sink, but he didn't even glance at himself in the mirror. He was ready to go, soot and all. This was just the sort of thing combined with his long shaggy hair and beard and huge physique that prompted people to continue to call him "Bear."

The girls glanced at each other. They really didn't want to be seen with him like this.

"Mr. Altman," said Eliza gently, "you have dirt on your face."

He looked at his reflection in the mirror.

"I guess I do," he said slowly, turning his head from side to side as if he could not quite believe the image staring back at him. "A washcloth, then, Miss Eliza."

With a basin full of soapy water, he scrubbed himself clean, then borrowed the family comb to untangle his thick black beard and hair.

As Eliza clipped out some knots for him, she thought a pleasant man like him might find a wife if he didn't look so ill-kept and wild all the time.

"Now, Mr. Altman, shall we go?" asked Eliza.

The big man nodded and offered Eliza one heavily muscled arm and Ruthie the other. While John and Josh ran ahead, the girls and Mr. Altman walked at a more leisurely pace up the packed dirt road. The sun streaked the sky with brilliant reds. Fluffy pink clouds floated over the woodlands and fields, and heat lightning sparkled above the horizon. The freshening night air felt almost cold after the heat of the day and the fires in the kitchen.

"Eliza, do you think Mama can see us?" asked Ruthie.

"I suppose. I'm not sure. What are your thoughts, Mr. Altman?"

For a time, he walked on in silence as though he had not heard their question.

"I've wondered about that myself. I don't know. I only know the Bible says to be absent from the body is to be present with the Lord. Your mother trusted Jesus, did she not?"

Both girls nodded. Jesus was very important to their mother.

"If it would make her happy to see you, then maybe she can see you from the glassy sea at the foot of the throne of God."

The McCaleys' yard was full of horses, wagons, and a few cars. Harmonies seeped from the house into the nighttime air.

Two brothers from a neighboring town, both tall and blond, were leading a spirited version of "Red Wing" as Mr. Altman and the girls slipped through the screen door and sat down on a back bench. The main rooms of the McCaley house had been cleared of nearly all of the furniture, and benches were set in the living room, parlor, and kitchen.

"Aren't the musicians handsome?" Ruthie whispered to Eliza. "Especially the younger one. Do you think we can get an introduction?"

"Don't be too forward, Ruthie. 'Friendly is fine; forward is foolish,'" returned Eliza, quoting one of Grandma's favorite sayings.

Eliza couldn't remember when she had enjoyed herself so much. The boys leading the music were talented and funny. She was surprised to hear Altman singing so beautifully, his voice deep and modulated.

She realized this man who worked the farm with her father had a vast amount of education. And although he had been with them for more than two years, she had barely given him so much as a thought before these last few months they had been studying together. She wondered again why this man was hiding out in the woods and farms of Ohio. And why wouldn't he talk about his family or himself?

Sitting beside him, listening to him sing, Eliza felt a stir of caring for Mr. Altman, long hair and beard notwithstanding. She had long suspected that her father was only cooperating with her learning in hopes that she would come to love Mr. Altman and permanently secure him as her father's farmhand. She was willing to make a lot of sacrifices for her family—and she was fond of Mr. Altman—but marrying him so her father could expand his farm was not something she intended to do.

Furthermore, when Eliza thought about the tiny primitive cabin where he lived in contentment, she would not be content. She would have to constantly battle dirt and insects. She would not choose to live like a pioneer. It was just too hard.

She also saw Altman was happy working on the farm; he was built for hard labor. He needed a woman who also wanted to live in the country and work the earth beside him.

These nine months since Mama died had thoroughly convinced Eliza if she was going to work so hard, she wanted it to be in the field of medicine, not in a field of corn. She wasn't afraid of hard work; she just wanted it to be work of her own choosing.

When the singing was over, John and Josh and Ruthie, full of high spirits, rode home on a neighbor's buckboard with a rowdy crowd of other youngsters. Eliza and Mr. Altman chose to walk home slowly under the stars.

Eliza shivered in the night air.

"I wish I had a coat for you," he said. "I could put my arm around you, but that would be a little forward, wouldn't it?"

Eliza laughed. "Yes, it would. And Papa would probably make you marry me. However, if you will loan me an arm to hang on to, I would appreciate it. I'm afraid I'll stumble over the ruts in the road."

Without a word, he took her hand and tucked it under his arm, holding her small fingers in his hand for a few moments.

"Mr. Altman, can I ask you a question?"

"You may ask."

"Who are you? Where are you from?"

She felt his muscular chest expand as he took a deep breath almost like a man in pain.

"I'm an orphan, Eliza, and an only child. My father died when I was a baby and my mother died when I was about ten. She worked herself to death."

"But how did you grow up?"

"Like you, I was forced to quit school when my mother died. I was put out to farmers for labor."

"But you have an education!"

"That I do. It was a hard-fought way to learn, but I got my diploma the same way you will get yours, studying on my own, taking the tests. From there, I put myself through various universities."

"But why are you here? You could be working somewhere else."

"I'm here to rest, Eliza, to recuperate from some heavy blows. Things I can't talk about just now. Maybe someday, but not just now. I beg you not to press me."

As they reached the door of the farmhouse, they paused to look at the thousands of glimmering stars that were scattered over the deep purple velvet sky.

"I'm sorry, Mr. Altman, I didn't mean to pry."

"Some things are hard to talk about, Miss Burger. You should understand that better than most."

"I do, and I apologize. It's just that you have been such a friend to my family—and to me—the best friend I've ever had, and I realized tonight that I know very little about you."

"Do you want to know more?"

"Yes. I mean … no. I mean … I don't know."

Eliza was never quite sure how it happened, but she suddenly found herself buried in Mr. Altman's arms, crushed against his strong chest with his lips pressed urgently upon hers.

His beard was softer than she expected. She did not struggle. It felt so good to be hugged and held by someone whom she trusted. She kissed him back fully and openly.

Suddenly, the man seemed to come to himself and released her.

"I'm sorry, Eliza. I don't know what got into me."

Eliza giggled.

"My apple butter perfume overwhelmed you. But if Papa would have seen you, he definitely would have made you marry me.

"Would that be so terrible, Eliza?"

Eliza hesitated. She didn't want to hurt him anymore that he had already been hurt, but it wasn't fair to let him think that she would even consider for a moment abandoning her dreams of a career.

"I think you should know, Mr. Altman, that I'm fully determined to go to nurse's college, so any romantic involvement between us is out of the question."

Without waiting for a reply, she went into the farmhouse and shut the door. Shaking, she leaned against it.

Mr. Altman had kissed her. She kissed him back and thoroughly enjoyed it. But she was determined it would be the last time that ever happened.

Papa and Cora and Little Betty were not yet home and everyone else was in bed. Eliza was glad. Mr. Altman's kiss had been such a momentous occasion that Eliza was afraid it was written all over her face.

She lit the lantern and looked at herself closely in the mirror. Her cheeks were pink and her eyes bright, but she was basically unaltered. She was still just Eliza Burger. Plain old Eliza Burger.

The clock chimed eleven and she figured Pa and Cora would be home soon. Still dressed, she laid down on her bed beside Ruthie and hugged herself hard. She could scarcely believe what had just happened. She wondered if Mama had seen it.

Around midnight, she heard a slight noise downstairs. Quietly, so as not to awaken the other sleepers in the house, she slipped down the steps. She thought it was Papa and Cora home from town and she wanted to hear what news they brought with them.

She was halfway down the steps when she saw that the kitchen lantern was lit and turned down to a low flame. But then she saw something that would forever change the course of her life.

CHAPTER 10

Eliza quietly crept back upstairs, undressed, and got into bed.

She lay in the dark in a state of shock. It had been quite a night and Eliza couldn't quite believe her eyes. Papa and Cora were unaware that she was on the stairs, or they would have stopped kissing.

It had been quite a night. First, she and Mr. Altman. Now Papa and Cora!

Why hadn't she noticed before? When she thought back on the last few months, she decided she must have been blind not to have seen this coming. But Mama had not been gone a year. How could Papa even consider marrying her sister?

Cora and Papa quietly came up the stairs with Papa carrying Betty. Cora pulled out the trundle bed and they tucked Betty into it.

"'Nite, sweet Cora," Papa whispered.

Eliza almost gasped. Papa called Mama sweet Margaret. How could he do this so soon?

Eliza heard her aunt murmur something in reply.

When Papa went downstairs, Cora undressed and climbed into bed on the other side of Ruthie. Although it had been a long day, Eliza could not sleep. She was churning with emotions. She decided she wouldn't say anything to Papa—or anyone—about what she had seen. Maybe it didn't mean anything, like the kiss she had exchanged with Mr. Altman.

The new house was starting to make sense. Papa was building it for Cora. Cora would live there permanently.

Suddenly, Eliza realized she could go to school. It was like a miracle! Her jail door was opening and soon she would be free to go wherever she wanted.

She added her freedom to the list of reasons why she couldn't, shouldn't encourage Mr. Altman, even though deep in her heart, she wanted to.

The first Thanksgiving without Mama was to be held at Grandpa and Grandma Knapp's trim, white-painted clapboard house.

Grandma confided to Eliza that it was very hard for her to even think about the approaching holidays when only a year before Mama was healthy and alive.

"I can't get over it," said Grandma, shaking her head. "Margaret took sick right after Thanksgiving, and she died before New Year's Day. Last year was hard enough on you kids. This is year will be tough, too, but somehow, we've got to make it better."

Grandma, Aunt Cora, and Eliza worked feverishly for several days before to make a good meal for what was turning into a crowd. Since the McCaleys were cousins, the eight of them were invited. Of course, Junior and Coppess would be there. Eliza had heard a rumor Coppess might be bringing a young lady to meet the family. In addition to the six Burgers, Bear Altman had been invited. Combined with Grandma, Grandpa and Aunt Cora, there would be twenty total.

Although Eliza and Mr. Altman continued to study together, they took pains to never be alone. He was a little more distant and Eliza appreciated it, although she often thought about how much she enjoyed the kiss they exchanged and wondered if he thought about it too.

Grandma and Aunt Cora roasted and stuffed two home-raised turkeys. Eliza baked four pumpkin and two apple pies. They fleshed out the meal with escalope corn, sweet potatoes, dinner rolls, potato salad, coleslaw, macaroni salad, chocolate pudding, and sweetened pears. Eliza also brought along the fixings for ice cream for the men and boys to turn after dinner. Eliza had learned if everyone was busy doing something, even turning ice cream, they had less time to think sad thoughts.

Grandma and Grandpa's big golden oak table was expanded to full length with three additional leaves. Coppess did indeed bring a young woman to meet the family. Miss Lucy Hoffman was blonde, pretty, and very shy. She blushed every time someone spoke to her. She and Coppess took a great deal of teasing, and everyone asked them if they had any announcements.

"Not yet," Coppess said good-naturedly. "I wanted her to see what she was getting into. I thought it only fair to let her take a look at the bunch of you before I asked her to make any decisions."

Everyone laughed and Lucy looked up at Coppess. It was obvious she adored him.

Over dinner, the conversation turned to the Burgers' new house and how soon they would move in.

"It's coming along pretty well," said Papa. "I really want to have Christmas in there."

The conversation buzzed on for a few moments, then Papa cleared his throat and tapped on his plate until everyone grew quiet. "I guess now is as good as any to make an announcement. Cora and I plan to be married the week before Christmas. It'll be just a little ceremony at the new house, and you're all invited. Afterwards, we'll take the train into Fort Wayne for a brief honeymoon and a little Christmas shopping, but we'll be back before Christmas day."

For a moment, the room was silent as the family struggled to absorb the news.

Eliza wasn't surprised. When she caught Bear Altman's eye, he winked at her, and she knew he wasn't surprised, either.

"Congratulations!" Eliza started clapping and the rest of the family joined in.

Suddenly, Ruthie burst into tears and ran up the stairs to the upper bedrooms.

"Well!" declared Grandpa, "I knew something was up. I think it is a very sensible move for both of you."

Eliza rose from her chair and gave Cora a big hug.

"Welcome, Cora. You've always been a part of our family. Now you will be even more so. I'm pleased."

Cora blushed and smiled gratefully at Eliza. "Will you stand up with me at the wedding?"

"Of course, Cora. I'll be happy to."

Eliza climbed upstairs to see to Ruthie with Grandma following.

They found Ruthie in their mother's bedroom, the one that was hers before she married Papa. Grandma had never changed anything in Mama's room, memorializing the days when both of her girls were at home.

Ruthie was sobbing, crumbled in pain on the bed, clutching Mama's decorative bed pillow. "Margaret" was embroidered across it with roses and forget-me-nots worked in silk ribbons.

"Ruthie, I miss Mama, too." Eliza said.

"Are we the only ones?" She shot an accusatory look at Grandma. "Has everyone else forgotten her?"

"Of course, we haven't forgotten her. A day has not yet gone by when I don't cry for my lost baby." Grandma put her arms around Ruthie and rocked her back and forth.

"But Ruthie, meals have to be cooked and laundry has to be done. Your mama would have wanted her children to go on and live and remember. Not die too. It's hard to live, but it is the best thing we can do for your mama is to live and take care of one another.

"Don't you think for a moment Cora doesn't miss your mama. Few sisters were ever closer than my two girls were. By marrying your pa, Cora is picking up her sister's burden and her life, not because she wants to cook and clean for her ungrateful nieces and nephews, but because she wants to do something loving for her sister and this is the best thing she can do. She's finishing the task your mama had to leave undone and she's doing it for your mama."

Ruthie wailed, "But how can Papa even think of getting married again?"

"You forget, child. Your pa married your mama after his first wife died. I believe he loved his first wife, and I believe he loved your mama, and I think he'll love Cora."

Grandma paused here for effect. "I think they'll be happy if you'll let them. It's high time for you to think about honoring your mother's memory by making your family happy instead of miserable."

Ruthie sat up on the bed and bit her lip, tears still cruising down her face. "It's hard, Grandma. It's so hard."

"Of course it's hard to think of somebody else besides yourself, but it's time you did," said Grandma.

A floorboard squeaked in the hallway. They looked up to see Cora standing in the doorway, her heavy face full of grief. Ruthie put her arms around her.

"I'm sorry, Aunty. I'll try to do better."

CHAPTER 11

For a time, Ruthie cooperated. She even helped Pa and Cora plan the small wedding ceremony.

Pa bought a new suit for the occasion and Cora had a stylish navy-blue dress made for herself of polished wool with white piping around the collar. It beautifully accented her dark hair and eyes, and she was almost pretty when she wore it.

With her own money, Cora bought new clothing for each of the children. It was the first store-bought outfits any of them ever owned.

Eliza's dress was rust brown serge. The color brought out the red in her hair. It had the new dropped waist style, and she was thrilled with it. Betty's dress was black velvet with a white lace bertha collar. It was purposely two sizes too big so she could get more use from it. Cora had a large matching bow made for Betty's golden curls, and when they tried the total ensemble on her, she looked like one of the expensive china dolls in the general store.

Ruthie's dress was the priciest of all. At her young age, it was clear she was going to be the real beauty of the family. Although Eliza's and Betty's dresses were ordered from the catalog,

Grandma and Cora took Ruthie to the dressmaker as a subtle way of extending an olive branch. Made from dove-colored silk and trimmed in cream braid; the soave jacket and skirt could also have suited a womanlier shape, but it looked charming on Ruthie's maturing figure. The dressmaker custom made a matching bow for Ruthie's thick brown hair.

The boys got new black wool suits from the catalog along with starched white shirts, exactly like Papa's. The twins had grown so much in the past year, their suits were actually bigger than Papa's.

The new suits for the wedding were considered their Christmas presents. The occasion provided an excuse to go to the photographers in Rockford for a family photograph after the wedding. Once that was done, the family would see Papa and Cora off on the train to Fort Wayne for their honeymoon.

The wedding day dawned cold and cheerless. The family had been up since well before 4:00 a.m. to complete chores and prepare for the guests.

Eliza and the girls had taken their baths and washed their hair the night before, but Papa and the boys would take theirs after the chores. Eliza pumped water for their baths the night before. She set the buckets to warm around the cookstove. The warming well water turned bright orange from the rust, but overnight, the iron settled on the bottom and sides. If she was careful, Eliza could ladle out the clean water without stirring up too much iron sediment.

As she stepped outside of the old clapboard house to do her chores, Eliza saw smoke coming from the new kitchen's chimney and the soft golden glow of lamplight spilling out of the window and onto the snow. Grandma and Cora spent the night in the new house and Eliza supposed Grandma was doing some last-minute baking.

Other than Cora's bedroom suite, the new house contained very little furniture. Papa purchased a new cookstove for the kitchen and a wood stove for the parlor, and they were in place. The kitchen table from the old house had been carried over to serve the guests after the ceremony, leaving Eliza and the family the old canning table from the work shed for meals.

Papa, Mr. Altman, Grandpa, and the boys loaded the wagon with the benches from the Stringtown Church and put them against the walls in the near-empty rooms. The new floors were swept clean and rag rugs were positioned at the doors to catch drips and hold boots while their owners enjoyed cakes, pies, and coffee after the wedding.

As Eliza fed and watered the chickens, she wondered how Mama felt about all of this. She couldn't imagine her mother begrudging Papa a new wife or her sister a new house, but it had not yet been quite a year since Mama's death. It just seemed too soon.

Eliza suspected the neighbors thought it was too soon, also.

The boys took it philosophically enough, and Betty was happy to have Cora as a new mama. Ruthie still struggled with the idea from time to time. Grandma said some of it might be her age with her newfound womanhood, but Eliza knew it was more than that. Losing her mother was a weighty adjustment for any young girl to make.

Eliza was mature enough to reason Papa, Cora, indeed the entire family, missed Mama beyond words to express their pain.

The new house was really Mama's, the one Papa always promised to build for her, but never did until now. Cora would clean it and care for Papa and the kids. Eliza knew from little hints Cora dropped, marriage to Papa and raising her sister's children was not the life Cora would have chosen for herself. She was only doing it for Mama, her beloved sister.

After breakfast, Eliza and the girls went upstairs to dress, leaving the kitchen for Papa and the boys to bathe and dress.

Eliza slipped her dress over her head.

"Please button me, Ruthie." She backed up to her sister who was sitting on the bed and not yet begun to dress.

"I see you are wearing Cora's "please like me" dress. I've decided I'm not going to wear mine. I don't like Cora and I'm not going to wear that ugly dress she had made for me. My everyday dress will do just fine for this occasion!"

"Ruthie, I don't know why you can't understand Papa and Aunt Cora are getting married as a sacrifice for us. They are doing it for you and for all of us. Aunt Cora would be perfectly happy living with Grandma and Grandpa, but Papa needs a wife and you and Betty and the boys need a mother. Cora has spent a lot of money so you can look pretty. She wants you to like her and get along with her. Maybe it's a bribe, but maybe it's love."

Ruthie snorted. "Maybe she just wants to live in a nicer house than Mama had. Maybe she thinks Papa is rich and she can have Papa's money too. Mama is barely cold in her grave and everybody but me has forgotten her."

"Ruthie! That's a horrible thing to say. No one has forgotten Mama. And Cora has a big heart, big enough to love even her ungrateful niece. You are not going to spoil this wedding. Quit sulking and get dressed!"

Betty was so beside herself with excitement she barely ate a bite for breakfast. Upstairs, she had taken off her nightgown, put on her panties and petticoat, and despite the chill of the upstairs room, was happily jumping on the bed trying to touch the ceiling.

"Quit jumping on the bed! Put your dress on and I'll button you next."

"I can't, 'Liza. If I stop jumping, I'll pop!" crowed the exuberant little girl.

Without warning, Ruthie pushed Betty down onto the bed. Her head struck the iron headboard with a dull thud. "Stop it! Stop it right now!" Ruthie hissed between clenched teeth.

Betty held her head and cried.

"For shame, Ruthie Burger! How could you be so hateful?" Eliza put her arm around Betty.

Ruthie looked frightened but defiant.

"Mama told her not to jump on the bed—lots of times! But she's forgotten everything about Mama. She even calls Aunt Cora 'Mama.'" Ruthie glared at them and then stuck her face up close to Betty's.

"She's not your mama. She'll never be your mama and you don't have to listen to her."

Betty cried harder. She buried her face into Eliza's bosom to shut out the vision of an angry Ruthie looming before her.

Eliza heard Papa's heavy footsteps coming up the stairs. Betty stopped crying and Ruthie was wide-eyed.

"Are you all right, baby Betty?" He put his work-roughened hand on her little blonde head and turned it toward him. She put out a quivering lip and sniffed.

"I reckon you'll live." His rough thumb wiped away her tears.

"Ruthie." He calmly turned to her.

"Go out to the woodshed. On your way, cut a switch."

"No, Papa! No! I'm too old for a switching. I didn't mean to hurt her. I just wanted her to obey Mama. Mama said not to jump on the beds."

He firmly placed both hands upon her shoulders. "Your mama also told you to keep your temper under control. You will not ruin this day, Ruth Margaret Burger. You will not dishonor the memory of your mother by hurting your sister and acting in this disgraceful manner. Go to the woodshed. I'll settle with you there. And, young lady, remember just because you have a new dress, does not mean you will be attending the party. Unless your attitude improves, you will be spending the day in the woodshed. Now get!"

Ruthie flew down the stairs, eliciting surprised yelps from John and Josh in the process of getting dressed.

It was a simple, midmorning wedding in the new brick house. About thirty friends and relatives watched as Eliza stood up for Cora and John stood with Papa. The ceremony lasted about ten minutes.

Pies and cakes were cut. People chatted with one another.

By noon, everyone other than the Burger family was gone except for Grandma and Grandpa Knapp and Bear Altman, who stayed to do the dishes, clean up, and haul the benches back to the church.

Papa loaded the family on the buckboard and drove in piercing cold and drizzle to Rockford, where the family sat for a grim-looking photograph.

Afterwards, Papa and Cora boarded the train for Fort Wayne.

Papa left instructions with Mr. Altman, Eliza, and the boys what was to be moved to the new house while he and Cora were gone. The transfer of household goods would be slow and orderly. His goal was for the clapboard to be empty by the time he and Cora returned from their honeymoon.

Even with the promise of a pitcher pump inside the house, it was hard for Eliza to leave the clapboard. They really didn't have a lot of furnishings, but all of the canned and dried food had to be carefully transported and shelved in the new pantry. To the amusement of her brothers, Eliza went through every corner of the old house, and cleaned it thoroughly.

While sweeping the dark eaves of the upstairs, Eliza found the cream can with her mother's notebooks still inside. She pried off the lid and reverently collected them.

By the feeble winter light, she flipped through one of the notebooks chosen at random. All time stopped as she read what Mama wrote.

March 1, 1913: 5:30 a.m.

Oh Lord, this day I pray for my daughter, Eliza. She wants to be a nurse, but her pa will never allow it. Father, for a beautiful young woman to dream of serving the sick and dying, such a desire must have come from You. Please make a way for her.

Eliza was thunderstruck. Her mother had prayed for her dream to come true. She clung to her mother's prayer through the dark days ahead.

CHAPTER 12

The week after the wedding passed quickly. With Papa and Cora gone, moving underway, and Christmas impending, Eliza barely had time to think.

Papa and Cora were due back on Friday, the day before Christmas.

The children could talk of nothing but the program to be held that same day at the schoolhouse on Fast Road.

"They are going to have a magic lantern show, puppets on strings, and music, and Santa!" John said. Ruthie, Betty, and the boys were beside themselves with excitement.

"Can we go? Please! Oh, please!"

Eliza had forebodings about letting them go. It was a year ago to the day Mama's sickness forced her to go to her bed permanently.

I'm not being fair. I don't need to remind the kids of Mama's loss again. They miss her every day. And they are so excited about going to the Christmas program. They have worked hard to move from the old house to the new and I hate to deprive them of the pleasure.

"'Liza, let me take the team and sleigh," John said. "I can pick up the McCaley kids and we'll all go together. Won't you let us go? It'll be great fun, Eliza! I'll be very careful. We'll be back before Papa and Aunt Cora get home. Papa lets Josh and I drive the team to town. If he were here, I know he would say yes."

She had to concede both John and Josh handled the team intelligently.

With great reluctance, she agreed to let them take the horses and sleigh.

Eliza couldn't put her finger on the exact cause of her unease. Maybe it was because of all the changes; she was clinging to anything familiar. Perhaps her nervousness was because it was the anniversary of the day Mama had to go to bed. Or nostalgia over leaving the clapboard and moving to the new house. Or because Aunt Cora would soon be living with them as mother. Or because Eliza intended to ask Papa if she could move into Rockford, work for Dr. Jackson, and attend high school classes.

But her uneasiness would not go away.

Little Betty added to Eliza's apprehension by awaking rosy with fever. Betty denied there was anything wrong with her. "I'm still going! They're going to have a magic lantern show and everything! Why are you so mean? If Aunt Cora was here, she'd let me go!"

"I'm sorry you can't go. I don't know what you have, and it won't do for you to be out in the cold. Tell you what. I'll read to you."

Bundled in a quilt, disappointed and tearful, Betty stood at the eastern window in the new kitchen and watched the rest of the kids glide away in the sled, the harness bells merrily jingling.

Eliza watched them go, her hand resting on Betty's blonde curls. "Guess what we're going to do today? We're going to make some cut-out Christmas cookies!"

The idea charmed the child enough to make her dry her tears. Since Eliza had some mending to do first, she let the little girl sort through the button box and admire the pretty trims.

As Eliza washed up the breakfast dishes, Bear Altman came to the back door. His boots were muddy, so he stood outside the door while Eliza wrested the milk cans out to him. He would haul them into the dairy and wait for Papa and Cora's train.

"The temperature is pretty mild today." He cast an eye at the heavy gray sky. "But I don't like the way those clouds look. The air has a feeling of impending doom about it."

He laughed lightly. "I'm probably exaggerating. But it does feel like we're going to get some wet weather. The cattle feel it too. They didn't want to go out to pasture this morning, even though the temperature is mild."

Eliza nodded in agreement. "I know what you mean. I thought it was my imagination."

"Do you need anything in town?"

Betty piped up. "Yes! I need some candy." She was still wrapped in her quilt, her blue eyes bright with fever. Betty was a great favorite of Mr. Altman's. She knew if she asked him for anything, she would likely get it.

His laugh was deep and rumbling.

"She's running a fever, Mr. Altman. I hope she's not coming down with something."

Without a word, Altman slipped out of his boots and stepped into the house. "Come here, Betty."

She shuffled over and held her arms out to him. He lifted her into his arms. She laid her head on his rough woolen coat, her blonde curls mixing with his black beard.

"Let me look at you, little miss." He gently placed a big hand on her forehead then touched her cheeks. "Nice fever you have. Is your throat sore?"

She nodded solemnly.

"How about your ears? Do they hurt?"

Again, she nodded.

He set her on the floor. "Sit next to the stove, Betty. I'll bring you something good from town."

To Eliza he whispered, "Try a drop or two of warm sweet oil in each ear and make her some hot honey tea to sip. Warm a cloth she can hold over her ears. Do you have any sour cherry jelly left from this summer? If she starts coughing, add some cherry jelly to the tea.

"When I go to town to pick up the folks, I'll go a little early and stop by Doc Jackson's to see if he's going to be out this way. He may have some sort of cough medicine for her. Do you need anything else?"

"No, I don't need anything else. But sweet oil, honey tea, and cherry jelly. What good ideas! Why didn't I think of those things?"

As she watched Mr. Altman drive the team down the road, Eliza shook her head in wonder. *How did he know those things would help?*

Midmorning the temperature began to fall as a fine dusting of snow sifted down. By noon, as Eliza fixed soup for herself and Betty, she noticed that, except for the tallest spikes, snow now covered the grass.

Although the new house was snugger than the clapboard had been, Eliza felt a decidedly cold draft from somewhere in the house. She pushed two chairs together in front of the cookstove, creating a warm makeshift bed for Betty.

Betty laid her head down on the table. "I can't eat the soup. It hurts to swallow."

Eliza carried her over to the chairs, bundled her in the quilt and laid her down.

"I'm going to mix up the Christmas cookies now. And if you are up to it, you can help me decorate them."

Betty watched as Eliza stirred up a batch of sugar cookies and cut them out with Mama's special cutter with the fancy fluted edges. Betty nodded off to sleep in the cozy kitchen as the scent of baking cookies filled the air.

The house was so much quieter than the clapboard Eliza couldn't tell if the wind had picked up.

The mantle clock's hands pointed to a few minutes before two as Eliza pulled the kitchen rocking chair to the east-facing window to watch for the kids' return. Between batches of cookies, she mended socks from the bottomless sewing basket.

In the stillness, it felt like Mama was here, just in the next room.

Mama? Are you watching me? Do you know Papa married Cora? Are you okay with that?

Eliza was startled back to reality as a strong gust rapped on the window. Snow was still coming down, but the wind was blowing harder. Eliza remembered her grandfather quoting an old truism: "Fine as a meal, snow a great deal."

Soon, drifts of snow made by a stout easterly wind formed sharp-edged drifts across the road. Eliza hoped the kids wouldn't tarry on the trip home.

Other than the ticking of the clock and the soft breathing of Betty, all other sounds seemed suffocated. Occasional gusts reached into the chimney and made the fire in the new cook-stove crackle.

As she patched socks and pants, Eliza grew anxious. By the time the clock chimed 4:30, she was frantic.

As early afternoon darkness gathered, Betty awoke from her nap. Her fever had broken, and the child was definitely feeling better, but Eliza was nearly sick with worry.

Where is Mr. Altman when I need him?

She knew he had stayed in town to bring home Papa and Cora, and now she thought perhaps the train from Fort Wayne was running late. Eliza was confident Mr. Altman, Papa, and Cora could take care of themselves, but something must have happened to the kids to make them late.

Eliza wracked her brain for ideas of what could have delayed the kids.

Maybe the sleigh turned over in the ditch. Maybe they got disoriented in the storm. Maybe they were skylarking.

She was responsible for them. She allowed them to go.

Every tick of the clock seemed to be urging her to go look for them. What would she do with Betty? How could she leave her home alone? As the nighttime gathered, Eliza made up her mind. She would go looking for them before it got any darker.

She was loathe to leave Betty by herself. She had heard stories of small children left alone who opened the cookstove and burned themselves. Or were scalded by hot water in the reservoir. Or went to the outhouse and were lost in the snow. She needed something to keep Betty busy, but what would that be?

Oh, dear God, what can I give her?

The idea came to her in a flash: Mama's treasure trunk was upstairs in Eliza's new room.

Eliza ran up the stairs and hesitated over the trunk lid. She ran her hand over its curved top decorated with a tracery of metal designs set between wooden slates. It wasn't a big trunk but held mementos precious to her mother.

On special occasions, Mama would sit in the rocker next to the trunk, her offspring gathered on the braided rug at her feet. She would lift out each item and tell the story of why she kept it. The latest item was one Eliza put in: the red satin ribbon off of Mama's coffin. It read, "Beloved Wife & Mother, Margaret Eliza Knapp Burger, Born April 19, 1880, At Rest Dec. 29, 1916."

As Eliza opened the trunk, the faint scent of lavender and rose slipped out.

On top was Mama and Pa's wedding photo. Mama looked so young. Papa did, too. Everyone said Eliza looked like her mother. It was only in their wedding photograph could Eliza see a resemblance.

There were other photos too. One of each of the babies, and Mama and Aunt Cora as little girls. Even then the two sisters looked very different from one another.

The most fascinating to Eliza was the photograph of Grandma and Grandpa Knapp on their wedding day. Mama looked like Grandma and Eliza looked like Mama. Eliza wondered if someday her little girl would look like Grandma Knapp too.

In a greeting card box was downy swatches of baby hair. Each was tied with a ribbon and labeled with the baby's name.

There was the strawberry-colored braid of Mama's hair cut off when she was twelve and had rheumatic fever. All her long, luxurious hair was thought to be sapping her strength, so it was cut off. Whenever Mama told the story of her near death, tears would come to Eliza's eyes.

If Mama had died, none of us would have been born.

Once her braid was cut off, she got better, but her hair never again as thick and wonderful.

Mama lived through that terrible fever. When she was with them, it was all that had mattered. If only she could have survived lockjaw, Eliza wouldn't have cared if Mama had been bald.

At the very bottom was Mama's china doll wrapped in a piece of material from her wedding dress. The rest of Mama's bridal gown had been made into baby clothing.

Mama never let the children look in the trunk by themselves. Eliza had felt a guilty pang when she had lifted the lid to put in the funeral ribbon.

In the year since Mama's death, she had never opened the trunk no matter how the other children begged. Now, it was the right thing to do. She hefted the trunk in her arms and carried it down the stairs to the kitchen. She laid an old blanket on the floor near the cook stove and set the trunk on it. "Come here, Betty."

The little girl came, her eyes bright with anticipation to see the wonders in the forbidden trunk.

"Honey, I have to go find the big kids. I don't like to leave you, but I know you're a big girl and I can trust you to not to open the stove. And if you have to go to the bathroom, use the chamber pot. Do you promise?"

Betty nodded solemnly.

"It's important you keep your word. I won't be gone long, but you must be very brave and obedient.

"See Mama's trunk? You can look in it while I'm gone. When you get to the bottom and find Mama's china doll, be careful not to drop it, but take it to Papa's bed, climb in there, and put it to sleep. You take a nap with it, okay?"

The little girl's face brightened at the thought of holding the treasured china doll. None of them had ever had anything but rag dolls so Mama's store-bought doll was something special.

"Promise me, Betty. I'm trusting you."

"I promise to be good and do what you say."

Eliza opened the trunk's heavy lid and straightened the prop. "Now be careful the lid doesn't fall on your fingers."

The little girl knelt down and reverently began to remove the items one by one, beginning with the funeral ribbon.

Eliza loaded the cookstove with as many logs as it would hold. She pulled John's woolen chore pants on under her skirt, and with a flash of inspiration, tucked her skirt and petticoats inside for additional warmth.

She put on her wool sweater, and Mama's on top, then John's chore coat. Last of all, she pushed all of her hair under his blue knitted cap and pulled on her gloves and his mittens. She wished she had a better pair of shoes or even boots, but her own shoes would have to do.

She peered at herself in the bit of cracked glass. Except for missing some stubble, she looked like John or Josh.

Eliza took a last glance at Betty. The little girl was totally engrossed in the wonders of the trunk.

"Bye, Betty," she called. "Remember your promise."

Betty did not look up. She just nodded.

Eliza pulled the door shut and started on the journey that almost ended her life.

Chapter 13

Eliza trudged the half mile east to the McCaley house. She hoped the children would be there. Maybe Mrs. McCaley knew their whereabouts. The McCaleys had a telephone and Mrs. McCaley listened into everyone's calls so she knew all the news. Someone may have talked about the school program.

The snow was heavy, making her trek slower than she expected. Walking east with the wind and snow in her face, Eliza fought her way up the road over ruts and drifts.

It was not really cold. She estimated the temperature was just below freezing, perfect snowman and snowball weather. That alone might explain why the children were so late. They were probably playing in the snow, unaware of the dangers or the lateness of the hour.

Stepping over the drifts caused Eliza to build up a sweat by the time she reached the McCaley's home. Eliza pounded on the door. The house was silent. She pounded harder, but still there was no answer. Cautiously, she opened the door and yelled for Mrs. McCaley. No one answered.

How odd! Where would everyone go in such a heavy snow?

The cookstove fire had been recently banked and the quiet kitchen was in a state of perfect tidiness. It was as if they'd cleaned the kitchen and then been swallowed by the earth. Eliza always admired Mrs. McCaley's skill at keeping her home organized. She wished she could do as well, but at the moment, she was frustrated as there was not a scrap of paper or a slate anywhere upon which to leave a note.

Eliza hated to go through the kitchen drawers, but finally began pulling them out one by one to find an envelope, a recipe card, anything upon which she could write.

She hit pay dirt in the oak secretary. Licking the lead of the pencil, she wrote on the back of a receipt:

Mr. and Mrs. McCaley,

The children are late coming home from the Fast Road School program. I have gone to look for them. Betty is alone at the house and not feeling well. Will someone please look in on her?

I will find my brothers and sister and your children and bring them home. Thank you for your neighborliness.

Sincerely,

Eliza Burger

The clock on the living room wall chimed five times as Eliza pulled shut the McCaley's door. During the short time she had been in the house, the drifts grew higher, and the wind blew sharper. The temperature was dropping as the sun steadily moved west.

Fast Road School where the entertainment was to be held was a good three miles south by southwest from the McCaley's place. With all of the snow, Eliza estimated that it would take her at least an hour to walk there. She would catch a ride home in the sleigh. She headed south on Eichar Road, knowing John would have to come that way to bring the McCaley children home. But it appeared that no one, not even a milk wagon, had been down the road since early afternoon. That puzzled Eliza.

What is keeping those kids? Surely the program is over by now! Why, oh why, did I let them talk me into allowing them to go?

Eliza trudged forward, keenly aware night was falling, and the cold was growing. She studied the landscape in the direction of the school, hoping to see a smudge of smoke coming out of the chimney. But the falling snow blurred distant shapes. Soon it was too dark to see much of anything. That the school building just ahead was enough to propel her onward although her fingers and feet were tingling from the cold.

The Fast Road school loomed ahead of her in the dark. She squinted, trying to see their sleigh and the horse. Where were all the people? As she entered the schoolyard, a hint of wood smoke in the air renewed her hope of shelter and rest.

As she reached the schoolhouse, her heart sank. The windows were dark. Everyone was gone. The good news was since no one was at the schoolhouse, it meant the kids had started for home. She hoped they made it.

But if they were going home, why didn't she meet them on the road? All she could surmise was they took the long way, perhaps taking someone else home.

Now it was Eliza's turn to hope she could make it home too. Walking was increasingly difficult, but she refused to consider it impossible.

No matter. I can still get warmed up and take a little rest before I start home.

Eliza knew most weather came out of the west, but this storm was coming due east. Eliza heard enough old timers' talk to know that a storm out of the east would likely be a bad one.

By poor planning, the school door faced west. It was locked up. No amount of beating or latch-pulling would open it.

Eliza was freezing now, and darkness was nearly total. The whirling wind and flakes made visibility almost nil. She searched the yard in the dark until she found one of the outhouses. Although the little outhouse had snow and wind sifting through the cracks, it provided a blessed relief from the direct assault of the weather. She rested on the edge of the toilet and thought about her situation.

If I follow the road home, the three miles might now take me several hours to reach home. I'm not certain I have that much stamina. But as the crow flies the house is little more than a mile from here. I'd have to go through part of the woods, but I played in those timbers ever since I was a little girl. I should be able to find my way through them in the dark. Furthermore, the wind might not be nearly as wicked among the trees as it will be in the clearing.

Although it had been a while since she spoke to Jesus, she thought now would be a good time to open up communication with Him.

I know I haven't talked to You much since You took Mama to heaven. And I've been mad at You a lot lately and have felt mean toward You. I don't know whether You will hear me now, but Lord, please give me strength to find the straightest path home.

She suddenly knew she should go the way the crow flies.

Thank You, Lord! Come with me. Let's go!

She pulled down John's woolen pants to reach her petticoat. With nearly numb fingers, she tore the bottom ruffle off of her petticoat and tied it tightly around her face, tucking it down into the collar of her coat. She pulled his knitted cap as low to her forehead as she could, leaving only her eyes exposed to the storm. It was the best she could do.

She took a piece of charcoal out of the ash bucket in the corner. With it, she wrote "Eliza Burger was here. Dec. 24, 1917" on the wooden wall.

Then she straightened her shoulders and prepared herself to face the storm.

CHAPTER 14

She pushed against the outhouse door, but a strong gust of wind fought her and held it shut. She listened until she heard it die down, then she stepped back and gave the door a running push with all her might. The door opened and Eliza fell face first into the snow, knocking the breath out of her. Stunned, she lay gasping. It felt so good to rest for a minute she was tempted to stay down and take a nap.

She knew better. She heard horror stories of people overcome with sleepiness in the cold and freezing to death. She forced herself to get up and locate her bearings before she headed into the night. She pushed what she thought was northeast, almost directly into the teeth of the storm. Between her and the woods was a field of corn stubble. The darkness of the night combined with the snow hid many surprises. The ground was uneven and full of holes. Between snow drifts and snags made of old cornstalks, she frequently tripped and fell.

After another unexpected fall, she lay exhausted in the snow. Leaving the road was a mistake; she knew it now. Someone might be looking for her. She thought about turning back, but she was not exactly sure which way the road was.

The best thing is to continue forward and hope I find the woods and eventually the house.

I might die out here. I wonder if I would go to hell.

Please don't let me die, dear God.

She rested for a moment, her eyes closed, her body almost warm. She jumped when something smacked her on the head. She felt for the object then recoiled in horror. It was a skeleton arm! What was a skeleton arm doing in a cornfield? Where had it come from? She held the ghastly object in front of her. It slapped her again.

Then she laughed out loud, an edge of hysteria in her voice. It was only an old corn stock! The skeleton arm was last year's harvest.

The thrill of fear warmed her. She threw the corn stock away. It swept into the howling darkness before her, swirling like a witch's broom.

Eliza stared into the night. The wind sounded as if it was laughing at her. Not the gentle chuckles of a spring breeze, but the malevolent cackle of a fiend bent on slipping its icy fingers around her neck and freezing the life from her. She stumbled to her feet. She had to keep moving or it would kill her.

Gusts moaned and swirled around her, looking like gigantic snow ghosts. They blew their frigid breath into her face and swept the field clean of snow in areas. Encouraged by their example, gaunt elbows of dead cornstalks tried to rise from the ground.

It came as a blessed relief when she finally reached the edge of field and what she hoped would be the relative safety of the forest. The trees stopped the wind and deposited huge drifts of snow between the trees at the edge of the woods. Eliza struggled to wade through them. At first, she wasn't sure which section of the woods she was in until she stumbled across a flat board stuck straight up out of the snow. She felt the edges with her hands. It was the old cemetery where Papa had buried his first wife and baby. Eliza put her face close to the board and recognized it as the baby's tombstone. She wearily sat down against it with her back to the wind. She wasn't too far from home now, and she hoped her little half-brother didn't mind her sitting on him.

Her heart was pounding as Eliza tried to catch her breath. In her exhaustion with the icy air whipping around her head, every respiration was a fight.

Somewhere, out in the darkness, over the screaming wind, in her confused and weary state, she thought she could hear someone crying.

The hands of time spun backwards to the night Mama died. The clapboard house was very still when something woke Eliza. She crept downstairs, stopping by her mother's bedside. She placed her hand lightly on Mama's forehead. At first, she thought Mama's fever had broken. Then she realized Mama was not breathing.

"Mama! Mama! Wake up!"

Papa was sleeping on the floor as not to disturb Mama. But when he heard Eliza's cry, he turned up the lamp and laid his head on Mama's chest listening for a heartbeat. He looked at Eliza and shook his head.

Eliza wailed.

She was hearing the same sound now and it was coming from her.

This was nonsense. Her mind was playing tricks on her. She knew it for sure now. None of this was real. She was at home in bed, warm and dreaming. She turned over and fell off the tombstone.

Shards of icy snow crunched against her cheek and woke her. She struggled to her feet. In a lucid moment, she realized if she stopped, she'd freeze to death. She knew that much. She wasn't sure if she was awake or asleep, what was real or pretend, but she knew she had to keep moving. It wouldn't be far now. She'd get home.

The darkness and whirling snow's hypnotic effect forced her constantly to keep her mind from drifting. Suddenly, a light appeared up ahead. Eliza battled her way to it. She stepped into a little light patch upon the ground and tried to see its source.

As she squinted, to her amazement, she saw her mother standing in a summer field filled with colorful flowers. A gentle breeze stirred her hair and made her curls bounce. Mama was younger. Her wrinkles healed like faded scars. She was laughing and smiling. She had a spring in her step Eliza had never seen.

Am I dead or just dreaming? She must have frozen to death.

It must be true. She could no longer feel pain or the cold in her hands and feet. In fact, she was warmer all over.

Mama suddenly seemed to notice her. She didn't appear to be surprised, only joyful. She smiled the bright welcoming smile Eliza knew so well and beckoned her to come.

Eliza spread out her arms and began to run to her mother.

"Oh Mama! Mama!" she cried.

There was a sudden flash of pain. Then everything went black.

CHAPTER 15

Robert was bone tired. Even though he stopped work early and came home, it had been a very long day out in the cold and snow, and his muscles and joints ached relentlessly.

He was troubled about Eliza. He didn't know why he should be thinking about her again, but he was. She laid upon his mind like a heavy wet blanket, and he unsuccessfully tried to push thoughts of her aside.

He thought of her more often than he wished, especially since that night in late August when he kissed her. He still burned with the shame for what he had done. He had no right to kiss her. Their friendship had been so warm and cozy; now they were stiff and formal with each other.

He lit a lantern and got down one of his books. The storm continued to howl outside his little shack, but he had a fire inside and he planned to stay close to it tonight.

He had trouble concentrating on the words of his book. On the pages, Eliza's heart-shaped face surrounded by wispy red curls and her bright questioning eyes appeared before him, leaving him restless and preoccupied.

He loved her. He had known it for quite a while. Of course, she wasn't interested in him. She was too young. Furthermore, she wasn't particularly interested in God either. Bear was determined to have a wife who was a passionate believer.

Loving Jesus and the Word was just one of the bonds he shared with his lost Rachel. In the end, it was the bond that mattered. Rachel was lost to this world, but he had assurance he would see her and their children again. For a time after her death, he hoped he would see her soon. But in the four ensuing years, he had learned to be patient with life, knowing death would come in God's own time.

Then came Eliza. He was surprised to find he could love a girl so much younger than himself. Not much more than a baby, really. Just turned eighteen. She acted older, maybe because of all of the responsibility thrust upon her at such a tender age. But she seemed to know what she wanted, and against all odds, continued to strive for it.

When the subject of God arose, he discovered Eliza had a perfunctory relationship with God. She was angry at Him for letting her mother die, but on the other hand, she knew people died from diseases and that death was just a part of life. Beyond that, she would occasionally go to church on Sunday, recite a blessing at meals, keep the Ten Commandments, and not bother God the rest of the time. Furthermore, she said she'd appreciate it if God didn't bother her with too many more demands.

He had tried to explain to her once God wanted to help carry her loads, but she laughed and said if God wanted to help, He was welcome to do some laundry.

No, Eliza was not for him. He wanted a believing wife by his side to share his faith. After the new year, when Silas and Cora were a little more settled, Bear had determined to move on and forget about Eliza. She was nearly finished with her studies and could take the final test for her diploma. Then his commitment to her would be finished too. He would go away and forget her. She didn't love him anyway.

Still, her auburn hair and pensive face with its quick smile seemed to be written into his book. Finally, he closed it and spoke aloud to God.

"Father," he began, "Lord of the storm, tonight I pray for Eliza."

Bear talked with God a long time about her, especially asking for His protection over her health and body. For some odd reason, her health seemed important tonight, so he carried his concerns to God as each presented itself in his thoughts.

Throughout the late afternoon as the storm raged on into evening, Eliza came often to his mind. He wished she wouldn't, but time and time again she came, so he prayed for her.

He ate a bite of supper and then opened the door to see if the storm had any plans of abating. A fine snow was coming down thick and fast. The easterly wind bespoke of a blizzard to him. He thought he should bring in more logs. The wood box was full, but he could feel the temperature dropping.

He dressed warmly for his brief trip to the woodpile. Falling flakes sparkled in the lantern's beam.

His cabin door faced south, away from Yankee Run, and he placed his woodpile as a windbreak on the west side of the cabin. He stacked the wood four layers deep and took his winter wood out of the eastern inside layer.

Normally, when Ohio winter winds turned playful, it was be-cause they had first run over the western United States, pick-ing up frisky habits. But these winds came from the east had stopped playing and turned deadly. Bear recognized their evil intentions. His lantern showed freezing rain falling earlier in the day combined with blowing snow effectively cemented shut the eastern face of his wood pile. Short of a large amount of shoveling and chiseling, he was going to get firewood out of the usually protected side.

He walked to the back of stack. The north and part of the west sides were also iced over. He walked along the western side feeling for loose pieces. His feet suddenly went out from under him as he tripped over a lump on the ground. His lantern flew out of his hand and the light guttered.

Disgusted with himself, he sat up and examined the lantern. Fortunately, he hadn't broken the shade. He straightened the glass and the flame glowed again.

What on earth tripped me up?

He held up the lantern and groped the dark object before him. It had give to it, so he pushed it over. To his amazement, it made a soft moan. He bent over the object and held his lantern so he could see.

By the lantern's golden light, he saw a pale face with a rag wrapped around it, topped with a man's woolen hat. It was one of the Burger boys! He heard a moan, so he knew the boy wasn't dead yet but wasn't far from it. Altman hoisted the boy over his shoulder and carried him into the house.

Heedless of the snow he was dragging in, he laid his bundle on the rug in front of the fire and knelt over him, peering into the boy's face. He recognized something wasn't quite right about the boy's appearance, but at the moment he was more concerned how much life was left in him. He needed to get the boy's snowy clothing off so the heat might revive him if he wasn't too far gone.

"Jesus, please let him live! Show me how to help."

When he pulled up the boy's pant legs, he was surprised to find winter shoes caked full of snow instead of boots. Why was he wearing shoes and not his chore boots? Eliza was the only one of the Burger kids he knew of whom Silas determined didn't need boots of her own but could share a pair with Ruthie. He pulled off the shoes and stripped the stockings from the foot and quickly appraised the situation. The three smallest toes on each foot were glossy white and had the look of frostbite. He pulled off the mittens and noticed his hands were in better shape.

He unbuttoned the jacket and pants and began to pull them off. Suddenly, even in the dim light, he could tell that the boy was wearing a dress. He loosened the rag over the boy's face and pulled the snowy stocking cap from his head. A cascade of auburn curls and hairpins fell out.

"Eliza!"

Dear God in heaven! This is Eliza! What is she doing by his woodpile in a blizzard nearly frozen to death? What brought her to his door on a night like this?

"Eliza! Eliza Burger! Talk to me! What were you doing out there?"

She answered him with soft moans and unintelligible mumbling. He couldn't make out anything. Once he'd freed her of her snow-covered wrappings, he carried her to his bed, and dress and all, tucked her beneath the quilt.

He went back outside, this time with an ax, and frantically chopped ice off of a section of the woodpile. He hurriedly brought in several armfuls, enough to last the night no matter how hard the wind blew. Then he checked on Eliza.

He brought the lantern close to the bed where he could access the damage. Her upturned nose and ears, spots vulnerable to frostbite, seemed okay. The rag she'd wrapped around her face probably saved them. There were some spots on tips of her fingers that looked bad. One in particular on her left hand might have to be pared off.

It was her toes that worried him most. He thought she'd lose both little toes and possibly the next ones, too. He would thaw them slowly and pray for the best. Gangrene was likely and he considered amputating now, while they were still numb, but he hated cutting flesh with any chance it might heal. But rotting toes were nasty too.

"Oh, Father, give me wisdom!"

He brought in a bucketful of snow. Taking rags, he tied handfuls of snow on her fingers and frozen toes. It wouldn't be good to let them thaw too quickly.

His textbook advocated rubbing the affected part with snow or a stiff brush to stimulate circulation. But Bear's real-life experience with frostbite revealed friction left a lot of damage on frozen skin. Nevertheless, he felt a pang of guilt for defying his textbook's wisdom.

Eliza remained in a twilight sleep. She shivered continually and muttered disjointed phrases about her mother in a field of flowers. Sometimes, she warned little Betty to stay away from the fire, and once she scolded John for tracking in snow. But in the hour or so that he slowly thawed her fingers and toes, she never opened her eyes or knew he was there.

By the wee morning hours, color returned to her fingers, and he was comfortable letting them warm naturally. He heated a pair of wool stockings in the warming oven and slipped them over her hands. The side of one toe still looked gray, so he kept it chilled, allowing circulation to slowly return.

He knew a couple of little tricks for defying the cold. He stitched rectangular bags filled with coarse pickling salt. When he was going to be in the cold for a long time, he heated these in the oven and placed them in the bottom of his boots to keep his feet warm.

He'd learned this from an elderly midwife when he was helping a woman give birth in an unheated shack. The poor girl used so much of her strength trying to keep warm she didn't have much left to push. He found them useful for sick folks trying to recover in breezy houses with little or no insulation.

Now he heated these bags and put one at the base of her neck. His big fingers trembled a little as he unbuttoned Eliza's bodice at her neck and waist. He slipped another heated bag under her left arm where her main arteries ran from her heart to the rest of her body.

He made himself a pot of coffee and put some beef bones on the cookstove to simmer. When Eliza regained consciousness, he'd start her on beef tea to make sure she had enough water in her system to stimulate her circulation.

Outside, the wind raised to a fierce howl. In spite of the thick log walls, he felt the chill of the falling temperatures and angry winter winds pounding on the cabin. During his last trip to the woodpile, there was so much snow in the air he couldn't tell if it was still snowing or just blowing around what had already fallen. But he could sense a blizzard pulled into the area and planned to stay a while.

He poured himself a cup of coffee and pulled a chair up beside Eliza's bed. He turned the lamp wick down to conserve oil and stared into the fireplace flames that rose and brightened as the outside currents pulled the fire and heat up the stone chimney. The fire was eating wood tonight. The ticking of the mantle clock could barely be heard over the screaming wind.

Nights like this reminded Robert of his mother. She knew the howling wind frightened him, so she would tell him stories about his father and their life before a hunter accidentally shot him.

"Your daddy was so proud of you when you were a newborn. He carried you downtown to show you off while I fretted at home. I did not want you out of my sight. Your father was such a talented doctor."

Talented doctor but a poor businessman.

As Robert grew up in Ohiopyle, Pennsylvania, he realized nearly everybody owed his father money for medical services rendered. When he was killed, a few paid up, giving Robert and his mother a pittance to live on while awaiting the townspeople's conscience to awaken.

Then the new doctor came to town, he expected prompt payment in full. This was a big change for the good people of Ohiopyle. Their former debts to Dr. Altman were conveniently forgotten.

Eliza muttered in her sleep and tossed fitfully. He smoothed the errant red curls away from her face, felt her cheek, and then placed a hand on her forehead.

"Mama?" she said.

"It's all right, 'Liza honey," he whispered.

She tried to open her eyes, but it was too much effort. She gave a slight smile and sunk back to sleep.

He sunk his chin in his hand and waited to see if Eliza needed anything. As the clock struck three, he dozed. In his broken, troubled dreams, he saw himself cutting off toes black with gangrene while Eliza screamed in pain.

CHAPTER 16

Eliza floated in a soft, warm haze. She couldn't get her eyes open, but she could see light through her lids. She could feel a comforting presence nearby and she was unafraid. Her mother had beckoned her to come join her in the fields of perpetual summer and Eliza had happily obeyed.

She felt a hand on her forehead. Mama's touch was so nice. She struggled to look at her, but her eyes would not open. She was so tired. Now that she was in heaven, she could rest.

It was dark the next time she awoke.

She opened her eyes. It took a moment for her mind to grasp the reality. She was not in heaven after all, but in an old cabin.

The last thing she clearly remembered was fighting her way through a blizzard to find her brothers and sister. Then she'd had a wonderful dream of Mama in a field of flowers. It seemed so real.

At the moment, she had a pressing need to relieve herself. Weakly, she threw the covers aside and discovered that she was still dressed, but her clothing was jumbled and loosened at her neck and waist. Her chemise and long underwear shirt were still in place, but she was confused as to why her dress was open and stockings were on her hands. She urgently needed to find the outhouse or even a chamber pot. Her head swam as she sat up and she steadied herself against the wall to keep from tumbling headfirst out of bed. She watched logs and rough furniture dance before her eyes. If she hadn't needed to go so badly, she would have laid down and forgotten the whole thing.

Gradually, her vision cleared. Her eyes lit on the back of a person sitting in a chair before the fire. His breathing was the deep, regular respiration of a sleeping man. There was something familiar about the thick black hair.

Then she knew. The man was Bear Altman, and this was his cabin. How had she come to be here?

The pressure in her bladder was insistent. She had to find someplace to go. Now.

The ropes supporting the mattress groaned and the corn husks in the tick rustled. Mr. Altman startled awake and turned to face her.

"Ah! Sleeping Beauty awakens!" He smiled. "You had a close brush with the death angel out there."

Suddenly, she saw two Bear Altmans as the room began to turn again.

He jumped to his feet and steadied her.

"You better lie back down. You've been a pretty sick girl, and you need to rest for a while."

She knew she couldn't get up on her own and her face flushed with shame.

"Mr. Altman, I need the chamber."

"Oh! Of course, you do! He stripped the socks off of her hands and helped her to her feet. She gasped with pain when she put weight on her damaged feet. He effortlessly carried her to the enameled chamber pot and gingerly set her down before it.

"Do you need help?" He seemed to be not in the slightest bit embarrassed.

Unable to speak, Eliza shook her head. She fumbled with her clothing while Mr. Altman held her around the waist and looked away. He gently but firmly supported her movements while she relieved herself and righted her clothing. When she was finished, he picked her up and carried her back to bed. He laid her on blankets, straightening them around her, and tucked her in.

The effort wore her out. She wanted to go back to sleep and forget everything that just happened, but her mind was uneasy as if it was trying to remind her of something important. Suddenly, she remembered what it was.

"Mr. Altman, my brothers and Ruthie. They didn't come home from school, and I went looking for them. They're out there, somewhere. We have to go find them!"

"I wondered what you were doing out in the blizzard. Rest easy. They're home safe and sound. Or at least they were when I when I went up to the barn to do the milking. I knew we were in for a storm, so I started milking early. John and Josh came home from school, and the McCaleys brought your pa and his missus home from the train station. They took over, so I came home. I had no idea you were out in the storm. If I would have known, I'd have come looking for you. You almost died out there, you know."

Eliza nodded. She knew she may have seen into heaven. She had nearly become a resident.

Mr. Altman fixed a bowl of warm water from the reservoir of the stove. He took a clean rag and carefully washed her face and hands, examining her fingers thoroughly as he bathed them. She lay quietly, allowing him to do with her what he wished.

"They look good, Eliza, real good. Do they burn on the ends? Especially the little fingers? They were frozen and I thawed them. Your fingers and your toes. They have a lot of bright color and that's what we want. Now I'm going to check your toes."

He reached under the blanket and carefully pulled out one foot at a time and looked at them closely.

Eliza whimpered. "They hurt."

"I bet they do. It's the circulation returning. Your little toes don't look very good. They're still kind of bluish, and I don't know if you'll lose them or not. We can't let gangrene get started, Eliza, so we'll do whatever is necessary if the color doesn't return soon."

She nodded weakly. She didn't want her toes amputated, but she trusted Mr. Altman completely. He always proved himself competent. If he said they needed to come off, then they needed to come off. She didn't have the strength to resist him anyway.

He poured a cup of steaming beef tea and fed her a teaspoonful.

"Each spoonful of liquid will save a little bit of toe," he told her with a wink. "Seriously, Eliza, you need a lot of warm fluids to renew the tissues. I know you want to sleep, but this is important too. So be a good girl and drink up."

She tried. He was patient and encouraging, but she was alternately feverish then violently chilled.

As Saturday dawned, the storm showed no signs of abating. The wind continued its concert of ferocious moans and screams. Mr. Altman reported a drift completely covered the northeast side of the cabin and he had to dig out the door to get to the woodpile.

"Do you know what today is?" he asked her.

She thought for a moment. "It's Christmas!" she said. "Oh, Mr. Altman, I want to go home! I've never spent Christmas away from my family."

"Unfortunately, I have. Many, many Christmases. And if I could, Miss Eliza, I would take you home today. But it is bitterly cold and it would be irresponsible of me to take you out in this weather. I'm not sure I could get myself through the snow and to the house, let alone take you too. I'm sorry, my dear. You'll have to put up with spending Christmas with me."

"I didn't mean it that way. I've never been away from my family this long and on Christmas … you know," she said, her eyes brimming with tears, "they probably think I'm dead."

"I've thought about that. I'd like to take them a little present of the news that you are alive. A little worse for the wear at the moment, but definitely alive. However, I'm afraid that present will have to wait."

When the feeble, cloud-shrouded light of day was at its brightest, Mr. Altman carried Eliza to the table he'd moved near the cabin's only window and set her on it. He lit a lantern and looked first at her fingers then her toes.

"The fingers look good, Eliza, but I'm not happy with the way your little toes look." He pointed out the blue-gray tips of dead flesh.

"Your body may slough off some of this, but I'm afraid to take a chance."

"What're you going to do?" Eliza grasped his arm.

"I'm going to pray for you right now and then wait for a few hours."

Not since her mother had knelt with her beside her bed and taught her to pray simple childhood prayers had anyone prayed with Eliza. Now, this large man with shaggy black hair and beard bowed his head and placed one of his huge hands on her toes.

Simply, like a much-beloved child addressing an understanding father, Mr. Altman asked God to be Eliza's Great Physician. He asked God what to do about her grayish toes and whether or not he should cut them off. Then he listened for an answer.

In the silence following his prayer, Eliza felt self-conscious sitting on the table. It had been a long time since she felt the presence of God, but now she felt sure the Lord God Almighty, Creator of the Universe, had entered this humble cabin on the banks of Yankee Run to look at her toes and make a recommendation.

Outside, the capricious winter wind continued to howl and tear at the logs. An occasional icy finger of wind pried loose a chink between the logs and let in cold. Mr. Altman kept a bucket of wet clay for just that reason. He stuffed the chinks with a mixture of clay and newspaper.

Through the tiny windowpane, Eliza could see bare trees swaying in the wind as if begging the skies for mercy. Inside, the fire in the stone hearth crackled and put on a brave but inadequate battle against the piercing cold. The clock ticked off the moments as God and Bear Altman held consultation over her extremities.

She was a little embarrassed to have God looking at something as insignificant as her feet. After all, they hadn't exactly been on comfortable speaking terms since Mama died. But Mr. Altman seemed to think God cared enough about her to extend His power from heaven on behalf of her toes.

After a lengthy pause, Mr. Altman picked up Eliza from the table and carried her back to bed.

"We'll give the toes some more time to heal, Miss Eliza. Maybe they'll slough off some of that dead flesh on their own. Meanwhile, my girl, plenty of warm fluids for you. And please don't hold back drinking because you're shy about relieving yourself in front of me. I know it's embarrassing for you; it would be for me, too, but we're both adults and we know about these things.

The fluids are absolutely necessary to throw off the effects of the cold and possible infection from your toes, so drink up!"

There was very little for Eliza to do but drink the beef tea Mr. Altman prepared. It warmed and nourished her all at the same time. He kept her feet and hands warm with the salt packs and woolen stockings. Although the storm continued to pound the tiny cabin and sift through cracks, Eliza stayed cozy.

He pulled his chair next to her bed and occasionally fed the hungry fire while they talked about everything and nothing. She found it surprisingly easy to talk to him about her dreams for the future and her grief over Mama's death.

He got down some of his medical textbooks from their shelf and read aloud the clinical description of Mama's illness. "The Latin name for it is *Clostridium tetani*. The common name for it is tetanus or lockjaw."

He read how it often begins with a puncture from a rusty nail.

"That's exactly how Mama sickness began! She was helping Papa in the barn when she scratched her back on a rusty nail. Several days later, she couldn't open her mouth or swallow her own salvia. She couldn't eat or drink or talk. All she could do was moan. It was terrible! We were helpless. Dr. Jackson could do nothing for her."

Mr. Altman nodded. He remembered coming into the house and seeing Margaret staggering around the kitchen and in pain with her mouth slightly open. He knew then there was nothing they could do but wait to see if the infection would run its course. Sometimes it took only two or three days for someone to recover. Sometimes it killed the patient outright.

Mama didn't give up easily. It took her ten days of pure agony to die. During that time, Grandma Knapp and Eliza rarely left her bedside. Helplessly, they took turns at night sleeping upright in the rocking chair just so she wasn't alone.

After she died, Aunt Cora and Eliza plunged into the work of caring for a grieving family and managing the day-to-day work of a household while suffering broken hearts themselves.

Each family member reacted differently to their loss, which was maddening to Eliza, who in addition to coping with her own grief, had to quit school, and assume all of her mother's chores.

Eliza had not spoken to anyone about any of this, but the words easily tumbled out to Bear Altman. He silently listened, nodding. He understood. Margaret had been his friend. She was his idea of what a godly woman should be.

She told him about the strange vision she had of her mother the night of the blizzard.

"Mr. Altman, I think I saw her in heaven. She was fine and so alive. Actually, she was more than fine; she was wonderful! And to think I've been angry with God for taking her to such a beautiful place."

"Jesus cried when he heard that his friend Lazarus died," Mr. Altman reminded her. "And He knew He would call Lazarus out of the tomb. No, Eliza, it is natural to hurt when you lose someone you love. But you must not let the pain of the loss rob you of your friendship with God."

"It did, you know. I've been angry with God for a year now. Maybe today, on Jesus' birthday, it's time to repent of it."

"Do you want me to pray with you?"

She shook her head. "No. I've got some other sins to confess too. I guess I need to start over to be a friend of God. I always trusted Mama's faith in Jesus to get me into heaven. That's not right, is it?"

Mr. Altman gently picked up her stocking-covered hand and held it gently. "No, Miss Eliza. It's not right. No one can repent for you, nor can they have saving faith for you."

"Do you mind, Mr. Altman? I need to think and pray for a little while," Eliza whispered.

"Not at all."

The big man moved his chair around to face the fire and give Eliza privacy. He folded his big hands in prayer as he watched the flames.

Three days after Mr. Altman found her in the snow, Eliza was still running a fever, but she was improving. He fixed eggs and bacon for the two of them, then sat on the edge of the bed while they ate breakfast. The storm had abated, and the wind had died. The sun shone brightly, turning the snow into a sea of glittering diamonds, but the temperature remained bitterly cold.

"Do you think you can manage by yourself for a few hours while I hike up to the house?" Mr. Altman's dark eyes searched her face.

"Oh, yes! I'm much better. Please tell them I love them, and find out if Betty is better and if she burned herself on the stove and …"

Mr. Altman placed a large finger on Eliza's lips.

"Shhh! Don't get worked up. I'll find out everything there is to know, and when I come back, you can ask me a million questions. Let's get you settled so I can get there and back before dark."

Mr. Altman made more broth for Eliza—this time from venison—placing it where she could easily reach it. He lifted down several medical textbooks and his Bible and stacked them on a chair near her bed. He warmly bundled himself against the frigid air, then brought in several loads of wood, which he stacked near the fireplace. It was nearly ten o'clock in the morning before he started for the Burger farm.

"Wish me Godspeed, Miss Eliza," he said as he went out the door.

"Godspeed, Mr. Altman!"

The cabin instantly seemed empty without him.

If I wasn't determined to be a nurse and he wasn't so shaggy, I could love Bear Altman, thought Eliza as she snuggled under the quilts. She knew she didn't want the drudgery of farm life that so obviously suited him.

The clock read 11:30 when Eliza awoke again. She gingerly got out of bed and used the chamber pot. Her feet were still very tender, but she tried walking a few steps before she sat down in front of the fireplace and watched the flames leap and dive.

For the first time, she noticed a small wooden trunk, not unlike her mother's, in one corner of the cabin. Curious, she hobbled over to it and opened the lid.

She expected to find Mr. Altman's clothes, but instead, there was a delicate pale blue woman's dress on top, folded carefully, the bobbin lace jabot only slightly crushed by the weight of the lid. A beautifully made cameo was pinned to the neck band and a hint of lavender escaped from the folds of the dress as she lifted it from the trunk.

She held it up to herself and discovered that the woman who wore the dress had been about her own size but with an impossibly tiny waist. A strand of black hair, not unlike Bear Altman's, was entwined around one of the silk-covered buttons down the back.

Under the dress were photographs. Eliza carefully laid the gown on the bed and drew out the cartes de visite. There were photographs of a man, a woman, and some children.

The handsome, clean-shaven, dark-haired man looked vaguely familiar. He had large, dark eyes, a strong chin, and even features. He was impeccably groomed and dressed in a well-tai-lored suit. The pretty young woman beside him had light hair caught up on top of her head. In one of the photographs, she was wearing the dress Eliza found in the trunk. There were three little children in the photographs, two boys and a girl.

Eliza supposed they were some of Mr. Altman's family. Perhaps he had a brother. Then it occurred to her that the man in the photograph might be Bear Altman himself. She hobbled over to the window and studied the image by its light. The eyes were very much like his, but could this handsome fellow be the same ill-kempt man who read schoolbooks to her and tended her father's animals? Was this woman his wife? Or perhaps sister? While Eliza felt a pang of jealousy, she rejected the thought. A man wasn't likely to keep his sister's dress. She must have been his wife.

She closely looked at the children. They seemed to have features that were a combination of the man and woman. Eliza was thunderstruck. Who were these people? Did Mr. Altman have a wife and family somewhere? She was surprised and chagrined how much the thought disturbed her. She had come to think of the man as belonging to her.

As she studied the photograph, a sudden realization swept over her: I am falling in love with Mr. Altman. She knew she needed to get away from him or all of her dreams and work would be for naught. And it didn't look like the man was free to love anyway. She carefully replaced the photographs and the dress and closed the lid. Although she felt rather guilty about looking through the trunk without permission, she had to know: Was that man in the photograph Mr. Altman? And did he have a wife?

CHAPTER 17

Swathing herself in bed covers, she turned up the lantern and enjoyed the first truly idle day she could ever recall. She read several chapters in the Bible, then read through a section in *Gray's Anatomy*. She was growing wonderfully drowsy when she heard Mr. Altman's voice booming "Hello!" outside the cabin door.

Eliza was happy to see him return safely from the frozen wilderness, but she was even happier he brought Ruthie with him.

Ruthie flew through the cabin door and sobbed as she threw herself on Eliza's bed and held her tightly.

"I couldn't bear it when I thought you were dead! Oh, Eliza! Don't ever go away again! And poor little Betty!" Ruthie cried as Eliza brushed the snowflakes out of the girl's dark hair.

"What about Betty?"

"When we thought you froze to death, she started wetting the bed again. She nearly drowned me! Mr. Altman had quite a time convincing her you were alive and would be back home in a few days."

"Did Betty get over the fever she had when I went looking for you?" Eliza's brow furrowed with worry.

"Oh, she's fine! Making a pig out of herself with Christmas candy. If you ask me, neither Cora nor Papa does a thing about it. But look!" She drew from her dress pocket a packet wrapped in brown paper. "Mr. Altman and I brought you some sweets. He said it might perk up your appetite."

Ruthie fed a crushed bit of ribbon candy to Eliza. "Don't do such a thing again, Eliza. If you die, I will die too." Tears filled Ruthie's eyes. Eliza gently stroked Ruthie's weather-reddened cheeks and held her sister until the girl was convinced this was not a dream and Eliza was very much alive.

For the next several days until the weather broke, Ruthie helped Mr. Altman care for Eliza. With Ruthie there, he could trek up to the farm to help Papa and the boys care for the stock during the deep freeze that followed the blizzard. The weather had taken a toll on the farm, and they had lost several animals that had to be butchered immediately.

Each day, Eliza regained more of her strength, although she had frequent violent chills and her hands and feet ached almost constantly.

"They're healing, Eliza." Mr. Altman examined her fingers and toes in the lamplight. "You have what are called 'chilblains.' They will probably hurt for some time to come. Maybe the rest of your life. But on the bright side, you still have all your fingers and toes to give you pain. I almost cut them off. I'm glad the Great Physician recommended I wait a little longer."

He taught Ruthie how to make willow bark tea for Eliza to drink and as a poultice for her fingers and toes until they could get to town for some aspirin.

"Willow bark is the pain reliever in aspirin," Mr. Altman told them. The poultices and tea did relieve some of the aching.

Although she still weak from the chill and frostbite, Eliza was deeply impressed that Mr. Altman prayed for wisdom as to her treatment and God told him what do to.

When I become a nurse, I'm going to ask Him for help with all my patients.

In the evenings, they sat by the leaping fire as the winter winds tore at the shingles on the roof and the log walls. Eliza, Bear Altman, and Ruthie read the Scriptures together in addition to working through Eliza's Latin textbook, which they brought back from the house. Being proficient in Latin was vital if she was to go to nurses' training.

Eliza was developing a deep hunger for God and longed to know Him better. She remembered how Mama loved to discuss the Bible with Mr. Altman, and she wished now she had paid closer attention to their conversations.

Ruthie read Mr. Altman's much-thumbed Bible to Eliza during the day while he was gone from the cabin. Eliza observed her sister taking a more active role in their conversations about God.

On New Year's Day, as they ate a savory stew by lantern light, Eliza commented, "Mr. Altman, I believe I'm ready to take my diploma test. How soon do you think I'll be fit to go to town?"

A smile flashed through Mr. Altman's dark beard.

"What a girl!" he said with admiration in his rumbling voice. "I would guess you could go in two weeks if the weather isn't wet or very cold. Weather conditions like those will be a trial for you for a while, maybe all your life. However, if you drink plenty of warm fluids and don't overdo, I think you could have your diploma very soon. And I suspect since the situation at home has changed, you might be able to go to nurses' training when the new classes commence next fall."

"What?" cried Ruthie, throwing her spoon on the table. "No, 'Liza! You're not going to go off and leave me with Aunt Cora. I can't stand her. Home will only be bearable if you're there."

"Ruthie, Aunt Cora's not so bad. And you know it's been my goal to go to nurses' college. If I get a chance to go, I will. But I'm going to have to get a job and make some money because Papa surely won't give me any."

Ruthie studied the chunks of meat and vegetables in her bowl. "Papa won't let you work for other people either, so that settles it. You're going to come home and stay home!"

Ruthie retrieved her teaspoon and stuffed another bite of stew in her mouth and chewed it emphatically.

Eliza's shoulders sagged. Poor Ruthie.

Eliza had no way of knowing at that moment she would never need her father's financial support again.

CHAPTER 18

Within twenty-four hours of New Year's Day, John, Mr. Altman, and Papa drove the sleigh and team back to the cabin in the woods. They swathed Eliza in quilts for the trip up to the house. She was still weak and experiencing a lot of pain, so once she was settled in her bed, Papa sent John into town to summon Dr. Jackson.

As Papa leaned against the doorjamb and watched, Dr. Jackson sat on the bedside chair and studied Eliza's fingers and toes. Finally, he rose to his feet, jammed his hands into his trouser pockets, and watched her with a mystified air.

"Eliza, for the amount of trauma your extremities experienced, they are in very good shape. You realize Altman not only saved your life; he saved your fingers and toes from amputation. Tell me, how did he thaw them?"

"Doctor, I really don't know." Eliza ran her hand over the bedding, smoothing it over herself. "I don't remember much of it. All I do know is he prayed for me and fed me a lot of beef broth and willow bark tea. Why don't you ask him? I would be interested to know too."

"Bear!" Pa called the big man from the kitchen into Eliza's room.

The big man shyly entered Eliza's bedroom and gave her a slight smile. She noticed he had combed his hair and his beard was trimmed.

"You did a masterful job saving this girl's life and her toes. How did you know what to do?" Dr. Jackson regarded him closely.

Bear Altman's dark eyes looked trapped. He turned his broad back to them and stared out the window. Nothing prepared any of them for his answer.

"Doctor Jackson, I am a trained, licensed physician. I spent about ten years practicing medicine in the Texas oil towns. When Eliza appeared on my doorstep more dead than alive, I knew I needed to act." Mr. Altman turned to face them. "Folks generally think of Texas as hot, but occasionally, a blue northerner blows in on unprepared people and then there's a lot of frostbite. When I found Eliza in the snow, I knew it was time to use what I knew to save her life and maybe her fingers and toes, too."

Dr. Jackson scratched his head. "I don't understand, Altman. Why are you working as a hired hand and not practicing medicine?"

"I got tired of trying to battle disease without ..."

Eliza thought she heard a catch in Mr. Altman's voice.

"... real cures or effective medicines. Many of the cures I learned in medical school didn't work or, in fact, made patients worse. For example, from my experience, rubbing a frostbitten area with snow tears the skin and invites gangrene. I know that's what the medical textbooks say to do, but I've seen too much failure with that type of treatment and had better success with slowly thawing the fingers and toes."

Dr. Jackson nodded thoughtfully. "I'm a fairly new doctor, Altman, but I, too, have seen similar things. There's so much that we don't know."

"You are so right. I was rather arrogant in those days. I thought I knew it all." Mr. Altman swallowed hard. "I knew God then, but I should have prayed before I made a diagnosis. I should have made God my partner in medical practice."

"On more than one situation, I've asked God for a consultation too." Dr. Jackson clapped his hand on Mr. Altman's shoulder.

Eliza was stunned. Bear Altman was a doctor! That explained why he had the medical textbooks.

What other secrets was he keeping?

Over the next few days, Dr. Jackson continued to check on Eliza until she suspected the real reason he came was not because she needed medical attention, but because he enjoyed the long talks Dr. Jackson and Mr. Altman had over hot coffee. The men relished each other's company and conversation. Dr. Jackson discussed some of his puzzling cases with Mr. Altman.

Eliza steadily improved. At first, she only felt well enough to be on her feet for a few hours a day. But by the end of the second week, she was almost entirely recovered except for occasional chills.

Her convalescence gave Eliza time to review her studies, and the frequency of Dr. Jackson's visits provided her with an opportunity to privately inquire whether he still needed someone to work in his office and be a companion to his wife.

"As a matter of fact, the young woman now filling the position is getting married and will be leaving soon. I have been wondering who I could get to take her place. Do you think you're well enough? Will your father permit it?"

"I think I'll be strong enough soon. As for my father, I don't really know. If you would be willing to try me, I'll ask him."

Eliza did not know how to approach her father. Not only was her working outside the home a touchy subject, but Papa was also behaving oddly Eliza suspected he was secretly drinking again. He had visibly aged during the days he thought Eliza had frozen to death in the blizzard. Now he was snappish to Cora, Eliza, and the children.

At times he dropped his hale and hearty persona and was curt with Grandpa and Grandma Knapp, Bear Altman, and the neighbors.

"He's had so many tragedies," said Cora, trying to explain away Papa's irrational temper tantrums. Cora was forgiving of Papa's bad temperament. None of the family had ever seen him like this, even in the darkest of times.

Eliza overheard Dr. Jackson and Mr. Altman privately agree Papa might be having a breakdown.

While she was concerned about her father, the tantalizing possibility of living in town and working for Dr. Jackson was foremost on Eliza's mind.

At first, she demanded God do this for her, but gradually she came to know that if it was what God wanted, He would work it out. She would do her part and trust God to do His.

Her desire to be a nurse had not changed since her Christmas Day prayer. If anything, she wanted it more. She now saw nursing as a path to help the hurting in Jesus' name and to be a servant. As she read the Word, the Holy Spirit encouraged her longing to help the sick, and she realized this was perhaps a call on her life as surely as some are called to preach or be missionaries. Therefore, she determined to be obedient as God made plain her path.

While she continued to regain her strength, a detail concerning her health niggled in her mind. Her time of the month was late—very late. By the first of February, it had not come. Eliza was worried. She whispered her concerns to Cora one night at the kitchen sink as they cleaned up following dinner.

"Talk to Dr. Jackson when he comes, Eliza. It might be because you took a chill. I'm sure everything will be fine," Cora told her.

It took some effort to get enough courage to ask him about it. However, Cora was right. Dr. Jackson reassured her that her condition was indeed common in women who had experienced a deep chill. He gave her two courses of powders to dissolve in water, which she was to drink while soaking her feet in warm water.

Although the powders did not change anything, his diagnosis erased the anxiety from Eliza's mind. She didn't know her troubles were only beginning.

CHAPTER 19

"I tell you you're going to do right by that girl!"

The clock chimed midnight, but it was Papa's yelling in the kitchen that awakened Eliza from a sound sleep.

Still in her nightgown, she ran down the stairs. The kitchen lantern sat on the new oak table. By its light, Eliza could see her father's face mottled with rage and poking the barrel of his shotgun in Bear Altman's chest.

Mr. Altman was barefoot, coatless, and hatless. He, too, was angry.

"Silas, have you been drinking? I'm not going to tell you again to quit pointing that gun at me. I didn't molest Eliza in any way. Let me remind you I saved her life. Now quit acting like a fool!"

"My daughter is pregnant, and we all know who's responsible. And you're going to do right by her!" Papa rammed the shotgun into Mr. Altman's chest.

"Silas Burger, put that shotgun away before you hurt somebody. If you weren't my friend and drunk, I'd lick you this minute in front of your wife and kids."

The big man put his hands on his hips and glowered down at Papa as if he were regarding a recalcitrant child.

"I'd like to see you try!" Papa said, poking him again with the shotgun barrel.

"I've had enough of this foolishness." With a quick twist, he safely pulled the gun out of Papa's hands.

"Now what's this about Eliza being pregnant?"

Eliza felt a touch on her shoulder. She turned. Cora and the children were standing behind her, looking frightened and confused. Clad only in their long underwear, John and Josh looked as if they were undecided whether to stay back or join the fray in the kitchen.

"Papa! What are you doing? What are you talking about?" Eliza stepped into the kitchen. "I'm not pregnant. I'm just recovering from the effects of being nearly froze to death."

She turned to Mr. Altman. "Mr. Altman, I'm so sorry. I don't know what's gotten into Papa."

As Papa rubbed his eyes with his knuckles, Eliza caught a strong whiff of alcohol.

"Come on, Silas," coaxed Altman. "Let's sit down and talk this over."

Papa made a sudden lunge for the shotgun, but Altman held it out of his reach.

"I'm not about to be hoodwinked again! You've lived here for almost three years and deceived us into thinking you were a hired man and nothing more. I'm not about to be fooled by you again. My daughter's pregnant and we all know who's responsible and you're going to do right by her!"

"Papa, I'm not pregnant!"

"John! Joshua! Hitch up the team. I'm going for the sheriff," yelled Papa. The boys shoved past Eliza.

"Stay where you are!" Mr. Altman ordered. Both boys froze in place.

"I don't want to see anyone get hurt. Cora and Eliza, take everybody upstairs while I try to talk some sense into him, although it's a fool's errand to try to reason with a drunk."

Cora shooed the protesting children upstairs, but Eliza stood her ground.

"Silas, you've got to settle down and get a grip and listen to reason. I never laid an improper hand on Eliza. You have to know that."

"You can't tell me you spent a week with my daughter and never touched her. She's got woman problems now—the kind that come when a woman is going to have a baby—and you're responsible. You forced my daughter and you're going to do right by her!"

"Papa, Mr. Altman did not rape me."

"You said you don't remember anything for a while. Who knows what he did then?"

"I know what I did—and didn't—do. I loosened her clothing so her blood could circulate and warm her up, but nothing more. Silas, it's you that has the problem, not me, and not Eliza. Her system sustained a terrible shock. She'll be fine if you'll quit upsetting her with this nonsense."

Papa plopped down on a chair and held his head in his hands. "I'm sorry. People are talking. They say that we don't know anything about you anyway —that Eliza is ruined because of this—that no decent man will ever want her ..."

"Silas, those are separate matters," said Mr. Altman. "But I give you my word that I did not touch Eliza improperly. However, people are going to talk. I wager folks are discussing your marriage to Cora too."

"I suppose." Papa sniffed.

"Life's been tough for you the last year." Mr. Altman put the shotgun back up on the hooks above the door. He pulled out a chair and sat down at the table with Papa.

Eliza and Mr. Altman's eyes met over Papa's bowed head. With a slight nod, he motioned for her to leave. This time, she tiptoed quietly upstairs and lay in bed, listening to the rumbling bass of Bear Altman's voice.

So the community was accusing Altman of raping her, when in actuality he saved her life. She feared she had yet to hear the worst of it.

Chapter 20

In the early morning light, it was as if the whole incident had never happened. Eliza lay in bed, tired from the drama of the previous night and not feeling well. She was happy thinking Bear Altman talked sense into Papa. Maybe now Papa would get better and go back to being himself.

After breakfast, Eliza lay down to take a short nap. She had just dozed off when Cora gently shook her awake.

Cora's dark eyes looked troubled and filled with foreboding.

"Eliza, Reverend and Mrs. Rutledge are downstairs to see you. They're in the parlor."

The Rutledges had recently come to pastor the Stringtown Church. They visited Eliza several times since the incident.

Cora helped Eliza button up her everyday calico dress and followed her downstairs.

The parlor door stood open. Eliza saw the Rutledges warming their hands in front of the new stove.

"My dear Eliza!" Rev. Rutledge greeted her solemnly. "Your father has asked us to speak with you."

Eliza sat down on the black horsehair sofa and held her head. It had begun to ache again.

Rev. and Mrs. Rutledge sat down on either side of her. Mrs. Rutledge took her hand. "Your father thinks that Mr. Altman forced himself upon you while you were unconscious. Is that a possibility? Was anything amiss when you woke up?"

"Mrs. Rutledge, my clothing was loosened around my neck and my waist, but I think that was necessary so I could get warmed up again. I want you to know Mr. Altman has always been a perfect gentleman to me. He never harmed me in any way, I assure you."

The blood rushed to Eliza's face and the room began to swim.

What was the matter with Papa and everyone? Bear Altman- saved my life. Why couldn't people just let it go at that?

Mrs. Rutledge slid her arm around Eliza's waist and Eliza sobbed on her shoulder.

"Your father is convinced otherwise. Would you be willing to undergo an examination by a doctor to prove your statements?" Rev. Rutledge asked.

"I'll not be examined by anyone! That is ridiculous! I hate to say it, but my father is not thinking clearly right now. I wish everyone would stop encouraging him in this nonsense."

Eliza wept. Mrs. Rutledge gently held her while she wetted the shoulder of the good woman's black wool dress with her tears.

"I believe you, Eliza," Rev. Rutledge said sympathetically. "I've talked to Mr. Altman, and I believe in his innocence too. I agree. Silas needs help and I intend to tell him that. But be prepared, Eliza. Silas is going to ask the sheriff to charge Mr. Altman with rape. I'm afraid he will do it too. You may have to provide evidence, so Mr. Altman doesn't go on trial.

"However, people will continue to gossip about you and Mr. Altman being alone in the cabin all that time. We can't stop that, although I certainly wish we could."

The Rutledges rose to leave. "May we pray with you?"

Eliza nodded.

"Oh God, heal Silas Burger's mind and quiet the gossiping tongues."

When they had gone, Eliza sat alone, tears streaming down her face. How far was Papa going to push this thing?

"Father," she prayed, "please tell me what is right to do. Give me wisdom."

Eliza heard Cora admit Bear Altman through the back door. Although his rough clothing was permeated with the smell of cattle and his boots were covered with frozen mud, he came into the parlor and shut the door behind him so they were alone. His big hands fumbled with his hat.

Eliza didn't look up. She was too humiliated to meet his eyes.

"Miss Eliza, I hardly know how to approach this. Your father has charged me with rape. The sheriff is here, and he is going to take me to jail. I don't have to tell you that I'm innocent, do I?" His expressive eyes pleaded for understanding.

"Of course not!" Eliza longed to soothe him as he comforted her when she was in pain.

"Your father says he will drop the charges if you and I are married. However, for your sake—and mine—I want your father to know I didn't harm you. If we choose this route, it will be a marriage in name only, I assure you. You'll be free to live where you want, do what you want to do. Eliza, I know what's important to you, and believe me, I would never stand in your way.

"But we don't have to get married. We can fight this charge, Eliza. I think we can win. It won't stop people from gossiping. The sheriff says I will have to go to jail until the trial. And even if I am proved to be not guilty, it won't convince your pa of the truth, and I'm sorry about that. I thought of your pa as my friend."

The man stood quietly waiting for her reply. She knew her reputation was ruined by her father's deluded charges and silly gossip in the neighborhood. Her life under Papa's roof was over, even if there was a trial and Mr. Altman was found innocent. This man had saved her life. She did not want him to suffer the indignity of being arrested and going to jail. She heard the voices of men out in the kitchen, and she knew it was the sheriff come to arrest Mr. Altman. The thought of this good man behind bars made her shudder.

"Mr. Altman, will you marry me?"

He looked startled. "Those are words I never thought I'd hear you utter. Yes, Miss Eliza, I will marry you."

CHAPTER 21

As Eliza dressed for her wedding, the upstairs bedroom was crowded with female friends and family members. Cora and Laura McCaley buttoned her into the same rust brown serge dress she wore for Cora and Papa's wedding just weeks before. There wasn't time or inclination to have another dress made.

Eliza was anxious to get the ceremony over and get away from the house. In the week since she asked Mr. Altman to marry her, she had not spoken to her father, nor had he said a word to her. She supposed in Papa's troubled mind he thought he was acting in her best interest, but she believed he was using her to trap Mr. Altman into being his permanent farm hand and that made her angry.

While she combed and styled her hair, Grandma, Cora, and the girls sat on her bed chatting with forced gaiety. Eliza never pictured her wedding day like this. She wanted to love the man she married, not be forced into marriage by her father. She truly liked Bear Altman, maybe loved him. If nature had been allowed to take its course, she might have voluntarily married him. Under the circumstances, she was resentful. She supposed he felt the same way.

Eliza took one last look at herself in the mirror. The next time she saw herself in the mirror, she would be a married woman.

Oh, Mama. I miss you.

A tear cruised down her cheek.

Since that fateful wintry day when she saw the apparition of Mama standing happy and carefree in a sun-dappled field, she had not wished her back to earth. Eliza imagined her mother watching from heaven. She wasn't smiling, but she was approving of her daughter's resolve to make the best of a bad situation.

From the top of the steps, Eliza heard the low rumblings of Mr. Altman's voice above the other murmuring tones. Only minutes before, she heard Grandpa's ol' Lulu popping and sputtering as it pulled into the yard bringing Rev. Rutledge from the String-town Church. She knew everyone was downstairs waiting for her.

Eliza squared her shoulders and descended the stairs followed by Grandma, Cora, and the girls. As she came into the parlor, the room became silent. Everyone turned to look at her. Grandpa reached out and patted her arm, and little Betty slipped her small hand in Eliza's.

Rev. Rutledge, his Bible in hand, stood in front of the stove. He cleared his throat. The parlor grew still. From the mantle, Mama and Cora's photograph peeked over his shoulder.

A tall, dark-haired man stepped up beside the preacher. He was well-groomed and wearing a tailored black wool suit generously cut to accommodate his wide shoulders. His immaculate white shirt was accented with a black tie. Clean-shaven with a strong jaw, he had full lips and straight, even teeth. He was the man in the photos she found in the trunk.

Eliza stared at him curiously. She guessed he was in his middle or late thirties; it was impossible to tell. His dark brown eyes, oddly familiar, watched her every move.

A thrill swept through Eliza. *He is so handsome! Who is he?*

Then he stretched out his hand to her. "Eliza, are you ready?"

"Mr. Altman? Is it really you?"

He smiled. "It's me. I didn't mean to startle you; I just thought I should trim the hedges for the occasion."

"You look … I mean, I didn't recognize you!"

"It's me," he said, grinning at her.

"It's going to take some getting used to, but I like it," she said.

Everyone in the room laughed, including Mr. Altman and Eliza.

"Children," said Rev. Rutledge, "if you're ready …"

Eliza took her place beside Mr. Altman.

"Would you take her right hand?" the preacher instructed him.

He lightly held her small hand in his.

As the preacher read the vows, Eliza studied his work-roughened hand. How tenderly he had cared for her when she was sick. She recalled the evenings he read to her while she mended, and how together they planted and harvested a garden.

"Sickness and in health, richer or poorer, till death do you part," intoned Rev. Rutledge.

Eliza knew this man would do those things for her even without the legalities. While he was a devastatingly handsome stranger, he was, in fact, her best friend and now her husband.

She learned during the ceremony that his given name was Robert, a name she far preferred over Bear.

Suddenly, the vows and prayers were over. Rev. Rutledge pronounced them man and wife. Mr. Altman did not kiss her. He shook her hand.

Guests were invited to stay for pie and coffee, but Robert Altman had other plans for himself and Eliza. He had hired a buckboard for the day. As soon as the ceremony was over, he climbed the stairs and carried down Mama's trunk packed with Eliza's few clothes and the cream can that held Mama's diaries and put them in the back of the wagon.

Papa followed him outside. "Altman, you don't have to live back in the woods anymore. Now that you're married to my daughter, you can move into the old house. It'll be closer for you to work."

Mr. Altman turned to Papa. "Silas—Mr. Burger—I've moved out of the cabin, and I won't be living there anymore or working for you."

"I don't understand, Altman …"

"I'm the one who doesn't understand. I don't understand why you would want me to work for you. Why would you want a man on your farm that would rape a helpless, nearly dead girl?"

Mr. Altman lifted Eliza onto the buckboard and climbed up beside her. He picked up the reins and whistled to the team.

Papa fumbled for the harness. "Wait a minute! Where are you taking Eliza?"

Mr. Altman reined in the horses briefly. "Mr. Burger, that is no longer your concern. Hang on, Eliza!" He lightly touched the whip to the horses' backsides. The harness jerked out of Papa's hand and the team briskly trotted out of the farmyard.

Eliza was breathless. It all happened so fast. As they drove toward Rockford, Eliza cast self-conscious glances at Bear Altman from her end of the seat. He was still bigger than most men, but with his trim haircut, the nickname no longer fit him.

Eliza didn't know where they were going. She hadn't made any plans because she assumed they would live in Robert's cabin on

Yankee Run. Eventually, she hoped to have a position with Dr. Jackson and his wife, but where would they go in the meantime? And would Robert remember his promise that they would be married in name only?

"I can't believe we just got married!"

The frozen ground sped past under Eliza's feet.

"Well, Miss Eliza—or perhaps I should call you 'Mrs. Eliza,'" said Altman with a wink. "It is all finished. You're on your way to your new home with Dr. Jackson and his wife. And I'm on my way to Chicago."

"Chicago! Why are you going to Chicago?"

"Eliza, America is going to war with Germany, and I've enlisted. Our boys in uniform will be needing doctors and I can serve. As a physician, I've been awarded the rank of captain. As my wife, you'll receive a monthly check from the government. It won't be a lot, but if you are frugal, you can live comfortably on it.

"And something else." He reached inside his coat pocket and brought out a little leather book and handed it to her. "It's a wedding present, Eliza. Take a look."

Curiously, she examined the book. There was the name of a bank on the front. She opened it and saw her name at the top of a page with a list of numbers beneath it.

"What is this, Mr. Altman?" she asked.

"It's a bank passbook. If you will notice, there is a tidy sum in there. It is now ours, yours and mine."

"Where did you get so much money, Mr. Altman?"

"Please call me Robert, Eliza. You forget, my dear, I was a physician for more than ten years before I came here. Boomtown wages are huge, although I personally paid an even bigger price for practicing medicine there."

Tears welled up in the corners of his eyes and he unashamedly wiped them away.

Eliza thought of the woman and the children in the photos and wondered if they were the price he paid, but now did not seem to be the time to ask questions about his past.

"I've been here almost three years, and as you know, I've barely spent a dime on anything but candy for your little sisters. The rest I have saved. I am placing it into your hands to manage any way you please. You can go to nurses' college, buy a house, run off to Zanzibar, whatever suits your fancy." Mr. Altman watched her reaction out of the corners of his eyes.

Eliza was dumbfounded. "I don't understand, Mr. Altman—I mean, Robert. Why are you doing this?"

"Whoa!" Robert halted the team in the middle of the road and looked at her squarely, his dark eyes searching her face. "You really don't know? Although you were pushed into marrying me, you will remember I promised you it would be a marriage in name only unless you wanted something different, so I'm giving you all of the options I can."

He raised the reins and expertly brought the horses back to a trot.

"Just so you don't worry, I have a room for myself tonight at the Big Hotel in Rockford, and Dr. and Mrs. Jackson are expecting you. Tomorrow morning, I'm scheduled to be on the early train to Fort Wayne and then on to Chicago. I expect to be shipped to somewhere in Europe when America actually joins the fight. Those who know say if the Americans join the war, it'll be over in a matter of weeks—maybe days. But if I don't come back, the money is yours all the same and you'll receive a widow's bonus."

Eliza was stunned. She thought she was giving up all of her dreams by marrying Robert Altman only to find herself completely cared for and all of her dreams within her reach. It occurred to her that if he didn't come back, she would lose the one man on earth who truly loved her. And perhaps the man she loved as well.

"Don't leave. I like you very much. In fact, I think I love you."

He smiled. "Eliza, I've loved you for a very long time, but I won't trap any woman into a marriage with me, especially not the woman I love. Understand, the money in no way obligates you to me. In fact, I'd say we're even. I saved your life, and you saved me from going to prison.

"We can write, and perhaps we'll see each other occasionally. After the war is over, if you choose me to be your husband, then …" Altman swallowed hard. "We'll consider other arrangements. But in the meantime, I have an obligation to our country, and you are invited to help out Dr. and Mrs. Jackson."

All too soon for Eliza, the buckboard pulled up in front of Dr. Jackson's house. Mr. Altman unloaded Mama's trunk and cream can.

"Ahh! The newlyweds! Come in!" Dr. Jackson greeted them at the front door.

Altman planned to leave immediately, but Dr. Jackson detained him. "Robert, you must come in for some coffee and cake. Mrs. Jackson is anxious to see you and we shall be deprived of your company for a long time, I fear."

Mrs. Jackson, wearing a delicate pink gown, sat on the sofa in the parlor. It was the first time Eliza met her, but she did not rise to greet them. Eliza was struck at how thin and pale she was. She did not look well.

For a while, the conversation centered on the war and Robert's assignment awaiting him in Chicago. Then Dr. Jackson changed the subject as one doctor seeking the opinion of another. "Robert, what treatment would you prescribe for a woman who still experiencing bleeding a year after a miscarriage?

"If it's not too much of an invasion of privacy, may I ask if the woman is Mrs. Jackson?" Mr. Altman asked.

Dr. Jackson nodded his head sadly. "We've tried nearly everything, Robert. I've written my professors at the medical school in Columbus, but no one has a clue. What's your opinion?"

"Mrs. Jackson, may I look at your hair and fingernails?" Mr. Altman asked.

"Yes. Of course." she said. She took out her bone pins and her pale blonde hair fell down around her shoulders.

How beautiful she would be if only she was healthy!

Mr. Altman moved a lamp close to her and studied her nails and her hair. He took her face gently in his hands and carefully examined her skin. Altman closed his eyes briefly. While others in the room may have thought he was thinking, Eliza knew he was praying.

"Here is a woman who is not eating very well and wearing her corset laced too tightly. You must be very careful with corsets, Mrs. Jackson. I have seen women die from compressing their livers with corsets. Tight corsets can have a disastrous effect on childbearing so you must give up the tiny waist of fashion for the sake of your health.

"Furthermore, because I suspect your blood needs enriching, I would prescribe a diet of more red meat, chopped finely and boiled until very tender, reserving the broth to drink as beef tea three times a day. Every day, you need at least one fresh egg and milk with cream. Also, plenty of green and yellow vegetables. Fresh ones, if you can get them this time of year. And fresh air. Bundle up warmly and take a very short drive every day the weather is fit. You must not get chilled, for as Miss Eliza will tell you, that can have dire consequences, too. But you need air and gentle exercise.

"Nothing I've suggested will hurt you. Food was meant to be our medicine. When God planted the Garden of Eden, he put the Tree of Life in it. Adam and Eve were invited to eat from it, and we are too.

"When the weather moderates, perhaps your husband might consider taking you to one of the teaching hospitals in Fort Wayne or Chicago. After a year of suffering with your condition, I think it merits a closer look."

"Well spoken, Robert!" Dr. Jackson seemed impressed.

The clock struck eight and Robert reluctantly looked at the door and then stood to his feet.

"I have a very early train tomorrow, so if you'll excuse me …" Robert picked up his hat.

Dr. Jackson extended his hand. "Robert, I shall miss you. I feel I have only just made a friend and now you must go."

"I shall miss you, too, Frank." Robert shook Dr. Jackson's hand and then Mrs. Jackson's.

Eliza escorted Robert to the door. With one hand resting on the shining brass doorknob, she slipped the other into his fingers.

"Robert, thank you for everything. I'm really going to miss you. I already owe you my education and my life. I'll be in your debt for any future success I have," said Eliza, looking up into his dark eyes. "But I do have a favor to ask of you: Will you write to me?"

He searched her face. "Do you really want to hear from me? You don't need me, you know. You have everything you need to fulfill your dreams. You have a good position here with Dr. Jackson, money, freedom from family responsibilities. Why do you want to hear from me?"

"Robert, just when I realize I love you, I'm losing you. Promise me you'll write."

He smiled down at her and lightly touched her upturned nose with one finger. "Alright, I will promise on one condition."

"Name it."

"I kissed you once on a starry summer night and you kissed me back. Do you remember?"

Eliza laughed. "Of course, I remember."

"Will you kiss me good night and goodbye?"

He opened his arms and she slipped into them. He kissed her gently, then with more heat. She felt his fingers slide down her back until both hands rested at her waist. He pulled her toward him, pressing her body into his.

Suddenly, he released her. "That kiss is certainly worth writing home about," he said with a smile.

"God keep you, Eliza," he whispered as he turned and stepped off the porch. Without looking back, he mounted the buggy and gave the reins a jiggle. Through the lacy curtains of the beveled glass door, Eliza watched his broad back and wondered if she'd ever see her husband and friend again. Would he survive the war? Or would she be a widow before she was truly a wife?

CHAPTER 22

At 3:00 a.m., the westbound to Chicago train huffed on the track at the Rockford depot. As Robert stepped aboard, the steam signal screamed followed by a lantern-waving conductor bawling, "All aboooard for Gary, Indiana, Chicago, Illinois, and points west!"

How well he remembered the wounded man he used to be. The man who got off the eastbound train in Rockford, Ohio, by accident with his heavy knapsack of medical reference tomes, a trunk, and weightiest of all, a broken heart.

He was an orphan who started a family only to have them all perish together. After their loss, Bear felt the need for family. His plan was to go back to Ohiopyle, Pennsylvania, where he was born and his parents died, to find if any of their family were still there.

He had fallen asleep but woke with a start when the train stopped in Rockford. He had asked a fellow passenger what stop this was.

The man said, "I couldn't hear the conductor very well, but he did say something about Ohio."

Half asleep and thinking he had arrived in Ohiopyle, Robert got off the train. When the cold air hit him after the train left the station, he realized his mistake. Looking back, he still wasn't sure why he stayed.

The day after their marriage, as the westbound train pulled out, Robert stood between cars and watched the gaslights of downtown Rockford disappear and a wintry Ohio landscape replace them.

He reached into the pocket of his wedding suit to stroke a lock of hair tied with a ribbon. It was a dead thing, this lock of hair, belonging to his beloved Rachel, who now resided in heaven and lived only in his memory. During the four years since her death, he carried Rachel's hair with him, carefully wrapped in her silk handkerchief. Now he felt guilty he still had it. He was, after all, married to Eliza.

He pulled it from his pocket and thumbed the baby-fine texture of the pale blonde lock. Helen Jackson had almost the same color of hair, and when he first saw her, she startled him. But beyond the color of her hair, the pampered Helen Jackson was nothing like his Rachel.

Rachel was smart and funny and no nonsense. He admired intelligent, ambitious women, and in that way, Eliza was very much like Rachel. Despite her delicate appearance, no one deceived Rachel. He had seen her competently match wits with con men, patent medicine salesmen, and run-of-the-mill flimflam men who are overrepresented in Texas boom towns. No one, not even he, ever got the best of Rachel. He learned not to pick fights with her.

She kept him brutally honest about himself. Since he was prone to exaggeration and pride, she deftly popped any ego inflation he attempted.

But she was gone along with her sparkling personality.

He sometimes imagined her rearing their three children in heaven, teaching them the life of Jesus as He lived it on earth. When lessons were learned, she probably would organize the children into one of those romps for which she was famous among the small fry.

He had no tangible mementos of his children, no locks of hair, no toys, no clothing. Everything that had been theirs was burned when fire swept through the town followed by the plague that claimed their lives. All he had was a few photos, which he kept in the trunk he'd left with Dr. Jackson for safekeeping.

Along with Eliza. He hoped she would be safe there.

Robert stared out the window. He liked Frank Jackson, but he had heard some disturbing rumors about him he hoped weren't true. Of course, folks in little towns liked to whisper about their neighbors. His rescue of Eliza certainly set tongues wagging. Spiced up their dull lives, he supposed. He wished Rachel had been there to size up Frank Jackson. She'd have told Robert in short order whether Eliza would have anything to worry about.

Rachel would have approved of Eliza. She would have instantly recognized behind the sweet expression on Eliza's heart-shaped face she was an honest, kind soul. Eliza was genuine, good, and spunky.

And Robert loved her. He hated leaving Eliza in Rockford and he hated leaving Rockford, Ohio and the Burgers.

He was still hungry for family. For a sense of belonging and kinship. The Burgers temporarily filled the void. They became his family. He not only loved Eliza, but he also loved them, too. Eliza was a tangible tie to them. For a while, they made him feel that he belonged somewhere in the universe. He had happily and gratefully taken on extra work because he considered himself family. Now all of that was gone.

Had he let himself be pushed into marrying Eliza to cement his position as part of a family? No, he loved her. He was devoted to her. He didn't intend to trap her. Silas definitely pushed the issue and maybe he had been too cooperative. Perhaps he should have fought to prove his innocence.

But if he loved Eliza, why was he still carrying Rachel's hair in his pocket? Rachel would have seen through his proclamations of love for Eliza. Carrying Rachel's hair in his pocket made a mockery of his love for Eliza.

He shivered in the cold. The landscape was starting to lighten. A new day was dawning.

Maybe he allowed Silas Burger to push him into marriage for more than one reason, but his need for family ties and love for Eliza didn't mean he would hold her captive. He would release Eliza, let her go, if she wanted to go. He'd said as much to Eliza. Then he made her beholden to him by giving her that large bank account. Leaving Eliza with a large sum of money was no risk. He knew well her sense of duty and responsibility. He had simply assured himself Eliza would wait for him, that the Burger family would someday welcome them both back into the fold. He realized he bought and paid for her as surely as men bought and paid for a woman out on Little Oklahoma. The evidence was in his pocket, in his very hand.

"Oh, God, forgive me."

"Sir, did you say something to me?" asked the porter.

"No, no. Excuse me. Where's the dining car?"

The porter pointed him to the car just before the caboose.

Robert made his way through the rocking train cars, through the smoker to the dining car. He ordered a cup of coffee and breakfast, then penned a friendly letter to Eliza, closing it with a couple of fateful lines.

"Leaving you at the Jackson's house was very hard for me, but you are so young, perhaps too young to be married, especially against your will. Know this, Eliza, if you should ever desire to be free, I will not stand in your way."

With his breakfast finished and letter in hand, Robert went to the caboose. He stood on the brake platform at the very back of the train and watched the sun color the eastern sky. He took the lock of hair from his pocket and held it hesitantly. Slowly, he untied the ribbon and the wind whisked away the strands of gold.

CHAPTER 23

Indoor plumbing was just as wonderful as Eliza imagined it would be. She relished the plumbing along with other luxuries available in the Jackson household. Every morning, there was the near miraculous appearance of shiny glass jugs of milk and cream, cakes of butter, and a basket of eggs in a box outside the back door—all appearing without any effort on Eliza's part except to order them.

To get meat, she only had to walk six blocks to the butcher shop and point out the piece she wanted. The Jackson's small household only required a minor amount of baking. Just bread, cakes, pies, and cookies twice a week.

But indoor plumbing was the best and Eliza constantly marveled over it. Water was at her fingertips anytime, day or night. Since Rockford now had electricity, the doctor was planning to bring that modern miracle to the house.

With all these conveniences, her days were spent in relative ease between cooking the good food Robert prescribed for Helen, taking messages for the doctor, and reviewing for her diploma test in a beautiful room that was all her own.

Her room was plainly furnished with a golden oak bedstead, dresser, and washstand, but to Eliza it seemed like a castle suite. In anticipation of Eliza's arrival, Mrs. Jackson had the room painted a bright periwinkle blue and hung white lace curtains in the windows. A blue and white hand-pieced quilt topped the bed, and a matching braided rug covered the shining floor. A blue and white oil lamp stood on the dresser.

It took Eliza only minutes to move in. She put Mama's trunk at the foot of the bed, set the cream can in closet, hung her work dress on a nail, and put her few pieces of underwear in one of the drawers. She was now unpacked and home.

In her quiet moments, she missed her family. Betty and Ruthie. John and Josh. Grandma and Grandpa and Aunt Cora. Even Papa.

But especially Robert. She hadn't realized how much she relied on him. She had found his black beard, mustache, and long hair off-putting because she sensed he was hiding behind them.

Seeing him smooth-shaven for a few hours changed her perception of her bridegroom. She thought him handsome.

She had no address for Robert, and she waited anxiously to see if he would write to her. In her memory, she saw him tall, strong, and capable, awaiting her in the dewy hours of the morning outside the back door with a hoe ready to help her in the garden. Or by lamplight, his shaggy head bowed over one of her textbooks, his deep voice clearly reading the words for her. Sometimes, the memory of his goodbye kiss rose to her mind. She wished she'd hugged him harder, kissed him longer. It would have been her right.

Each day, she jotted little notes to him, telling him her thoughts and activities. She found she could say things to him on paper she had not nor could not say in person. But when she wrote, it was as if he sat on the edge of her bed, listening like he had in the cabin during the storm.

Now he was gone. Like a penny dropped into the ocean, leaving her with a nagging apprehension he had disappeared from her life forever.

Twice a day, she walked down to the little post office to collect the doctor's mail and look for a letter of her own. Aunt Cora had written her, and she received a letter from Grandma Knapp but none from Robert. By the end of the second week, she was uneasy, questioning if something awful happened to her bridegroom.

To calm her anxieties and occupy her mind, she continued to review all of her lessons in preparation for her diploma test, touching the books Robert had touched and sometimes, inexplicably, wanting to cry.

The Jacksons did not regularly attend church services, although they were members of Grace Methodist Church of Rockford. On the first Sunday morning at the Jackson's, as the bell tolled calling worshippers, Eliza walked to the church on the corner. This church drew a much bigger crowd than the little congregation meeting at the Stringtown Church. Eliza felt invisible and alone. But after the service, as she shook hands with the elderly preacher, Rev. Broadrick, he introduced himself and promised to visit.

"There are quite a number of young women about your age in our congregation, Mrs. Altman. A few of them are young brides too. If you would like, I shall ask them to stop at the Jackson's to introduce themselves."

"Thank you, Reverend. I should be most grateful to meet them."

The prospect of making new friends and meeting up with some of her former school friends cheered her. Perhaps knowing other believers would make her move to town less lonely and help assuage her yearning for her family and Robert.

By the first week in March, her body fully recovered its natural rhythms. Despite the fact she had not yet heard from her husband, she was more optimistic, confident she eventually would.

When the dressmaker came to measure Helen Jackson for clothing that would fit without a tightly laced corset, Eliza took the opportunity to walk through the melting snows to the high school and timidly knock on Mr. Cook's door.

"Ah, yes, Miss Burger, isn't it?" he asked when he saw her.

"Yes. Well, no. It's actually Mrs. Altman now." She was still not accustomed to her new name.

"I've brought back the books I borrowed, and I was wondering when I could take the test for a diploma."

Mr. Cook studied her critically over the top of his glasses. "Are you quite certain you are ready? It is a very rigorous test. I don't want to have to administer it more than twice per student."

She straightened her shoulders and looked him in the eye. "Yes, Mr. Cook, I'm certain I'm ready."

"Very well, then, Mrs. Altman. Come back tomorrow at 8:00 a.m. and I will administer it. Be prepared to stay all day. You will need several sharp lead pencils and you will only be allowed brief breaks at 11:00, 1:00, and 3:00. Also, bring your own lunch."

He turned back to his work. "Good day, Mrs. Altman," he said without looking up.

Eliza was so nervous that she barely slept all night. She asked God to help her remember all she had learned. By daybreak, she felt relaxed and confident.

The test was every bit as grueling as Mr. Cook promised, but Eliza discovered she knew almost every answer. Robert had indeed been a very good tutor. It took her until 3:30 to complete the test. Then she paced the hall as Mr. Cook and his secretary graded her work. Finally, the secretary stuck his head out the door. "Mr. Cook will see you now, miss."

As she entered his office, he stood gazing out the window behind his desk. Eliza could read nothing from his back.

"Well, Mrs. Altman, I have something for you." He handed her a roll of paper. She opened it. It was a high school diploma with her name on it.

"I passed! I'm a graduate!" Eliza was ecstatic.

"Indeed, you are, Mrs. Altman. Congratulations. You did remarkably well on the test. If you had been a regularly enrolled student, you would have placed at the top of the class."

He lifted his pointer finger as if to motion for her to wait. "I also have something else for you."

He placed her mother's gold watch in the palm of her hand. "I believe our contract is complete." Mr. Cook actually smiled at her.

"Thank you so much, Mr. Cook. I really appreciate your help and ..." she would have continued, but Mr. Cook held up his hand.

"That will do, Mrs. Altman. I am an educator. I am only doing my job."

He sat down and resumed working at his desk before she left his office.

Eliza stood alone on the steps of the school and watched a pair of robins collecting odd bits of dry grass to build their nest. She was now a high school graduate! She reached an important milestone, but she hadn't pictured her graduation like this. Papa and the family should have been here. Robert should be smiling proudly at her. Even Grandma Knapp and Aunt Cora would have congratulated her. Maybe they would have had cake at the house.

But save for the robins, occupied with their own ventures, she was celebrating alone.

She wished she could somehow make peace with Papa. She had been willing to forgive him for forcing her to marry Robert. In fact, she almost wanted to thank him.

If she hadn't been so certain becoming a nurse was God's path for her, as well as the hope she and Robert might someday have a life together, she would have begged Papa to forgive her and let her come home.

She sank to the school steps and looked at Mama's watch. It had stopped ticking. A tear slipped down her cheek and splashed on her diploma.

"Mrs. Eliza."

She looked up to see Dr. Jackson holding the reins of his prancing team.

He beckoned to her. "Come. I'll take you home." He extended his gloved hand and pulled her up beside him onto the buggy seat.

"How'd you do on the test?" He glanced at her from under the rakish derby he had pulled down to shade his blue eyes.

She held up her diploma.

"Congratulations! What an accomplishment. This calls for a celebration. Pick your poison. What shall it be? Ice cream? Pie? Cake? Candy? Chocolates?" He smiled broadly at her, his strong white teeth beneath his mustache providing a pleasing contrast to his dark skin.

"Chocolate!"

He laughed. "Chocolate it shall be! I will drop you off at the house to start dinner and then I shall go purchase your treat. Before Robert left, since he was so sure you would pass, he asked Helen and me to have a little celebration in your honor when you actually got your diploma. He insisted on leaving the money to pay for a treat of your choosing, so the chocolate is really from him. He's a good man, that husband of yours." Dr. Jackson smiled at her.

"I think so, too. But he hasn't written to me. I don't even know where to send him the news that I've graduated." Eliza looked anxiously at Dr. Jackson.

"Are you afraid he's already forgotten his pretty wife?"

Eliza nodded ruefully.

"I think you have made a lasting impression upon Dr. Altman as you do on most men you meet. Perhaps I can find a way to notify Robert for you and that will be my present to you," said Dr. Jackson mysteriously.

When Eliza burst into the house proudly carrying her diploma, she encountered Helen clad in her frilly, lace dressing gown. The dressmaker had been fitting her new wardrobe to her all day, so she hadn't bothered to get dressed. But when Helen heard that Eliza had her diploma, she insisted on tightly lacing her corset and putting on one of her prettiest dresses.

"Frank likes me in this." She spun so Eliza could see how the peach dress accented her delicate coloring and small waist. "But it's going to be the last time I wear it. The dressmaker says the newest styles are fuller through the waist and shorter in length. Since I'll be loosening my corsets anyway, I'm going to have an entirely new wardrobe."

As Helen studied herself in the mirror, she caught sight of Eliza's reflection. She critically considered her auburn hair, heart-shaped face, and slim shape.

"I've just had an idea, Eliza. You don't have many clothes. I will have the dressmaker alter my old clothing to fit you. And that shall be my gift to celebrate your accomplishment."

"Are you certain? That is such a generous gift! Thank you!"

Eliza didn't care if the dresses were out-of-fashion or hand-me-downs. The worst of Helen's clothes were nicer than Eliza's Sunday dress and she was thrilled to have more than two dresses at the same time.

After supper, while Helen and Eliza shared the chocolate fudge that Dr. Jackson bought, he retired to his office with the door shut, and where he remained for about forty-five minutes. Suddenly, he burst through the door.

"Eliza! Come quickly!" He excitedly beckoned her to pick up the telephone receiver laying on his desk.

Never having used a phone before, she cautiously held it to her ear. Sounding far, far away and very faint, she heard Robert's voice.

"Congratulations, my dear Eliza! I'm so happy for you!"

"Where are you?"

"I'm in Chicago …"

"I'm talking to you, and you are in Chicago! How can that be?"

He laughed. His voice sounded tinny and faint but was music to Eliza's homesick soul.

"I just want to tell you…" he began again, but static obliterated his words, then the line went dead.

"It was Robert!" she said, staring into the receiver in amazement. "All the way from Chicago. He was trying to tell me something, but I lost him."

Later, after the household had gone to sleep, Eliza lay in bed, wondering what Robert wanted to say. Was he being sent to Europe? Was he coming home? Was he ill? Would his next words have been I love you?

The next day, Eliza received her first letter from Robert. She carried it to the Jacksons from the post office, hidden in her pocket. At the first opportunity, she ran upstairs to her room, threw herself across the bed, and carefully eased open the envelope.

Robert's handwriting was strong and angular. Written aboard the train from Fort Wayne to Chicago, it was a newsy missive full of his trip, the sights, and the people he met. He closed it with words that nearly made Eliza's heart stop.

"Leaving you at the Jackson's was very hard for me, but you are so young—too young to be married, especially against your will. Know this, Eliza, if you should ever desire to be free, I will not stand in your way."

What did Robert mean by this? Did he think she was too young for him? Was he already sorry he had married her? She had just begun to fall in love with him; now the one person whom she loved outside her immediate family seemed to be turning her away.

She sobbed into her pillow. If her family wouldn't speak to her and Robert didn't want her, she would still dedicate herself into becoming a nurse. And she would keep all of them at arm's length where they could not hurt her anymore.

Especially Robert.

CHAPTER 24

"Ah! The graduate," Dr. Jackson teased as Eliza laid a plate with his breakfast on the kitchen table. When Helen slept late, Dr. Jackson took his morning meal in the kitchen. The morning following her graduation was one of those occasions.

Eliza blushed as she poured his coffee. "I've wanted my diploma and the opportunity to become a nurse for so long, all of this seems like a dream."

Dr. Jackson appreciatively chewed his food. "Eliza, you are a very good cook and you're competent at everything you do. Cooking and housework are hard for Helen. She tries, you know, but she doesn't have any real interest in learning it or doing it. Her family is well-to-do, and she never did any of that before. I think she thought if she married a doctor, she wouldn't have to learn, either. I'm a disappointment to her, you know." He stabbed a sausage and bit into it.

"Anyway, since you're not going to be going to high school, I'd like to pay you to work here full-time, keeping the house, my office, and as a companion to Helen. She really likes you, and working in my office and riding with me on calls will help you discover if you truly want to pursue a career in nursing after all."

He picked up his coffee cup, crossed his arms, then tipped back his chair to study her. "What do you think, Eliza?"

Eliza flushed with excitement. "Dr. Jackson, that sounds perfect."

"First thing, when it is just us, here in the kitchen or in the parlor, I'm Frank. In the office or out with a patient, I'm Dr. Jackson. Do we have an understanding?" He grinned broadly and extended his hand.

She happily placed her hand in his.

"A bargain."

To her surprise, he didn't shake her hand but squeezed it and held on. He laughed as she struggled to free her fingers from his grasp. "You're strong," he observed. "I like strong women."

Eliza was perplexed by this. Was he teasing? Or just being friendly? After the false accusations she and Robert faced because he saved her life during the blizzard, she was cautious about jumping to conclusions by misconstruing his intentions.

Over the next month, they worked side by side in his office. Dr. Jackson taught her to grind powders, roll pills, and make plasters. He regularly updated her on the conditions of various patients, and she was surprised to discover he was a natural teacher and was very generous loaning her his medical textbooks.

Helen often retired early. Sometimes Eliza and Dr. Jackson sat up later to discuss treatment of the patients they saw during the day. Dr. Jackson often emphasized what a practical and valuable learning opportunity these discussions were for Eliza.

"You won't always have a doctor handy to make a proper diagnosis. In small rural communities, peoples' lives may be in your hands. You may be called upon to make life-or-death treatment decisions and you can learn a lot when we talk over our cases. You may save a life from a situation we discuss."

While Eliza considered her relationship with Frank Jackson to be friendly but professional, she was often vaguely uncomfortable when it was just the two of them.

Sometimes she felt his eyes following her. There wasn't anything he did that was untoward—until one day when in a seemingly accidental move, he brushed against her breast as she was holding a child during a treatment.

Eliza gasped in alarm. Did he do that on purpose? Or was it an accident?

"I think of you as a younger sister," Frank Jackson told her later that evening as they packaged powders. "You are a lively, intelligent young woman, and Helen and I want you to think of us as family. I want you to feel free to talk to me about anything at all. I know the circumstances surrounding your marriage are difficult, and you must be terribly lonely for your family. But do know, dear Eliza, I stand ready to be your true friend and ally through this."

His words sounded sincere, and the Jacksons had been very good to her, but Eliza was uncomfortable in a way she couldn't put her finger on.

Eliza flushed. "Thank you, Frank. You and Helen have been very kind to me."

She recalled Mama and Robert Altman discussing the Scriptures around the stove after supper while Mama mended, and Papa slept in his chair. There was a different feel to the situation. They exchanged no actions, looks, inflections of voice—nothing that could be interpreted as anything but pure friendship. Eliza felt there was something wrong in Frank Jackson's attentions, but just what it could be was beyond her imagining.

Eliza wrote to the Lutheran Hospital School of Nursing in Fort Wayne and discovered they had some correspondence classes she could take until classes resumed in the fall. This gave her great peace of mind. Living with the Jacksons was only temporary. Within five months, she would leave for Fort Wayne and devote herself entirely to her studies, and whatever was bothering her about Frank Jackson would be far behind her.

In spite of her misgivings, Eliza was happy with her situation. Yet, as often as she stepped out on the porch to shake a rug or sweep, her eyes strained to the southeast section of the streets, the direction Papa's wagon would come if he came to town.

Daily, she checked the mailbox for some word from Robert. Whenever she saw his strong script crawling across the face of an envelope, a little thrill shot through her.

Grandma and Grandpa Knapp, Coppess, and Junior were the only ones in the family who flaunted Papa's edict against visiting her. They stopped to see her on their weekly visits to town and brought her cookies and a tantalizing whiff of home and family.

According to Coppess and Junior, Papa was drinking. Occasionally, he was mean to Aunt Cora.

"I told Papa, 'Neither Junior nor I remember our real mother, but Cora has been a mother to us. If you so much as lay a finger on her again, I'm going to lay you out proper!'" Coppess clapped his fist into his palm.

"He hasn't hit her since, but he talks rough to her and the kids. I'll tell you, Eliza, I've never seen Papa like this. If it wasn't for John and Josh, the farm would go to ruin."

Eliza's heart ached for Papa and her family, and she longed to comfort them. At the same time, she was angry with Papa for his behavior. Her loneliness and anguish were somewhat assuaged in prayer and Bible reading. Yet there, the Holy Spirit niggled at her attitude of unforgiveness toward her father. She knew, somehow, she must forgive Papa.

But what Papa was doing to his family was evil, almost unforgivable. And it was wrong of him to force her to marry Robert so he could have him as a permanent farm hand.

What Papa had done out of selfishness God turned for good—at least so far for her. Even if she had not benefited, she still would need to make peace with Papa. But how? And how could she help Cora and the children?

CHAPTER 25

It pleased Eliza to see Helen Jackson's health steadily improving. The two women soon became fast friends, although they were very different from one another. When the doctor went out on night calls, they would turn up the lamp in the living room and take turns reading aloud from Helen's magazines and doing fancy sewing. Helen had a pump organ, and they often sang together as Helen played, although Eliza was careful to see Helen didn't overdo.

It was watching Helen, cheeks rosy with excitement from the music and exertion from pumping the organ, that made Eliza realize how alone Helen was in Rockford, far away from her happy circle of friends and family, no longer pampered and cared for. Eliza understood loneliness and longing for family. She was becoming an expert at it.

As the weeks passed, Helen joined Eliza more and more as she did the housework. It pleased Dr. Jackson immensely when one day Helen cooked an entire meal on her own.

Dr. Jackson also noticed the improvement in Helen's health and homemaking ability and was prepared to take advantage of the opportunity to further procure Eliza's help with his practice.

One morning as Eliza sterilized his instruments after he was out on a delivery, he surprised her with a request.

"Eliza, I have some new books I'd like you to study on the care of pregnant women, birthing, and infant care. You could be a big help to me in many of the deliveries."

"Oh, thank you! I've wanted to learn more about birthing!"

Eliza was excited. That area of medicine held special interest to Eliza. She didn't want Woman to suffer needlessly when giving birth.

Helen Jackson enthusiastically undertook to study the subject with Eliza, for she often told Eliza that she hoped someday she would be strong enough to have lots of children.

Eliza found the information on childbirth and infant care fascinating. Although the textbooks sternly warned against placing too much credence in "old wives' tales," she often wished she could talk over her newly acquired knowledge privately with Grandma Knapp and Mama. They knew little secrets and Eliza knew some of those time-honored remedies were effective. She wished now she'd paid closer attention when the women discussed such matters.

Eliza's first solo delivery came late one stormy evening when Mrs. Hileman went into labor with her first child. As Dr. Jackson hitched up the team, Helen helped Eliza pack her nurse's bag with clean sheets and towels.

"Oh, Eliza, I wish I was going too. Do you think Frank would take me?" Helen's pale blue eyes looked childlike. "I've been studying the textbooks."

Dr. Jackson seemed both surprised and pleased. "But Helen, it's raining. Do you think it's wise for you to get chilled?"

"Maybe you're right." Her pink mouth took on a charming pout. "Do you think I can go next time if the weather is good?"

"Perhaps so, my dear," he said, kissing her on top of the head. "Keep the coffee pot on for us, would you? As cold and wet as the weather is, we're going to need something to warm us up."

A savage north wind greeted Eliza and Dr. Jackson. They drove directly into it, rendering the buggy cover useless.

"Grab the oil cloth from the back!" Dr. Jackson shouted over the wind. Eliza's frozen fingers fumbled in the dark as she fought to open it and cover herself and Dr. Jackson.

"Move over here next to me!" Dr. Jackson barked. They wrapped themselves together in the oil cloth. He whipped up the horses to a fast canter to shorten the journey.

The buggy rattled over the bridge north of town. Above the howling wind, Eliza could hear tinkling piano music and laughter coming from Little Oklahoma as they swept past it on their way into open country.

There is an unending party at Little Oklahoma. I wonder what goes on in there. What is so funny they are always laughing?

Frederick and Maude Hileman's baby girl was born a few minutes after midnight. By the time Eliza and Dr. Jackson returned to town, the frolics at Little Oklahoma were more subdued but still happening.

The wind died, although the rain was still steadily falling on the canvas buggy top. The steady staccato reminded Eliza of the tin roof on the old clapboard house and the cozy warmth of sleeping with her two little sisters. For a moment, she dreamed she was snuggled in with them, hearing the rain making music …

"Whoa there!"

She awoke with a start and felt Dr. Jackson's arm around her waist steadying her on the seat.

"Oh, I'm sorry! I drowsed off." She was glad he could not see her blushing.

He laughed softly. "A doctor's hours take some getting used to." He didn't remove his arm.

"We're almost home now. I think I'll just hang on to you until we get there."

As they climbed the back porch steps, they could see through the window the lamp was burning low. Helen was sleeping soundly on the sofa. They took off their muddy shoes and wet coats and quietly tiptoed to the warmth of the kitchen cookstove. Wafting from it was the seductive aroma of coffee, waiting and hot.

"Coffee, Eliza?" Dr. Jackson reached for the blue enameled pot.

He poured the steamy fluid into thick, white china mugs while Eliza topped each with fresh cream. He opened the firebox door and heaved in a few more chunks of wood.

"Pull up a chair, Eliza." He left the stove front open so they could watch the flames while they dried off.

"Heard from Robert lately?" His tone was casual, conversational.

"Oh, yes! I get a letter almost every other day. He really likes what he's doing. He's working such long hours doing induction physicals on new recruits. He definitely believes America is planning for war with Germany."

"Since not many soldiers are having babies, he's probably not working the same hours we are," Dr. Jackson observed. "You know, Eliza, you were very good with Mrs. Hileman. You were businesslike, but gentle and compassionate. I think you'll make a good nurse. And since Helen is feeling so much better, I'd like you to attend more deliveries and even some of the prenatal checkups. Would you like that?"

"Oh, I would, Doctor!" Eliza was so excited she almost spilled her coffee.

"It's Frank. Remember? We had a deal." His eyes flickered across her face.

"Frank?"

Both Eliza and Dr. Jackson startled.

"Helen! Did we wake you? It's wicked weather and we were both soaked to the skin."

Dr. Jackson is almost babbling. He acts guilty as if we were doing something shameful.

"Well, get out of your wet clothes, bank the fire, and come to bed." Helen yawned. "I'm tired."

"I'll take care of the fire," volunteered Eliza.

"Well, good night then." Dr. Jackson seemed reluctant to go.

Eliza poked the logs to the back of the firebox and added some long-burning green wood to hold the fire until morning.

Frank Jackson is so nice to me. He is unselfishly helping me like Robert helped me. I wish I could figure out what it is about him that bothers me.

Perhaps if she could talk to someone who knew him, someone who would say Dr. Jackson's attentiveness was nothing more than older brother kindliness he claimed. She could tell herself that, but her own voice wasn't convincing.

Dear God, give me wisdom. I have committed to working here and I have no other place to go. What am I supposed to do?

Eliza decided to avoid private contact with Dr. Jackson as much as possible until she understood her sense of caution and foreboding as she continued to pray for guidance. The closest way she could describe it was the dark feeling of impending disaster she had on the morning she allowed the children to take the sleigh to the Christmas program.

She confided her fears to Robert in a letter. However, upon rereading it, she thought she sounded childish, paranoid, and ungrateful for Dr. Jackson's guidance. She put the letter in the stove and watched its edges curl and blacken.

She wrote nothing about her concern to Robert in her next letter. Instead, she wrote enthusiastically about the possibility of caring for new mothers and their babies.

While my enjoyment of maternity care is tempered by the knowledge so many things can go wrong during birth and postpartum, I find nothing as thrilling as handing a freshly washed newborn to its mama and seeing them get acquainted for the first time. Perhaps I should specialize as a maternity nurse. Is there such a thing?

By mid-summer, Eliza could see Helen was robust. Eliza was delighted when Helen told her that a new baby was due in early April.

Eliza's joy for the Jacksons was tempered by a disappointment of her own. As the country prepared for a possible war, un-married students were given preference for admittance to the nursing college. The nursing college in Fort Wayne declined her application for attendance on that basis. They recommended that she apply elsewhere, continue her correspondence classes, or consider joining the Salvation Army or Red Cross.

While Eliza was devastated by the news, her disappointment was tempered by the knowledge that her skill and reputation as a competent midwife-nurse was growing. There was a lot she didn't know, she avidly read all the new textbooks Dr. Jackson ordered for her. She continued to apply to nursing colleges elsewhere.

She wrote Robert seeking advice.

I am loath to wait another year to start school, but there seems to be no remedy for the situation. Other nursing colleges are also giving preference to unmarried applicants. Also, I am reluctant to leave Helen during her pregnancy. What is your guidance? She has come to depend upon me for much of the household planning and labor. If I left now, Dr. Jackson says it might cause her undue emotional strain and endanger her pregnancy. On the other hand, I may not be able to find a school that will take an old married lady. Should I consider the Red Cross or Salvation Army? I'm not considering a divorce or annulment. Those options are not on the table.

Robert's next letter was filled with helpful counsel.

I am praying you will know what to do and that you will have God's peace whatever transpires. Seek and ye shall find, dear Eliza. Knock and ask. Shall we believe together the door will open in God's own time?

Helen's pregnancy was progressing so well Eliza felt free to occasionally stay in the homes of families to provide further care for a mother who experienced a difficult birth or to care for a sickly baby. Her familiarity with housekeeping amply prepared Eliza to assume the new mother's share of chores, too. Even though it was hard work, she thrived on it while she continued to seek admittance to various schools of nursing.

Her search was proving futile. Every door was shut as America readied for war. Would she have to wait for proper training until the war in Europe was over?

Newspaper reports indicated the war would be over in a short time if the United States joined the fight. It was looking more and more she would be forced to wait until then.

She resigned herself to living in the home of Dr. and Mrs. Jackson, much to the delight of the couple. The coming child provided them with a point of mutual interest, and the tension between Eliza and Dr. Jackson was muted by his newfound interest in his growing family.

Late in September, Eliza knew a storm was brewing as her fingers and toes ached with the changes in the weather. As she kneaded bread dough in the Jacksons' kitchen, she heard the wind lashing icy rain against the side of the house and the window. The leaden sky reflected Eliza's sense of foreboding. Sudden weather shifts often brought babies, and she dreaded even the thought of going out in such a storm. She made a cup of hot honey tea for herself and Helen and swallowed several aspirin to dull the aching in her extremities.

Helen had just joined her at the kitchen table when a frantic knocking sounded at the back door. Through the glass, Eliza saw Elroy Cooper and her heart sank. His wife, Bella, was due anytime. So even before she opened the door, Eliza suspected what errand brought him to the doctor's door.

"Come in, sir!" Eliza held open the door. Dripping with icy rain, Elroy stepped in on the braided throw rug, his tattered hat in hand, a week's growth of whiskers covering his chin. He wore a thin, ragged coat Eliza knew would scarcely protect him against the storm.

"I've gotta keep moving, miss. Would you tell the doctor that Bella's got pains and we need him right quickly?"

"Dr. Jackson is out on a call and not expected back for some time. I'm afraid I shall have to come with you," Eliza explained. "Helen, please give Mr. Cooper my tea while I get my supplies."

She quickly gathered her equipment and outdoor wraps and pulled Helen aside to whisper a hurried message. "Helen, please send Frank out to the Coopers as soon as he gets in. He's mentioned to me before that he is worried about Bella Cooper. I don't know what her problem is or what I'll encounter but do send him out!"

"Don't worry, Eliza! You're a wonderful midwife. I've heard Frank say you are as good as he is during a delivery." Helen smiled reassuringly at Eliza as she helped her tie a woolen scarf around her head. "I'll keep the teapot hot for you. Stay warm and dry."

Elroy Cooper lashed up his team of skinny horses and headed his decrepit wagon directly into the storm. Eliza had heard many stories about Elroy's treatment of Bella, but she was touched at his rush to be back at her side. She shielded her face from the rapidly falling ice, unaware Cooper was driving in the wrong direction until she heard him shout "Whoa!" to the team and felt the buggy stop.

She peeked from around the icy scarf. They were at the ferry crossing for Little Oklahoma. Before Eliza could protest, Cooper jumped off of the wagon and boarded a skiff for the island. A man quickly rowed Cooper to the other side.

Eliza climbed out of the wagon. She stood on the muddy bank with ice and wind swirling around her and shouted into the storm, "What do you think you're doing, Mr. Cooper? Your wife is in labor! Get out of that boat and take me to her this instant!"

Cooper and the oarsman laughed.

Over the wind, Eliza heard him say, "That little spitfire doesn't know you very well, does she, Elroy?"

"Don't get all upset, miss. I need a bottle for comfort. You wouldn't deny a new father a little comfort, would you?" Elroy Cooper shouted through the wind.

"Yes, I would! Get back here! I'll not wait while your wife is in labor for you to get drunk!" Eliza stamped her foot but instantly regretted causing the teeth-clenching pain that shot through her from her still-healing toes.

Eliza climbed up on the wagon, wet, angry, aching from the cold. She sat for a moment wondering what her options were.

Elroy Cooper can find his own way home!

She snatched up the reins, turned the team around, and drove to the home of laboring Bella.

The Cooper's house is not as snug as Papa's barn, Eliza observed as she heated water on the kitchen cookstove to wash up after the ninth little Cooper was born. Little drifts of snow filled the corners, and a frosty draft was ever present. All of the children were barefoot and poorly dressed against the cold. Eliza couldn't understand while they weren't dead from exposure. In the short time she had been there, she had not been able to get warm. Her fingers and toes ached abominably, and the chilly house did not help.

Like the other young Coopers, Bella and Elroy Cooper's newborn baby girl had a frail, bird-like look. Of all of the people in the household, only Bella's identical twin sister, Stella, appeared healthy, plump, and rosy-cheeked. Eliza thought Stella was what Bella would look like if she weren't so worn out with childbearing and worry.

To Eliza's knowledge, Stella had never spoken an intelligible word in her life. She was only able to communicate with guttural sounds and hand motions. But Bella seemed to know what her sister was thinking, and the communication between the two was uncanny.

On the other occasions when Eliza saw Stella, she was happy and smiling like a thirty-five-year-old child. Today, however, Stella looked unhappy as she sat on the bed beside Bella, gently stroking her sister's hair.

Dr. Jackson arrived about an hour after the baby was born. Elroy Cooper, well lubricated with drink from Little Oklahoma, caught a ride to his home with Dr. Jackson and he was in a particularly ugly mood.

He staggered into the bedroom to see his wife. Stella hooted fearfully at him from the head of the bed and almost assumed the fetal position.

"Get out of here, you moron!" Cooper snarled at Stella. "Get away from Bella! And don't you touch the baby, either!"

Stella snuggled close to her sister, holding her ground. She bit the knuckle of her clenched fist until a little trickle of blood ran down her arm.

Elroy slapped Stella and pushed her out of the bed. Stella landed on the floor with a thud.

"What do you think you're doing, man?" Dr. Jackson shouted. "You can't just push someone around like that!"

Eliza helped Stella to her feet and put her arms around her to comfort her. She could feel Stella's breaths coming in short, convulsive sobs. Then Eliza felt a stab of pain as Stella sunk her teeth into her shoulder.

"Ouch! She bit me!" Eliza touched her shoulder. Fortunately, she was wearing enough layers of clothing and Stella had not broken skin.

What was going on here?

Elroy Cooper ignored Eliza. He focused his bloodshot eyes on his wife.

"Bella ..." he began hesitantly.

She turned her face away from him. He stamped out of the room and slammed the door. The children scampered to the corners, made themselves as small as possible, and watched their parents and aunt with frightened eyes.

There was no doubt in Eliza's mind: Something bad was going on in the Cooper house.

Dr. Jackson's eyes met Eliza's over Bella. "I hear you had a disagreement with Elroy." He smiled and shook his finger at her. "You know, if he had been sober, he might have had you charged with horse theft! As it was, by the time I picked him up, he couldn't remember what had happened to his team and wagon, but the oarsman at Little Oklahoma told me."

"Doctor, do you know what's happening in this house?"

"No, I don't know. Do you want to tell me about it, Bella?" Dr. Jackson's piercing blue eyes studied the tired woman's face.

"It's bad, Doctor, real bad! When Elroy gets to drinking, he don't know what he does! He's buying that cheap hooch out there at that whorehouse and then he gets mean to us all!" Bella's toothless mouth puckered grotesquely as she sobbed.

"I'll talk to him before I leave, Mrs. Cooper. You have my assurance on that."

When Dr. Jackson finished attending to her medical needs, he took Elroy outside behind the house. Through the thin walls, Eliza heard only brief snatches of conversation but what she heard unnerved her. Bella and Stella heard it, too, and the women held each other and sobbed.

"Doctor, you just got to get rid of it for me," Eliza heard Elroy say. "It isn't right to let it be born. You've seen how she is. She can't even speak like a human. If she had a baby, it wouldn't be no smarter than her."

"So why'd you rape her?" Dr. Jackson demanded.

"I know I done wrong. I just didn't expect her to get pregnant," whined Elroy.

"You have nine children, man! What did you expect would happen?" Dr. Jackson's voice was angry.

"Alright! I was drunk and I wasn't thinking. But what's done is done. I don't want the baby. Stella don't know nothing, and Bella will shoot me if she finds out."

Elroy was pretty convinced of this last point, and a glance at Bella's face convinced Eliza that it was a possibility.

"Besides, Doctor So High 'n' Mighty, I heard about you and that gal …"

Eliza strained to hear the rest, but the wind carried the sound away and they could hear no more.

Stella cried inconsolably in Bella's arms. Bella's face was set like stone.

Eliza didn't know what to do. She rocked the new baby girl and wondered why God allowed such things to happen.

Two weeks after the birth of the Cooper baby, Eliza saw Elroy Cooper drive his dilapidated wagon into the yard. As he walked across the yard, Eliza could tell by his gait he was sober, or nearly so. He rapped sharply on the back door. Eliza opened it and the man boldly stepped in without an invitation.

"Tell the doctor he's needed, girlie. Stella's took ill." Cooper turned on his heel, mounted the wagon, and drove his bony team away.

Eliza watched him go. She didn't know exactly how far along Stella was, but Eliza was sure if Stella's baby was coming, it was too early and it would not live.

The ride to the Cooper's farmstead was much different this time. Dr. Jackson had recently bought a new Ford automobile, and he drove it when the roads were dry as they were this day. As they bounced into the rutted, weed-covered yard, Eliza saw children peeking from behind the curtains. Over the popping car engine, Eliza heard Stella's screams.

Dr. Jackson and Eliza helped Stella deliver a tiny stillborn baby girl. The little body fit in the palm of Eliza's hand. She studied the baby, awestruck by its miniature perfection. Why had it died? Had Dr. Jackson done something to cause this as Elroy Cooper had begged? Given Stella something? Eliza had to know.

Later, as they left the house, Stella was sitting up in bed. She rocked a dirty sock in her arms, crooning a wordless melody to it. Eliza thought it was one of the saddest sights she had ever seen.

"Why did that baby die?" Eliza asked as they drove back to Rockford through the autumn countryside.

Dr. Jackson swallowed hard. "Babies die, Eliza. They're fragile. In this case, considering the circumstances, I think it's for the best."

He avoided looking at her.

"I have a question, Dr. Jackson: Did you do something to cause Stella's baby to be born early?"

His knuckles turned white on the steering wheel. Suddenly, he whipped the wheel to the right and pulled he car off of the road. The car came to a shuddering halt as the engine sputtered and died.

"It wasn't right, Eliza. I know that. But God help me, I didn't know what else to do. I've been out to that house more times than you can imagine, setting broken bones, binding up bruises, everything under the sun. The sheriff and I have had long talks about what goes on under that roof. If Elroy is put in jail—which is where he certainly belongs—there will be no money in that household and those women and children will go hungry. Hungry, Eliza! Do you know what it is to be a hungry child?

"And then there's Stella. She couldn't begin to take care of a baby, which just puts an extra burden on Bella Cooper. A baby that is starved might grow up to be as bad off as Stella or worse. Is it right to let it happen? Elroy asked me to do something, and I did. I'm not proud of it, Eliza."

Dr. Jackson's eyes looked desperate for understanding.

"You had no right to play God, Dr. Jackson."

"It's 'Dr. Jackson' now, is it, Eliza? I thought—no, I hoped—you would understand."

Eliza was afraid he was going to cry.

They sat in silence. Eliza was confused. Dr. Jackson had many good arguments for aborting that baby, but Eliza felt none of them were good enough to take the life of a child. Although the baby girl was unceremoniously buried behind the Cooper's house, Eliza still felt the weight of the infant on her heart.

It was a sleepless night for Eliza. Alone in her room, she wrote a long letter to Robert and told him of the incident.

Questions flooded her mind for which there were no good answers. Yes, she had to admit the tiny baby might be better off dead than growing up in the Cooper household, but who was to say? Not Dr. Jackson. Certainly not her.

Who knew the future? Only God. If He had allowed the child to be conceived—even in such a repugnant fashion as rape—then God had a purpose for her life.

Eliza wrote to Robert:

If it is in my power, I will never allow such a thing again regardless of how noble the purpose seems to the participants.

It was past midnight when she finished her letter, but sleep was still far from her. A cup of warm milk might help her, she thought. She drew the quilt over her flour sack nightgown, and with her hair in a long braid, she quietly slipped down the back stairs to the kitchen. By the light of the cookstove's fire, she warmed a little milk in a saucepan and poured it into a mug.

Eliza jumped as Dr. Jackson's voice came out of the darkness. "Is there enough for me, too?"

"Where are you?" she asked, clutching the quilt modestly around her.

"Here. In the corner."

She heard the rasp of the chair legs as he stood up.

"Can't sleep?"

"No."

"Eliza?"

"Yes?"

"I'm sorry about today. I was wrong. You were right. I shouldn't have done it. I gave Elroy a package of herbs and I guess, somehow, he got her to take them. Mixed them into her food, I suppose. Anyway, the deed's done and I was wrong."

Eliza said nothing.

"Am I forgiven?"

"You're asking the wrong person for forgiveness, Dr. Jackson."

"Eliza! Eliza! Always so proper! Do you ever let your guard down?"

"Good night, Dr. Jackson." She started for the stairs.

In an instant, he blocked the door. "Don't go! Stay with me, Eliza. I need you tonight. I need you to comfort me."

"Please move out of the way, Dr. Jackson!"

His voice was husky. "It's Frank, remember?"

She turned to run but he trapped her and pulled her to his chest. She fought against his grasp. In the struggle, he knocked the glass of milk out of her hand. It shattered as it hit the floor. Eliza felt the warm fluid running around her feet.

"I love you, Eliza. I need you. I need you like a man needs a woman. Do you know what I mean?"

Suddenly, he released her.

"I'm sorry. I apologize for that, Eliza. Twice today I've done something I regret. No need to tell Helen about this, you know. With the baby coming, this would upset her."

Eliza could hear his footsteps ascending the back stairs. She stood frozen to the spot, afraid to move for fear of stepping on broken glass. There was no longer any question in her mind. She needed to leave the Jacksons. She needed to find a new place to stay.

Oh, God, You brought me here. I can't stay any longer. Show me where I should go.

She sat down on the steps and thought. She would talk to Rev. Broadrick. Perhaps he could suggest something. And maybe Grandpa and Grandma Knapp would take her in.

God would provide, she decided.

Another thought struck her as she lit the oil lamp and wearily cleaned up the milk and glass. Maybe Robert would have an idea.

Chapter 26

Eliza's cheeks burned. She was aware Dr. Jackson was eyeing her thoughtfully as he answered the early morning phone call.

The three of them had just set down to breakfast when the phone rang, and Eliza was hoping the call was one Dr. Jackson would make without her.

He had been particularly eager to please both women this morning, but Eliza did her best to avoid him. Although she didn't feel she could explain why to Helen, Eliza decided after last night, she would never again sleep under Dr. Jackson's roof.

He replaced the receiver and turned to her. "Busy today, Eliza?"

"Yes, I am." She avoided his eyes.

"You may want to change your plans. Your Aunt Cora is in labor. Your father specifically asked that you come with me, Eliza. I think he may want to make peace."

Doctor Jackson finished his coffee in one swallow. "No better time than at the birth of a baby."

Aunt Cora having a baby? Eliza was dumbfounded. She hadn't heard this bit of news.

"Better pack a bag to stay, Eliza. Cora is older and this is her first baby. She's likely to have a hard delivery and there's no telling what condition she or the baby will be in afterward."

The doctor strode toward the office door to pack his equipment.

Helen followed him into his office. "Frank, please don't leave Eliza out on the farm. Our baby is due soon. I want her here with me."

As she ran upstairs, Eliza heard Dr. Jackson promise Helen he would bring Eliza back as soon as possible. But Eliza's heart soared. How beautifully God was answering her prayer! She threw all of her personal items in her nursing bag before packing the essentials for delivering and caring for a newborn.

She was going home! Papa asked specifically for her to come. She was excited to be with her family again. She had been so homesick.

The weather was dry, and the roads were passable, so Doctor Jackson drove his automobile out to the farm. They silently drove the fifteen minutes it took to travel the three miles that had separated her from the ones she loved so dearly. How could she have stayed away so long?

As they motored up Springtown's dirt road, Eliza strained to catch a first glimpse of the farm. The old clapboard house looked lonely and abandoned, but the new brick house seemed welcoming. Papa had truly built a beautiful home for his family.

"Dr. Jackson, I don't intend to go back with you," she said as she stepped from the auto. "I will send someone for my clothing. You explain to Helen why. I caution you to tell her the truth as I will be sending her a letter telling her what happened and why I am no longer in your employment."

Dr. Jackson's handsome face hardened. "Suit yourself," he snapped as he picked up his doctor's bag. "I'll see to it no nursing school will ever accept you. And after all the rumors about you and Robert's snowy tryst, you will be branded as a scarlet woman by your neighbors as well. My patients will believe me."

Dr. Jackson's threat was like a spear thrown into her heart. She expected him to be repentant and embarrassed. She was caught off guard by Dr. Jackson's plans to retaliate.

He has faced this before. How many other women has he blackmailed into silence?

He would not ruin her homecoming. She deeply inhaled the fragrance of the farm, the wood smoke, the warm, sweaty smell of cattle and horses combined with a heady whiff of manure. She was home!

She heard a woman screaming in the new house.

"Aunt Cora!"

Ruthie flew out the back door, threw her arms Eliza, and squeezed her tightly. "Oh 'Liza, why did you ever leave me? Why won't you hug me? Don't you love me anymore?"

Another scream came from the house. Eliza broke away from Ruthie. "Ruthie, Aunt Cora needs help!"

The girl put her fists on her hips and gave Eliza a look of disgust. "All anybody cares about is Aunt Cora!"

Dr. Jackson met Eliza at the back door. He crowded in front of her, throwing a sharp elbow into her ribs.

Aunt Cora was in bed, sweaty and disheveled. Her beautiful dark hair hung loose, plastered in ringlets to her head. The bed sheets were bunched up in wrinkled wads.

Swiftly, Dr. Jackson examined Cora then pulled Eliza outside the bedroom door. "The baby's turned wrong. It's breech."

Eliza's heart sank. This was the first breech birth she had ever attended, but she had read extensively about them and knew that Cora could be in for a long, hard labor and a difficult delivery. She and the baby might not survive.

"What do you want me to do?" Eliza asked.

Dr. Jackson shoved his hands into his trouser pockets and frowned, his face furrowed and worried. "Nothing. Sit with her. Comfort her. Keep her in bed. There's nothing to be done."

He looked as helpless as Eliza felt.

"It's going to be a long day," he told her as he went out to the kitchen for a cup of coffee and then retired to the barn with the rest of the men. Although the men competently attended their animals when they gave birth, the moans of a woman in labor left them nervous and feeling helpless and guilty.

It was indeed a long day. Eliza timed Cora's pains with Mama's gold watch. They were two minutes apart, yet they produced nothing. Eliza held Cora's hand between contractions and read aloud from her favorite book of poems. When the pains came, Eliza prayed for her, silently lending all the support she could.

Toward evening, frantic pounding was heard at the kitchen door. "Is Doc Jackson here?" It was one of the McCaley boys.

"What's the trouble?" he asked.

"Your misses called and said an automobile flipped off the bridge just outside of town. Four or five people are hurt bad! They want you to come and bring help!"

"Eliza, you're on your own," Dr. Jackson told her as he picked up his bag and threw on his coat. Then he said quietly so no one could overhear, "Do what you can for Cora, but I'm afraid we may have to do something drastic if the baby doesn't arrive by morning."

Eliza clinched her fists. She had read descriptions of the use of the entomology wire whose function was to dismember a live baby to save the life of the mother.

"Oh, no! I'll pray!" she whispered.

For the first time, she doubted she were meant to be a nurse. After yesterday, she didn't think she could bear to see another dead baby, especially not Cora's.

"Praying's about all any of us can do," said Dr. Jackson. "In the meantime, try to make her comfortable. Her heart is weakening from the strain, and you understand I'll do what I have to do to save Cora's life."

Grandpa and all four the Burger brothers loaded in Dr. Jackson's automobile to see if they might be of help at the accident site. They took along lanterns to light the scene, but Eliza suspected they were grateful for something to do while they awaited Cora's baby.

With the men gone and the chores finished, Grandma and the girls slipped into Cora's room to wait with her. By the glow of the kerosene caboose lantern that had once been Eliza's study light, they talked quietly while they sewed on tiny things for the baby and worked on the ever-present mending. Eliza hovered over Cora and prayed for wisdom.

Cora's eyes, rimmed in a bruising purple, were sinking back in her head. Her breathing was increasingly shallow, and she seemed beyond caring whether or not the baby was born. Eliza was afraid she was giving up. Grandma was too.

"I know you've had some medical training, Eliza, but she's got to have more help than just laying there. Can't we do something to get my new grandchild born?" asked Grandma.

Eliza hesitated. Dr. Jackson had specifically said to keep her in bed, but Cora wasn't getting anywhere.

"Let's get her on her feet for a little while," Eliza suggested.

With Grandma on one side and Eliza on the other, the two women half walked, half dragged Cora back and forth across the bedroom, pausing only when her labor pains came upon her.

"Does walking seem to be helping?" Ruthie anxiously looked up into Cora's face. "I don't think I want to have any babies."

As nighttime settled over the farm, Cora was lost in her own world. Exhausted from straining and pain, her breathing was labored. She said nothing, although an occasional groan escaped her lips. Grandma and Eliza, with Ruthie taking turns, continued to support her steps back and forth across the planking floor which squeaked in protest with every step.

Around midnight, Eliza sensed a change in Cora. She rallied her strength, and when the pains came, she pushed with them. Suddenly, there was a rush of water. It took the efforts of all four of them to get Cora back on the bed. Propped on the edge and supported by Grandma, Ruthie, and Betty, Eliza delivered the baby boy despite his backwards arrival.

He was a big baby. Because his skin was so blue, Eliza was afraid he was dead. She cleared his nose and throat, rubbed his chest, and flicked his feet until he issued a weak cry. And praise God, he turned pink! Relieved, Eliza held him up for Cora to see, but she was too exhausted to respond with more than a faint smile.

While Grandma and the girls settled Cora into bed, Eliza closely examined her new little brother. Even to her untrained eyes, something seemed amiss. The boy's spine seemed to be curved to the right and his whole body leaned slightly in that direction. Saying nothing, she handed him to Grandma to administer his first bath while she attended Cora's needs.

As the clock downstairs chimed one, Eliza tucked the baby into the oaken cradle that was the first bed for all of them. Cora was sleeping soundly in the big bed beside her newborn's cradle.

Eliza was so exhausted she could barely stay awake; however, someone would need to sit up all night with Cora and the baby. There was too much risk of the baby choking on leftover mucus, so Eliza took the first shift.

She looked back toward the forest and the cabin where Robert had saved her life. She supposed Papa had decided to stay there for the night. He never wanted to be around when Mama was having a baby. Eliza assumed he felt the same way when Cora was in labor.

Eliza looked down at the tiny sleeping boy and wondered if she and Robert might someday have children too. Suddenly, she remembered: His letter was in her pocket!

His words were timely. They resonated with the cries of Eliza's own heart. Her conflicts were unknown to him, but he wrote about the pain life had inflicted upon his soul, all those things he kept hidden from prying eyes. For the first time, he wrote about his past and the family he lost.

Cholera swept through the entire town. I somehow survived cholera as a youngster, so I could attend cases without fear. I left our home early in the morning to provide whatever comfort I could to the sick and to direct the rapid burying of the dead. My wife and children were healthy, asleep in their beds when I last saw them. Our home was in the best section of town, far from the disease, so I thought. However, when I returned home after nightfall, I found my house empty. I learned my wife and children were already buried in one of the mass cholera graves outside town. This is the nature of cholera. A person may be healthy at sunrise but dead by sundown.

For years, I could not forgive myself. While I was caring for others, my own family perished. Then one day, I realized God, the Great Physician who loved Rachel and the children more than I, had been at their bedsides. He cared for them when I could not. Yet it was and still is a bitter pill.

Memories of the faces of young children and woman in the photos in Robert's trunk sprang up in Eliza's mind. They were Robert's wife and children, beloved by him still, but gone.

Her new little brother stretched in his sleep. She already loved him and shuddered at how close they had come to losing this precious child.

She thought of Stella singing wordless lullabies to a dirty sock. Life was so short, so precious.

Eliza did not want to be away from those she loved any longer. She wanted to come home, but where was that? Here? Or with Robert?

She would forget whatever differences lay between herself and Papa, especially when one breath was all that stood between forever ending the quarrel by saying words of love.

Knowing Papa as she did, she supposed he still thought what he did by forcing Robert to marry her was right. No amount of arguing would convince him to the contrary. To the end of her life, she would forever regret it if she didn't tell Papa she loved him one more time. They had lost enough loved ones and would likely lose more.

Then there was Robert. He had told her more about himself in this one letter than he ever revealed in all of their conversations and letters combined. He trusted her with his past. It was true he never said he loved her in any of his letters. He signed them "Fondly, Robert." But Eliza knew she loved him, and if God granted her another opportunity, she would tell Robert face-to- face.

It was near daybreak when Dr. Jackson, Grandpa, and the boys pulled in the driveway. As tired as he was, Dr. Jackson sprinted in the house to see how Cora was faring. He was relieved that the baby was born alive, and Cora had survived.

He, too, was concerned about the baby's spine tilting to the right. "I think he laid crooked in the womb, Cora. If you massage him gently on that side, it might stimulate it to grow faster and eventually catch up to the other. Beyond that, all we can do is wait to see if he grows out of it."

Cora's brown eyes filled with tears as she looked up from the bed where she nursed her newborn whom she named Arthur.

"I was so careful! What did I do wrong?"

"Nothing! These things happen. Only God in heaven knows why. But I must say you are very lucky to have given birth to an otherwise healthy baby. For a little while there, I did not expect either of you to survive."

Grandpa and the boys started the chores as Eliza walked Dr. Jackson out to his auto. She planned to ask him to bring her trunk and cream can out to the farm. Resting his foot on the running board, he heaved his bag in the back and turned to face Eliza.

"You did a fine job with Cora, but another doctor would have fired you for disobeying orders to keep her in bed." His eyes looked tired, but angry. "I expect my orders to be followed, to the letter, Eliza."

She started to protest, but he interrupted her. "Don't bother to explain. You were wrong to go against my orders. This time it turned out alright. Another time, you might not have been so fortunate, nor would another physician be so forgiving."

He climbed in the auto. "Helen wants you to be on hand when her time comes. I give you my word we will never have another incident like last night. Eliza, I don't want to lose your help in my practice because you may have misinterpreted something I said." He slammed the door.

Eliza watched him drive down the frozen mud road. For a second, she doubted herself. Maybe she had misinterpreted what he said.

She thought it through. *No, I know what he said and what he meant.*

"How's Cora?" She heard Papa's voice behind her and whirled around to face him.

"She's tired. She had a very rough time."

Eliza wanted to hug him and scold him all at the same time.

Papa avoided her eyes as he slowly rubbed his day's growth of whiskers. "How's the baby?"

"He's fine. He is a little bent to the right, but Dr. Jackson thinks that maybe he'll outgrow it."

"Then it's a boy."

"Yes. He's a fine boy. A big one too. Do you want to see him?"

Papa nodded.

She led him to the kitchen stove where Ruthie and Betty watched him sleep. Papa reached into the cradle and lifted him out. He opened the soft blankets with his work-roughened fingers and stared at his new son.

"He's a big'n, isn't he?" Papa's eyes glistened with tears and pride. "He don't look bent to me. He looks like he's got the makings of a farmer!"

He wrapped the baby back up and carried him into the bedroom where Cora lay sleeping, her breathing so shallow she looked like a corpse.

"Is she alright?"

Grandma rose from the rocker beside Cora's bed and motioned them to step out of the bedroom. She followed him out and firmly shut the door behind her.

"Silas Burger," Grandma said with fire in her eyes, "Papa and I have been good to you for more than twenty-five years. We cared for those two motherless boys of yours just like they were our own. We gave you two daughters in marriage. One of them is dead and gone, and that can't be helped. But this one in there nearly died giving you a son. I want you to know if she is ever put through that kind of hell again, I will personally come hunting for you with a shotgun!"

Grandma snatched the baby from Papa, went back into Cora's room, and shut the door in his face.

"I guess I deserved that," Papa said. "I've been kind of ornery to Cora. She's so forgiving it's easy to be mean to her."

He eyed Eliza. "I suppose you have a thing or two to say to me too."

"I do, Papa. You were wrong but I love you." Impulsively, she hugged him around the neck, his whiskers scratching her cheek.

"Are you home to stay?"

"Robert and I don't have a home yet. I don't know where home is."

"You always have a home with me, Eliza. You and Robert both," Papa said quietly.

The following weeks saw Cora slowly recover from her harrowing experience. Despite his rocky beginnings, Arthur proved to be a robust baby and the apple of everyone's eye.

Eliza was happy to be home with her family, but she was restless, too. The house and the yard and the forgotten garden all held memories of Robert. At every meal, she missed his quiet, steady presence. He had been gone more than a year now. It was too long.

March came in like a roasting lamb with warmer-than-usual temperatures. Eliza and the girls took advantage of the heat to wash all of the sheets and quilts and hang them out in the sunshine. To make certain no bugs had taken up residency in the bed frames, they wiped them down with a mixture of a cup of kerosene to a gallon of hot water, even painting the cracks and crevices with a feather dipped in the cleaner. They opened the upstairs windows and washed down the walls, the floors, and all of the woodwork.

Two weeks to the day of Arthur's birth, Dr. Jackson stopped to check on Cora and the baby and to ask Eliza to come back to town. Cup of coffee in one hand and the other pushed deep in his pocket, he stood next to the cookstove and told Eliza how much Helen missed her.

"She says she's not going to have the baby unless you come back to town to help her, Eliza. Her mother's here with two servants to do the cooking and cleaning, so it's not like they can't manage without you. She just says she'll feel better if you're with her. What do you say, Eliza? Are you ready to come home?"

Eliza eyed him thoughtfully. "I don't think Cora is ready for me to leave. She's still very weak, and although the girls are good workers, neither of them can manage without some help. I think I ought to stay here a little longer. Besides, Helen isn't due for a little while yet."

"No, she's not. I just don't think everything is going as well as it was. She's not very big. She's eating okay, but the baby's not growing." His brow furrowed with worry.

Eliza did not want to commit. "Dr. Jackson, I just can't leave Cora yet. She's just too weak. Stop back in another week and we'll see how she's doing. And if Helen really needs me before then, I'll consider coming."

"You know I'm sorry, Eliza." Dr. Jackson looked embarrassed. "I promised you it would never happen again."

Eliza was less than convinced.

Later that evening as Eliza blew out the lamp for the night, she heard the creaking of a wagon pulling in the yard. Peering into the darkness, she recognized Elmo Winter, Dr. Jackson's handyman, hobbling toward the back door with a lantern in his hand.

"Miss Eliza! Dr. Jackson asked me to fetch you back to town! Miz Jackson is having her baby!"

Eliza gasped. "Oh, no! It's too early!"

"I know!" said Elmo. "Dr. Jackson says he's real worried about her. He doesn't think the baby will live."

Eliza ran upstairs, snatched her bag, and threw her clothing into it. She stopped briefly to tell Papa where she was going and why, then ran down to join Elmo for a wild drive through the night.

CHAPTER 27

Eliza stood in the hall outside the Jackson's bedroom holding the tiny body of Helen's baby while listening to her desolate sobs. A perfect miniature little boy bigger than Stella's little girl, who never drew breath. Eliza had no words to assuage Helen's grief. None exist in any language.

Eliza bathed and dressed his body in the smallest gown and bonnet she could, find although they were still too large.

"My baby! My baby!" wailed Helen from the bedroom. Eliza could hear Helen's mother trying to comfort her.

Dr. Jackson paced the hallway, his face etched in grief. "It's all my fault!" he muttered under his breath. "God's punishing me!"

Still holding the dead infant, Eliza approached him. "Should we let her see the baby?"

He shook his head. "No. It's better if she doesn't see it. Put it in a basket on the back porch until the undertaker comes."

"Frank … he's a beautiful baby. I think she should see him."

His face, thrust in hers, became a mask of anger. "Are you contradicting me again?"

"Yes, I am. Look at him. He's your son. His little body is dead, but he had a soul, and it is in heaven."

Dr. Jackson's eyes lost their fire as they dropped to the blanket-wrapped bundle. He took it from Eliza's arms and pulled back the blanket; his face melted in tears. "He was so perfect. Just too tiny to live. Why did he die?"

He wiped his tears and opened the door to their bedroom. He paused at the foot of the bed.

Helen Jackson's mother was outraged. "Frank! What are you doing in here with that thing?"

"He's not a thing, Mother Woodward. He is our baby. I think Helen should have a chance to tell our son goodbye." He looked questioningly at his wife. She opened her arms and Frank laid the tiny bundle in them.

In the week following the graveside service for Baby Boy Jackson, Eliza alternated her time between the Burger household and the Jacksons.

Helen's mother planned to stay on for another month, but Eliza wasn't sure Mother Woodward was any help. She nagged Helen daily about her food intake, encouraging her to diet away her "baby fat," and if she got a hint Helen was crying or had been, she demanded Dr. Jackson give Helen frequent sedatives so she wouldn't grieve the loss of her child. She was so overbearing both Dr. Jackson and Eliza were relieved when one evening, just at twilight, a man named Carver came to request their services delivering a baby in Little Oklahoma.

They followed him in the car down to the boat launch of the Saint Marys River where Dr. Jackson parked.

The launch, located in a clearing at the edge of a dark woods, was dank and slippery with mud. As she neared the ferry boat, Eliza was assaulted by the foul odor of raw sewage floating in the river and besieged by starving mosquitoes.

Located offshore in the Saint Marys River channel, Little Oklahoma blazed with light. Rinky-tink jazz and raucous laughter floated across the water as if carried on the reflections of the waves.

Once Eliza and Dr. Jackson were aboard, Carver launched the ferry. Eliza was going to Little Oklahoma! She felt the thrill of the forbidden. For a fleeting moment, she thought she should cover her eyes as she did when she was a child.

Above the blasting music of the band, laughter, and shouting on Little Oklahoma, Eliza heard someone screaming in the darkness. Eliza supposed this was their patient.

The oars dipped into the dark water propelling them closer to screams. Eliza saw the outlines of a powerfully built man on the dock waiting for their boat.

"Carver! Is that you?"

"It's me, Butch!"

"Do you have the doctor?"

"Yeah. He's here in the boat along with his…" Carver turned to Dr. Jackson. "Why exactly do we have this girl along?"

"She's my nurse."

Eliza was pleased he gave her that designation.

"Hurry up, Carver! Prissy isn't doing very well. Her screams are bothering the customers. I told the band to play some loud music to drown her out."

A few more strokes of the oars brought them to the dock. Butch grasped Eliza under the arms and effortlessly lifted her out of the boat, then hoisted up Dr. Jackson and Carver.

They hurried along the garishly painted railings of Little Oklahoma. Bright lights blazed through windows surrounding the crowded, smoke-filled salon. Inside, men kept company with scantily dressed women and girls with painted faces. Even in the dim, flickering lamp lights, Eliza could tell that some of the girls were little more than children.

Some huddled over drinks, exchanging loud talk and laughter. Others gambled on the roulette wheel while a few couples danced to the music of the band. The music changed tempo, the lights dimmed, and the women and girls lined up on the stage and danced.

Eliza tried not to stare, but she was curious. She had heard about these girls and women from her friend Glen Franklin.

"Money means nothing to them. They purchase the most expensive fabric and trims we have. And they always invite me to come see the show at Little Oklahoma."

As the screams began again, they increased their haste into the two-story hotel behind the bar where the women and girls of Little Oklahoma plied their trade and slept. Butch led them to a small room on the second floor. He pushed open the door ahead of them.

It was not a woman in the bed but a pretty little girl not more than twelve or thirteen years old. She wore a clingy, dirty nightgown. The bedcovers were wadded up, exposing a filthy straw mattress beneath her. She screamed as a labor pain gripped her.

"Shut up, Prissy!"

Before Dr. Jackson could stop him, Butch dealt the girl a powerful smack on the head. She fell back, stunned into silence.

"What are you doing?" yelled Dr. Jackson. "Get out of here!"

"I told her to shut up!"

"I don't care! Get out!" Dr. Jackson shoved the swearing man out the door and shut it firmly behind him.

The girl softly moaned, thrashing side-to-side on the bed.

Dr. Jackson glanced in the pitcher and poured the water into the bowl. "Eliza, get her and that bed cleaned up best you can. I'm going to scare up some hot water and soap, if they have such things on this floating hellhole."

Dr. Jackson stepped out and suddenly Eliza was alone with the girl.

She whimpered, "Whiskey. Get me some whiskey! I don't want any more pain." She grabbed Eliza's hand. "Make it go away! Make the pain go away!"

"We'll do our best." Eliza gently washed the girl's face and hands then began to give her a bed bath, all the time fervently praying for wisdom.

"What's your name, dear?"

She spoke with an Irish accent. "They call me Prissy but me name is Bridget."

As each new pain began, Eliza noted it on Mama's watch. Eliza knew better than to touch her during contractions. She waited until the pains subsided, then continued to bathe the girl and remake the bed with clean sheets.

"You're doing fine." Eliza noted the telltale bulge on the girl's perineum. "The baby will soon be here."

"I've got to push!" panted the girl.

Where is Dr. Jackson?

The girl seized the metal bars of the bed and began to strain.

"Take it easy!" Eliza warned. "Push slowly or you'll tear."

The girl was deaf to Eliza's instructions. She pushed with singleness of purpose. Eliza saw the top of the baby's head. She used her hands to support the skin.

"Slow down! Don't push so hard."

Eliza carefully delivered the baby's head, then eased out the shoulders. The rest of the baby boy easily slid out.

He was a small baby but perfectly formed. As Eliza wiped the mucus from his face, he let out a lusty cry, and his wrinkled skin magically turned a healthy pink.

"It's a boy!" No matter how many times she witnessed a birth, she was awed by the miracle of it. She gently laid the baby on the girl's stomach.

The girl acted as if she had been scalded. She pushed the baby away with such violence Eliza was afraid she had hurt the child. "No! Get it off of me! I don't want it!"

Eliza snatched up the tiny child and held him to her breast. Instinctively, he turned toward her, mouth open, searching nourishment.

Prissy turned her face to the wall.

"He's a fine baby …"

"Let it die." Her voice was expressionless. "I don't want it."

Dr. Jackson came back in time to deliver the afterbirth and apply a few stitches to the area where the girl had torn during the birth, while Eliza gently washed the baby, marveling at the perfection of his tiny fingernails and toenails.

As Dr. Jackson worked, Butch and Carver strode in without announcement or permission and watched the doctor stitch up Prissy, who to Eliza's surprise, showed no signs of embarrassment.

"How is she, Doc?" Butch wanted to know.

"The question is 'How *old* is she?'" said Dr. Jackson, glancing up from his work.

"She's eighteen," said Butch quickly.

"She's not a day over fifteen and I will speak to the sheriff about her. I've warned you about this before, Butch."

"Now, Doctor." Butch dropped a meaty paw on the doctor's shoulder and confidentially leaned into his face, "You don't want to get Prissy into trouble, her being a new mother and all. What would I do with a baby? But if you and the young woman was to forget this …" He looked meaningfully at Dr. Jackson. "… it would be well worth your while."

"We've been over this before, Butch. When I suspect a prostitute to be underage, I report you. Now, get out! I threw you out of this room once today and I'll throw you out again! I'm here to care for a patient. Let me finish my job!"

Butch and Carver withdrew sulkily. "Don't tell this guy anything, Prissy," Butch ordered as he shut the door behind him.

When he finished, Dr. Jackson drew a chair up beside the bed and sat down next to the girl. "Where are your parents?"

"I don't want to talk about it." Her eyes dull with pain.

"You need help, Prissy. This is no kind of life for a girl. It's not only the occasional slap from Butch; it's all the rest. Maybe you're too young to know, but there are diseases you can contract, terrible things can happen. And then there is the baby. What are you going to do about him?"

Prissy looked away. Eliza saw a tear slide down the girl's face and disappear into the pillow.

"Please, mister doctor, take it. Don't leave it here. Take it with you, please!"

Prissy grabbed Eliza's dress. "Please, miss, don't leave the baby here! Please!"

"Why don't you want him?" Eliza asked.

"I can't keep him. I know what happens …"

"Shut your mouth, Prissy! I told you not to say anything to him!" shouted Butch from the other side of the door.

"Prissy, I don't know what brought you to Little Oklahoma, but you can't stay here," Dr. Jackson told her softly. "I have someone who'll take care of you, help you get resettled somewhere safe and help you start over with your baby.

Prissy soundlessly wept, shaking with fear and despair. "Promise me that you'll take the baby," she whispered.

Dr. Jackson stood up and studied her. "I promise," he mouthed.

"Bring the baby, Eliza." He gathered up his instruments and shoved them in his bag. When he jerked open the door, Butch and Carver were leaning against the wall.

"Where do you think you're taking that baby?" Butch demanded.

"He will require further care. I'm taking him back to my office where I can better provide for him. His mother can collect him in about two weeks. She's welcome to come visit him whenever she likes."

"You can't take that baby," Butch argued. "It stays here."

"Not this time, Butch. We are ready to go back to Rockford. Miss Prissy is to have complete bed rest for two weeks. She is not to have gentlemen callers for three months."

"Three months!" protested Butch.

"Three months. And get one of the other girls to stay with her tonight. I'll look in on her tomorrow."

"Ahh! That's fine, doctor."

Butch evidently thought Dr. Jackson would not report him. He pulled a wad of bills from his pocket and thrust them into the doctor's hand. "We don't want any witnesses that a baby as born here tonight."

"Hide him in your bag, Eliza," Dr. Jackson whispered. Prissy didn't have any clothing for him, so Eliza wrapped him in one of his mother's petticoats. As Eliza prepared to tuck him into her bag, Prissy put her hand on Eliza's arm.

"Let me kiss him goodbye."

Prissy kissed the baby on the forehead.

"Take him away. Don't let Butch have him."

As Carver rowed them to the Rockford shore, Eliza cuddled the baby in the bag shielding him from the night air.

Eliza's heart bled for him and Prissy. What would become of them? She silently prayed God would watch over her and her baby.

What am I supposed to do for them? How can I help that little girl and her baby?

Carver put them ashore, and Dr. Jackson drove them to the house. He let Eliza out at the door. "Eliza, feed the baby and dress him. I'm going for the sheriff. I'm not going to let Butch do to Prissy like he has done to other girls."

"What do you mean?"

"I'll explain later, but I've got to hurry before it's too late." Dr. Jackson started his car and sped off in the night.

Eliza carried the baby up the steps and quietly let herself in. She did not want to disturb Helen if she or her mother was asleep.

Eliza dressed him in a soft flannel gown and diaper from the stack of baby clothes she and Helen had sewed for her baby. Eliza sterilized a baby bottle and nipple, and he greedily began his first meal.

"I thought I heard the rocking chair squeaking," said Helen. Dressed in her lace wrapper, she stood watching from the doorway.

"Are you having trouble sleeping …"

Helen's eyes froze on the baby in Eliza's arms.

"Eliza, where did you get that baby? Who does he belong to?"

Eliza started to tell her about Prissy and Little Oklahoma, but Helen stopped her. "I don't care where he was born or who his parents are. Let me feed him."

"Don't put yourself through this, Helen. He isn't ours to keep."

"I don't care. I just want to feel a baby in my arms."

Helen took the child from Eliza and sat down in the rocker. Eliza rested on the sofa while Helen crooned gently to the baby while giving him his bottle.

"He's a perfect little baby, Eliza! I can't believe she didn't want him. What kind of a monster would not want her own baby?"

"A frightened one," said Dr. Jackson, coming into the parlor. "One who thought her baby was going to be thrown into the river."

By the time Dr. Jackson returned with the sheriff, Prissy had already disappeared from Little Oklahoma. All that remained to prove she ever existed was the baby in Helen's arms.

"Butch and Carver even had a new girl sleeping in that bed. The sheriff and deputies are looking for Prissy now, but likely as not they'll never find her," Dr. Jackson said, rocking back and forth on his heels, his hands stuffed in his front trouser pockets. "They likely are taking her to Fort Wayne or Chicago—anywhere to get her out of here so they can keep her. I hope the trip doesn't kill her."

According to Dr. Jackson, Prissy wasn't the first girl to give birth on Little Oklahoma's sordid shores. Only last year, he had been summoned to deliver the baby of woman-child who was perhaps younger than Prissy.

"When she saw that baby, she was like a little girl with a dolly. I was afraid to leave her with it. She was too young to be in the clutches of the likes of Butch and Carver, so I went to the sheriff. The next time I saw her, at the jail, she was black and blue, bleeding profusely, and denying she ever had given birth. Her baby was nowhere to be found. The sheriff and I suspected foul play at the time. Of course babies are in the way in a place like Little Oklahoma. They're bad for business.

"About a month later, the remains of a baby were found downstream of Little Oklahoma. I couldn't prove it was the baby I had delivered. The girl was gone, sent somewhere else, or dead.

"Prissy obviously thought her baby was in danger, too."

Helen snuggled the baby closer. "What's going to happen to this little boy?"

"The sheriff will pretend to look for Prissy. He won't put any real effort into it because Carver and Butch will pay him off. As for the baby, he'll be put up for adoption, I guess."

Helen's eyes were shining. "Please, Frank, can we? I know he's had a bad beginning and all, but we can overcome that, can't we? Please?"

As Eliza wrote Robert later: "I knew they were going to keep the baby when I heard Dr. Jackson say that they had to keep him because his eyes were the same color blue as Helen's. As you know, all babies' eyes are blue at birth."

Robert's next letter brought her a photograph of himself in uniform. Under the circumstances, a wedding photo was not taken, and she did not have another picture of him. He looked thinner than she remembered, although he was spare before he went. He had grown a neatly clipped black mustache. He looked unbelievably dashing. The dark eyes she remembered so well were luminous and expressive. It seemed it had been a long time since she watched his broad back driving away after their wedding. She had truly missed his friendship. Eliza was glad for the photo, because sometimes in her dreams, Robert looked like Dr. Jackson.

CHAPTER 28

Eliza stared at the headline on the *Rockford Record*: "War Declared!"

A double stack of papers bound with twine lay on the boardwalk next to a newsboy who shouted the headline to passersby. She barely heard him as the big, black letters seared in her brain.

Eliza dreaded this moment. It was one thing for Robert to be in Chicago. At least he was safe there. It was quite another thing for him to be far, far away in Germany where he could be shot, captured, and killed. And what of the unknown diseases?

In one of Robert's previous letters, he told her of the frothy insouciance of the recruits, their boasts of beating the kaiser in a few weeks and coming home heroes before it was time to make hay at the end of June.

To Robert, they sounded naive.

"I wish such a thing were true," he wrote, "but I do not think Kaiser Wilhelm is so foolish as to provoke the sleeping giant of the United States without adequate preparation. I hope I am wrong, but I fear the work of the Pale Horse may be aided by unknown weapons. I have heard rumors …"

Robert had not elaborated. As Eliza stood with a gathering crowd of Rockford citizens, she wondered what he meant by "the work of the Pale Horse may be aided by unknown weapons." She splurged and bought a paper for two cents and tucked it under her arm as if to hide the truth from herself.

The Rockford Post Office was alive with bragging talk of war. Men stood in clusters talking what seemed like pure foolishness to Eliza, unaware of the stricken expressions on the faces of their wives who hugged their sons close to them. As she stood in line to ask for Dr. Jackson's mail, Eliza thought of the little boys she helped bring into the world. Would the love, pain, and sacrifice required to bring those children to life be forfeited to assuage the ego of a distant megalomaniac?

"A letter for you, Mrs. Altman," said the postmaster. "Looks to be from that soldier husband of yours. God bless America!"

Wearing his postman's hat, he looked very military when he saluted her.

Once on the sidewalk, Eliza tore open Robert's letter.

I have been given a week's leave of absence, Eliza, but I am told that I must take it before the middle of the month. I can come home, but I think it better you come here, if you wish. Will you be afraid to travel on the train all the way to Chicago or will you think it as an adventure? If I know you, and I think I do, I suspect that you will enjoy the novelty of a train trip and seeing a big city like Chicago. There is much I want to show you. If you wish to come, I will reserve rooms for us at a moderately priced hotel. Please understand you are under no obligation to come.

The noise of the street receded from Eliza's senses. She saw Robert's dark, smiling eyes before her, then she felt a nudge from God.

She walked over to the bank and withdrew one hundred dollars. Never in her life had she held so much money in her hand.

Trembling, she tucked it into her purse and strode over to the Rockford depot and bought a ticket for Chicago on the morning train.

Chapter 29

Through the smoke and steam of the Chicago train platform, Eliza scanned the crowd for someone familiar. Taking the porter's hand to steady herself, she stepped off the train and looked around her. Where was Robert with his dark hair, broad shoulders, and expressive eyes? Would she recognize him after more than a year? Would he recognize her?

Perhaps she had been hasty in coming. She sent Robert a telegram apprising him of her arrival time. What if he had not received it? What if he couldn't come?

She envied the stylish, bustling travelers, all of whom appeared to know where they were going. When she dressed this morning, she thought she looked pretty. As she looked around, her fussy, ruffled ensemble, remade from one of Helen Jackson's dresses was styled quite differently from the tailored clothing of the city women. Eliza felt like a country bumpkin with no idea whatsoever of what she was doing. Grimy from travel and rumpled, this was not at all the way she wanted to meet Robert. For a moment, she wished she was back in familiar Rockford, Ohio, where she knew people and she didn't look so out of place.

"May I help you, miss?" The porter touched his hat with a chocolate finger.

"Someone … was supposed to meet me."

"Don't you worry, miss. The railroad handles travelers every day and we take care of each one of them. If your party doesn't come for you soon, I'll take you somewhere safe to wait." He set Mama's trunk on the platform next to Eliza. She sat down on it.

"Watch your pocketbook, missy," he whispered to her. She snatched it up off the trunk and hid it in the folds of her skirt.

"Mrs. Altman! Mrs. Robert Altman!"

Eliza saw an earnest young man about her own age in a military uniform, cap in hand, calling at random to the unloading passengers. He looked past her until she waved her hand to capture his attention.

He fumbled with his cap, then suddenly remembered his manners. "I'm Corporal McCoy, one of your husband's orderlies." He extended his hand to her.

"Captain Altman is unable to meet you, so he sent me to escort you to your hotel. He doesn't know how soon he can get away from the hospital."

"Is Robert alright?" Eliza anxiously searched his face as she shook his hand.

The young man grinned. "No, ma'am! He's angry at the General. Captain Altman wanted to come meet you himself, but since he is going on leave, the army is squeezing every bit of doctoring out of him. We're at war, you know, ma'am, and we're all going to be shipped overseas."

"Robert, too?"

The man's eyes darted nervously, trying to evade hers. "I think the captain will have to answer that one."

Corporal McCoy easily shouldered her trunk.

Then Eliza knew: Robert was going to war. These next few days might be the last time she would ever be with him.

Alone in her hotel room, she watched amazed at a river of humanity bobbing beneath her window. Although it was well past sundown, ragged little children peddled pencils and newspapers and shined the shoes of the legions of servicemen and nattily dressed businessmen who bustled under the golden glow of the streetlamps. Some men escorted brightly painted ladies wearing elaborate and daring dresses. Eliza suspected some of these women might be right at home on Little Oklahoma. Perhaps poor Prissy walked the streets of Chicago on the arm of a soldier.

In spite of the constant excitement and noise wafting up from the street, exhaustion from the long day of travel soon overtook Eliza. She reluctantly dressed in her flour sack nightgown and curled up in the large mahogany bed. The shadows of the couples on the street loomed large and danced on the wall opposite her bed. Bits of gay laughter and conversation drifted to her ears.

When would Robert come? Perhaps she had been hasty buying her train ticket, but she wanted to see him, to tell him that she loved him—and get his help finding a new living situation for herself. What would happen here? Would Robert still love her? Would he have changed? Could she bring herself to tell him that she didn't want to go back to the Jacksons? Would he blame her for Dr. Jackson's attentions?

Oh, Father God, help me to know what to do and where I belong.

It seemed to be only a moment later that the shadows of the night's revelry on the wall was replaced with full sunlight. Mama's little watch read 7:00 a.m. Eliza leisurely turned over and yawned. Her stomach rumbled.

Will Robert come for breakfast? And if not, where will I eat?

Eliza carefully looked through her small selection of dresses. She was looking for something plain, but well designed. She had seen no one in Chicago wearing calico, mostly dark gabardine with decorative piping. She had nothing comparable, so she dressed in Helen's made-over peach silk dress. Would Robert think she was pretty? Had he ever thought of her as pretty?

"Sorry, miss, no one has asked for you and there are no messages either," said the man behind the lobby desk. "We would have sent a bellhop to your room to notify you if someone asked for you. And we deliver all messages."

He seemed a trifle miffed as if she had questioned the hotel's reputation.

"Would you please check again for a message?"

He put his hand inside the message box with her room number and rattled it around the edges so she could see that it hid nothing.

"See? I'm sorry, miss. There is nothing for you. You can check back later."

Eliza searched the faces of the servicemen in the lobby. Some smiled encouragingly at her, but none were Robert. Perhaps he would be too busy again today to come. Perhaps he would come after breakfast.

She went back to the desk and the long-suffering clerk looked dismayed to see her again so soon. "No message yet, miss."

"I just wanted to say that I would be in the hotel restaurant should a message arrive."

"Very good, miss. Should a message arrive—or a person—we shall find you. I promise," he said, as if he thought she would extract a vow from him if he didn't voluntarily offer it.

Although she had never eaten in a hotel restaurant, it was her only option. She was flabbergasted at the cost of the food when she read the menu. If she hadn't been so hungry, she would have gotten up and left. While she studied the menu, looking vainly for an inexpensive breakfast, a white gloved hand tapped her shoulder.

"Mrs. Altman?" A dignified waiter with a pencil-thin mustache hovered over her. "A message, ma'am." He laid a sealed envelope on the snow-white tablecloth next to her.

She tore it open and unfolded the plain white card.

Eliza,

Will you meet me in the hotel restaurant at noon?

I am anxious to see you.

Fondly,

Robert

She slipped the note in her purse and tugged on the strings to close it. Did he really want to see her? It had been so long since they had seen one another.

Her eyes fell on a dark-haired soldier eating breakfast with a beautiful red-haired woman. Tendrils of hair curled around her creamy throat, partially obscuring the swell of her breasts as they strained at the low-cut bodice. Their laughter and conversation were intimate. It was obvious that the man was totally smitten with his companion. He could barely eat, and he certainly couldn't take his eyes off of her generous bosom.

Robert was far handsomer than this soldier, and these were the woman in Chicago Robert saw every day. Eliza suddenly felt plain and homespun; her appetite vanished.

"Just coffee," she said to the waiter as she shut her eyes to block out the vision of the couple. Eliza turned in her chair to face the other direction so she could drink her coffee.

Perhaps the army had dramatically changed Robert. Perhaps he no longer loved the simple country girl she was. Maybe one of these sophisticated women was more Robert's style. But she had put her life in God's hands. She would trust.

For the remainder of the morning, Eliza wandered around the lobby visiting the gift shops and book stalls and watching the people. She was dazzled by the sheer quantity and variety of everything. She realized there were more people in the hotel than in all of Rockford. Although she was amply entertained by the sights and sounds, the hands of the clock moved incredibly slowly toward noon.

At 11:45, she took a table near the restaurant door where she could watch the entrance.

Robert appeared. She spotted him before he saw her. She wanted to wave her dinner napkin and shout, "Over here! Over here! Here's where I am!"

Robert paused to speak to the maître d'. Apparently, army life was good to him. He looked very dashing in his uniform. His hair and mustache were neatly styled. He walked with an air of confidence that Eliza had not seen before. His dark eyes scanned the room. They briefly rested upon her and then went on.

Eliza was stunned. He had not recognized her. As his eyes swept back across, Eliza timidly waved at him.

Puzzled, he fixed his eyes on her, then flashed with recognition. He strode across the room to her, took her hand. "Oh, Eliza! I am so happy to see you! I didn't recognize you for a moment! You've grown up from a pretty little girl into a very beautiful woman!"

Eliza blushed. "You look wonderful, too, Robert."

"Have you eaten lunch?" he asked, not releasing her hand, his eyes hungrily devouring her.

She shook her head. She was momentarily tongue-tied.

"Then let's order. I've so much to show you while you are here. Since you've come to me and we have a whole week together, I want to show you all the wonders of the big city. How do you like it so far?"

By the time their food arrived, the conversation became more relaxed, but did not have the easy intimacy they had enjoyed in the days when their friendship was young.

However, Robert didn't allow time for awkwardness to develop. Much to Eliza's relief, he had planned their day to be tightly packed with sightseeing and entertainment. They rode cable cars and elevated trains to destinations Eliza never dreamed existed.

She was particularly thrilled with Lake Michigan. She had never seen such a large body of water. She loved watching the sunshine dancing on the waves.

Navy Pier made her proud to be an American as she marveled at the huge warships under construction. Her heart was stirred to see the stars and stripes flying over the vessels. Young sailors and shipbuilders looked so jaunty and brave as they crawled over the superstructure.

"All these boys!" Eliza said. "With that kind of manpower, surely the war won't last any time at all."

Robert regarded the troops sadly. "There will be some fine men and boys aboard these boats. I fear a lot of them won't be coming home to their mothers and sweethearts and wives. Eliza, I've looked into the faces of our soldiers and sailors, and I can tell you that most of them are unprepared for the realities of war. They're training them with wooden rifles. Some of the boys think war is going to be like hunting coons in their cornfields back home.

But unlike raccoons, the Germans will be shooting back with real bullets. There are new weapons over there, weapons like chlorine gas bombs and machine guns. I fear some of these boys won't be ready to meet their Maker when the bullets start flying."

Robert shook his head sadly. "I wish I could have told each one of them about Jesus when I gave them their physicals."

Eliza studied Robert's strong profile. A stout lake wind ruffled his glossy black hair. Eliza shivered and moved closer to him. He put his arm around her, and she snuggled into the shelter of his body. They stood quietly together watching a ship on a trial run while the gulls dove and screamed in its wake.

It was nearly 11:00 p.m. when Robert walked Eliza to the door of her hotel room.

"I really enjoyed today, Robert! I've seen more today, had more adventures, done things I've only ever dreamed of doing. Thank you." She gently squeezed his hand.

"We have tomorrow too," he said. "Actually, we have a whole week, I hope. You are going to stay the whole week, aren't you?"

"How long can we afford it?" Eliza was thinking about the expensive lunch they had in the hotel.

"If we conserve a bit, we can afford all week. Then I have to report back for duty." He touched her nose slightly with his index finger.

"Then I will stay until you send me home."

She was enjoying every moment of her adventure and didn't want it to end. Not so soon. Maybe not ever.

She smiled up at Robert. She hoped he would hold her and kiss her. He squeezed her hand and released it, then took the hotel key and unlocked her door.

"I've checked into the hotel for the week too. They only had one empty room. Oddly enough, it's next to yours, but I don't want you to be nervous about it," he said, holding his hands behind his back. "So this is goodnight. Would you like to meet for breakfast?

Eliza agreed to meet him at 7:00 a.m. She shut the door behind her and leaned against it.

My husband is so wonderful, so kind, so handsome! Seeing him again with more maturity makes me know I truly love him.

Being with him again, something new awakened in her.

I want to be Robert's wife. But how do I tell him?

Chapter 30

The week passed all too quickly for Eliza. In the late afternoon of her last full day as she washed out her underthings in the sink, she hated to think that tomorrow the train would take her back to Rockford and uncertainty. Eliza enjoyed her time with Robert and the vacation from the tension of living with Dr. Jackson's subtle and not-so-subtle advances.

Eliza wanted to discuss their future. But so far, he hadn't mentioned anything about any future plans. Eliza suspected he was avoiding the subject. It was almost as if he didn't think he was going to have a future with her, or any future at all.

She wanted to hear his thoughts on what she could do while he was away. Since nurses' colleges were only available to single women, she valued Robert's advice on her next career move.

Also, she was looking for an opportunity to tell Robert about her concerns with Dr. Jackson. There were times during the week, quiet, intimate moments, when she could have poured out her heart to Robert, occasions when she might have looked into his eyes and said, "I love you. I am sure I want to be your wife."

Something held her back. She had nagging doubts if Robert would welcome those words or sentiments. And she didn't want unpleasantness to spoil a single moment of the time they had together.

But tonight could be their last night together until eternity. They would have only two more meals together, supper tonight, breakfast tomorrow. Then they would say goodbye, perhaps forever. Pressing upon her heart was the need to tell him how she felt. She wanted to hold his hand, look into his dark brown eyes, and say, "I am your wife. Stay with me tonight."

Dear God, if there is a way Robert and I can have a future together, please open the door. But if it is not to be, help me to graciously accept it.

Eliza carefully hung her flour sack underwear on hangers and hid them in the closet. If Robert did come in her room, she didn't want him to be greeted by flowered drawers with Baker's Secret still faintly imprinted across the seat.

He had given her instructions to dress warmly, and she hopefully suspected they were going to be by Lake Michigan. She brushed her hair and, instead of coiling it on top of her head as she usually did, she loosely braided it and tied a forest green bow around it at her neckline. She slipped into the dark green dress Robert purchased for her earlier in the week. He had seen it in the window of a big department store and insisted she try it on.

"Do it for me! It'll bring out the color in your eyes."

He was right. It did. When she viewed herself in the three-sided mirror, she was amazed to see this particular shade made her eyes sparkle and her hair gleam. The dress was expensive, but it fit her so well Robert insisted upon buying it. Eliza couldn't get over the tidy stitching and intriguing buttons that perfectly suited it.

She put on several layers of petticoats beneath the dress and a made-over coat of Helen Jackson's and prayed that she would stay warm in the night air off of the Lake.

She heard what sounded like a puppy whining and scratching on her hotel room door.

"What on earth…" Eliza said as she opened the door. She caught her breath.

Robert stood there, smiling mischievously and wearing his dress uniform. He looked so handsome that she could hardly believe this was the same man the folks back in Ohio had nicknamed "Bear."

"Ready?" He offered her his arm.

"Absolutely." She slid her hand into it.

They took a cab down to the wharf and stood in line with a brightly dressed, high-spirited crowd waiting to board *The Belle of the Lake*. The three decks of the old paddlewheel excursion boat were lit with colorful Japanese lanterns. The boat tugged at its moorings and groaned to be launched as a ragtime band entertained the crowd with spritely tunes from the upper deck. The tantalizing aroma of hickory smoke and roasting pork drifted over the throng.

Eliza and Robert, jostled and pushed by their fellow passengers, were swept on board. A steward in an immaculate white uniform directed them to the dining room where a banquet was spread.

Eliza had never seen such an assortment of meats, salads, pastries, and confections. She had to look at everything before choosing a single mouthful of food.

After they ate, they sat out on the deck drinking cups of hot coffee while a barbershop quartet sang nostalgic love songs from the gallery. Then the mood on the boat changed. The band played one waltz after another as the moon rose over the water with opalescent clouds hurrying across the sky with stars peeking between them.

Eliza felt Robert's nearness, his arm around her shoulder, the rise and fall of his breathing. She tried to memorize every detail of the moment and absorb the pleasure.

He cleared his throat. "I have something for you, Eliza." He reached into his trouser pocket and brought out a velvet-covered box and opened it. Even in the dim light, Eliza could see a narrow band, gleaming and gold.

"It's too dark out here for you to see it, but it has a ruby in it. Something about that fiery red stone reminded me of you."

He smiled at her. "As you know, I'm probably going to be sent somewhere overseas. I wanted you to have something to remind you of me. It's not a wedding ring, Eliza. It's my way of saying thank you.

"You and your family have meant more to me than you can possibly know. I came to your home a shattered man, broken by grief, without any dreams. The only thing I had were memories that broke my heart. Your mother and pa were good for me. Your brothers and sisters too. But helping you survive your own heartbreak when your mama died and helping you reach for your goals were healing to me. Your stubborn courage in the face of all kinds of obstacles, not allowing yourself to be turned to the right or the left, have been an inspiration to me. God used you to heal me, Eliza. Whatever may come, I'll forever be grateful to you."

Gently, he took her hand in his and slipped the ring on her finger.

"If I die overseas, no one else in the world will remember me if you don't, Eliza. Thank you for giving me my life back, even if it is only for a little while."

Eliza stood on her tiptoes and gently kissed him. His arms slipped around her as he returned her kiss, gently then with growing passion. He held her to his chest. She could feel his heart beating through the layers of her clothing.

"I've wanted to tell you for so long that I love you," she whispered. "When you left me with the Jacksons on our wedding day, I wanted to call out then I loved you, but then I was afraid you—" His mouth covered hers and her words were forgotten.

It was nearly midnight when the vessel docked, and they disembarked. A horse-drawn buggy took them back to the hotel and they walked silently through the halls to their rooms, hand in hand. The gas jets were turned low in the hallway, leaving them just enough light to read the numbers above the doors.

"This has been the most wonderful night of my life," Eliza whispered, her back leaning against the door of her room. "I've been hoping, dreaming, even praying ever since we were married this moment would come. That I could say, 'I love you' and that you would love me in return."

She looked deep into his eyes. In them, she read love and desire.

He kissed her passionately as a warm rush swept over her.

"I have something else to say, Robert." With both hands, she pushed against his chest so she could look him fully in the face, so he would look at her and know she meant the words she was about to speak. "I want to be your wife."

He laughed. "You are my wife."

"No, Robert, listen to me. I want to truly be your wife. I want you to stay with me tonight. In my bed."

He blinked. "Eliza, you can't be serious!" He withdrew his arms and stared incredulously at her.

"I've never been more serious in my life."

This was not going the way she planned.

"Do you know what you're asking?"

"Of course, I do!"

"You can't!"

"But I do!"

He put his hands on his hips and turned his back to her. "Eliza, I can't. Don't misunderstand. It's not that I don't want you. I do want you." He slapped his forehead. "I'll probably kick myself every day that I said no, but I can't do it. It's just not right. This may only be a moment of passion for you, but I could damage you for the rest of your life."

He turned to face her. "Eliza, I could leave you with a baby."

"I know," she whispered, and once again she pulled him close to her. He came unresisting to her arms.

"It could be the end of your career. You might never go to nurses' training."

She kissed away his objections. Taking the room key out of her pocket, she placed it in his hand.

He drew away from her and stared at it. Suddenly, he unlocked her door and pushed it open with his foot. Eliza went in ahead of him and sat down on the edge of the bed. His eyes, dark and unfathomable, briefly flickered over her body. He deliberately shut them.

"I can't." He dropped the key on the carpet and shut the door behind him.

CHAPTER 30

Eliza didn't know when she had been more humiliated in her life. For a while, she wrestled with the sheets and blankets on her bed then finally gave up all pretense of trying to sleep. She threw them aside and began to carelessly stuff her clothing in Mama's trunk. She encountered her underwear, still damp, hanging in the closet. Still holding them, she sank to the closet floor and cried, forgetting that the wall between their rooms was paper thin.

"Stupid! Stupid! Stupid!"

She had ruined everything. She should have never invited him in. Even in the dark, she felt her face turn red with shame.

They had planned to meet for breakfast, but Eliza didn't think she could face him. Her train didn't leave until 1:00 p.m., but she could check out now and wait at the station. She need never see him again.

She would just leave him a note with the ring. It would say, "Robert, this is goodbye forever. I am returning your remembrance ring because I want to forget you. Eliza Burger"

For a few angry moments, she savored the satisfaction of cutting him to the core. Then she slipped the ring back on her finger.

Even when she hated him, she loved him. She could never do something so spiteful to Robert.

"Eliza!"

She jumped. Her name had come out of the dark.

"Eliza! Can you hear me?" It was Robert's voice through the wall.

"I know you're there, Eliza. Why won't you speak to me?" His voice had a catch in it.

"I'm here."

"Eliza, please don't be angry with me. You probably are, aren't you?"

"Yes."

"You know I love you, don't you?"

Eliza began to cry again.

"Eliza, I do love you!" His voice pleaded for understanding. "You don't know how hard it was for me to walk out of your room. I would never hurt you for anything. You have to know that!"

She didn't answer.

"I suppose it's time to tell you."

For what seemed like an eternity, there was silence on both sides of the wall.

"I owe you an apology, Eliza. I think I trapped you into marrying me. A doctor would have confirmed you were not raped. I know that would have been distressing for you, but it would have been over in a moment, and you would not have been forced into marriage.

"But I wanted you, Eliza. I wanted your whole family. You've always had someone. You can't know what it meant to me to be part of your household. When your mother died, I felt like I was kinfolk. I could ease the pain you were feeling because I knew what it was like. I'd been through terrible losses myself.

"If you hadn't shown up at my door during the blizzard, I'd have waited for you, courted you properly, but your pa pushed the issue and I jumped on it. I knew as soon as I agreed to marry you, I was wrong, so I joined the army to give you a little time to think, knowing full well my bank account would keep you obligated to me. Since then, I tried to give you back all the freedom I stole from you.

"Can you forgive me?"

"Eliza?"

She didn't know what to say.

"Eliza?" His voice was pleading.

"Of course, I forgive you. I have a confession of sorts to make too."

Eliza told him in detail about Dr. Jackson's overtures. "I was afraid to tell you about him because I feared you might think I'd encouraged him. I didn't, you know."

"I believe you. I'd heard rumors about Frank, but we both know how folks like to gossip, so I didn't believe them without further evidence, but I do now. What do you want to do, Eliza?"

"I want to go to nurses' training, but as long as unmarried women get admission preference, I don't suppose I'll get in for a while."

"Do you want a divorce?"

"No! No! If it's a choice between becoming a nurse and being your wife, I want to be your wife—even if it's in name only."

"That's the sweetest thing you've ever said to me. If you were here, I would kiss you."

"If I were there, I would kiss you back."

"Eliza …" Robert's voice quavered slightly.

"Yes?"

"Think about it. Pray about it. I'll do the same. If we are to be together, let's make our decision in the cold light of day. I never want you to ever regret becoming my wife."

"Alright, Robert. I'll meet you in the cold light of day. Good night."

Eliza sat in the closet and prayed for guidance, but nothing changed her mind. She felt called to be a nurse, but she felt equally called to be a wife to Robert Altman.

I give it to you, Lord Jesus. Let my path be confirmed by two or three witnesses.

She felt an unbelievable peace that stayed with her until she heard loud pounding and yelling at her door.

"Mrs. Altman! Mrs. Robert Altman! Are you in there, ma'am?"

A man's voice was calling her. She awoke in the dark, laying on the floor, disoriented and confused.

"Mrs. Altman!"

"I'm coming!" she shouted back and fumbled for the closet doorknob. She was blinded by the daylight. Her rumpled bed told the story of the troubled night before.

Still clad in her nightgown, she opened the door a crack and peeked around it. A red-garbed bellhop stood at her door, envelope in hand.

"Mr. Altman asked me to give you this when he checked out," said the boy, waiting for a tip.

"Checked out?"

"Yes, ma'am. He just left a few minutes ago."

"What time is it?"

"It's five minutes to 12:00, ma'am. And may I remind you that check out is promptly at 12:30." He doubtfully eyed her flour sack nightgown.

She slammed the door and tore open the envelope.

Dear Eliza,

The hotel clerk says you have not checked out, but I have knocked on your door several times. Why won't you answer? I waited for you until my time ran out. I must be back at the base at 1:00 p.m., so if I leave now, I'll just make it. I ran into an officer from the base who tells me that rumor has it—and there are lots of rumors in the army!—that my unit will be shipped out today. I suppose I will be going with them.

I felt sure I heard from God last night, but you have not come down this morning, and now I am confused. Do know that regardless of whatever transpires between us, that I do love you.

Your husband,

Robert

Shipped out! Today!

Eliza frantically pulled off her nightgown, threw it in the corner, and pulled on her clothing. Her underwear was still dampish, but it scarcely mattered. Her hair uncombed, she grabbed her purse, and ran down the stairs and to the lobby desk. The bellhop was idling behind the counter.

"How do I get to the army base?" she breathlessly demanded.

"Are you trying to catch your husband?" he asked.

"Yes!"

"He's still out front waiting on a cab. He was going to take the train but there was a derailment—"

Eliza didn't wait for his explanation. She ran for the revolving door. Ahead, she saw Robert's dark head just disappearing into a cab.

She pushed through the door. "Wait! Stop!"

"You'll have to take the next cab, miss!" said the driver, putting Robert's bag in the trunk.

"No!" She banged her fist on the glass. "Robert! Wait!"

Robert turned toward her. His eyes, swollen as if he had been crying, grew wide at the sight of her. He opened the cab door.

"Eliza!" He took in her disheveled appearance.

"I overslept! Oh, Robert! Please don't go!"

"Honey, I have to! I have to report for duty in an hour!"

"Let me ride with you!"

"Cabby! Can you take me to the base, then bring my wife back to the hotel?"

"Sure, Mack! Anything for one of our service boys or his missus."

Eliza slid into the backseat next to Robert.

"I'm staying in Chicago, Robert. As long as you're here in the city—two hours, two days, whatever—I'm staying."

"It may only be two hours." He looked pensive.

"I know. I read your note."

"You're a mess. You know that." He lightly touched her nose.

She giggled and vainly tried to smooth her wild locks. "Yes, but I'm your mess."

He kissed her over and over again until the cab pulled up in front of the army base. Eliza saw servicemen and their sweethearts and wives openly embracing and kissing in front of the gate. Nearly all were crying.

As the cabbie retrieved Robert's bag from the trunk, Robert kissed her one more time.

"Go back to the hotel. I'll let you know as soon as I know what I'm doing. You'll hear from me today."

"I'll always love you," she whispered, her heart breaking at the sight of her tall, handsome husband going through the gates with other servicemen. He turned and waved at her from behind the gate.

She rented the room for an additional day. It gave her an opportunity to properly pack her clothing. She knew she would be going somewhere tomorrow; she wasn't sure where. Maybe back to Rockford, maybe to a rooming house. She had no idea what tomorrow would bring. All she knew was God had led her on this path and would show her where to go next.

By six, her packing was done, but she had heard nothing from Robert. She slipped outside to the street and bought some bread, cheese, and an apple from the little delicatessen on the corner. She took them back to her room for a picnic in front of the window where she could watch and wait. At seven, the lamplighter lit the gaslights in front of the hotel and crowds of servicemen and pretty ladies began to appear.

She now understood their frantic gaiety. They were laughing in the dark because if they didn't, they would be crying.

If my life was not in God's hands, I would be crying, too.

The chambermaid came in at 8:30 to light the gas and turn down the bed. Eliza drew the curtains and lay down on the bed. Something had happened. Robert promised to send a message, but something had prevented it. He must have been shipped out and couldn't get a message to her before he left. She would somehow find out for certain what had happened to him in the morning. She was disappointed, but there was nothing to be done. She tried to formulate some sort of plan, but her mind was numb with spent emotion and grief.

With the street noise as a lullaby, she drifted off into a fitful sleep. She dreamed she was on a battlefield tending wounded soldiers with Robert. Suddenly, bullets exploded all around her. Robert's blood splashed on her. She caught him as he fell.

"No!" she cried.

The bullets came again. She was hit, too.

More bullets, then the battlefield receded, and the hotel room came into focus. She shook herself and heard pounding on her door.

She stumbled to it and flung it open.

Robert stood before her. She threw herself in his arms. "It's you! You're here. You're really here." She pressed him to herself to make sure he was not a dream again.

She felt his rumbling laughter bubbling up from his chest as he enfolded her in his arms.

"I'm real and I've got news! Listen, Eliza. Because of my age and the fact that I am a married man, they're not sending me overseas. I'm to be permanently stationed here in Chicago at the

Soldiers' Home at Camp Douglas. And you, my dear, are going to be permitted to live there with me."

"Oh! Before I forget, you also have a job at the base hospital. They need a woman there with maternity care experience for the officer's wives. It looks like the army may even be willing to provide you with further training. What do you think of that?" Eliza could scarcely believe what she was hearing. "Are you sure? Are you sure they won't change their minds?"

"Well, my love, anything's possible, but as of this moment—he flipped open the lid on his pocket watch and glanced at the time—"10:12 p.m., that's my orders."

He bent down and kissed her ardently. Suddenly, he lifted her in his arms and shut the hotel door behind them.

The End

END NOTES

1. From the mid-1800s and into the twentieth century, spiritism—the belief in reincarnation, automatic writing, Ouija boards, and the like—enjoyed a revival with notables such as Thomas Edison, May West, Marie and Pierre Curie, Queen Victoria, Arthur Conan Doyle, Mary Todd Lincoln, and many others.Germans had a form of spiritism in their folktales. They believed in ghosts, demonic manifestations, fairy creatures, and the Mahr.Every time someone says, "gesundheit," they are wishing someone good health, although there was a belief that a person's spirit left them when they sneezed, and "God bless you" was a way to return their spirit to them.

2. Eliza's Cloud Biscuits RecipePreheat oven to 450 degrees.Measure 1 cup of buttermilk or 1 cup of milk mixed with 1 tablespoon of apple cider vinegar. Let stand until milk curdles.In a large bowl add:2 cups all-purpose flour3 teaspoons baking powder¾ teaspoon saltMix together dry ingredients.Add 5 tablespoons melted butter or lard and 1 cup milk.Stir to mix. Drop by tablespoonful onto a greased baking sheet. Bake at 450 degrees 12 to 15 minutes until lightly brown. Serve hot.

3. Grandma's Sugar Cookie RecipeSince the recipe calls for nutmeg, these cookies hint of a German origin. What makes these cookies both soft and crisp is the balance of baking powder and baking soda. Although this recipe has been halved for modern bakers, it still makes a lot of cookies. These may not be exactly like Grandma's, but they are close.Preheat oven to 350. Set aside ½ cup buttermilk or ½ cup heavy cream mixed with 1 tablespoon apple cider vinegar.In a large bowl, add:2 cups granulated sugar1 cup butter (softened)3 eggs1 tablespoon vanilla½ teaspoon salt1 teaspoon baking soda and 1 teaspoon baking powderteaspoon nutmegCream together then add 5 cups of all-purpose white flour, alternating with the buttermilk/heavy cream.Mix, roll, and cut with cookie cutters. Be skimpy on the flour or you'll have tough cookies. Sugar may be sprinkled on unbaked cookies. Bake 8–10 minutes at 350 degrees on a greased cookie sheet. Or, if you prefer, omit sprinkling with sugar and spread with your favorite buttercream frosting when they are completely cool. Store in a lidded container.

4. Eliza's Egg Noodle RecipeThis recipe has been cut in half for smaller modern families.Ingredients:1 cup of flour, plus more as needed1 egg (beaten well)½ teaspoon salt2 tablespoons milk½ teaspoon baking powder (optional)Add salt to flour and mix together. If you want fat noodles, stir in the baking powder. Add egg to flour and mix until a soft dough forms, adding more flour if necessary. Turn out dough on floured surface and knead several times. Allow dough to rest for half hour. Cut the dough into two pieces for easier handling. Roll out dough to desired thickness. Cut dough to desired size noodles. Allow them to dry at least two hours. Noodles may be cooked in boiling water or broth.

www.ingramcontent.com/pod-product-compliance
Lightning Source LLC
Chambersburg PA
CBHW060342310726
48976CB00003B/680